Dangerous Aspects

By Colin Winston Aldridge

Kempton
M A R K S

A Kempton Marks book

Text Copyright © Colin Winston Aldridge 2008

The cover original artwork was created and donated by:
Mair Llewellyn ©
www.TickhillClinic.com
MairLLLL@aol.com

ISBN 978-0-755205-05-9

Kempton Marks
19 The Cinques
Gamlingay, Sandy
Bedfordshire SG19 3NU
England

This book is dedicated to: Lucy Maud and Sydney Roland who by any measure were great parents.

I would like to thank the following kind people for all their help in the creation of this book:

My wife Janet who read and re-read every word many times over and without whose encouragement I would have been easily distracted.

My three North American editors who along the way kept the story, spelling and grammar firmly entrenched in American English;

Jayne Denker of New York State,
Chris Traxler of Philadelphia
and my good friend Kat Miller of Utah.

From the world of EFT a special thank you to Tam & Mair Llewellyn for their kind and supportive response. And to Gwyneth Moss for contributing the ABC of EFT as the penultimate page.

Foreword

The book you now have in your hands is both an unusual and very special book. It is two books in one, or rather a book with two stories. Unusually, too, it is an attempt to do two things at once which actually works well for both.

It is a novel about a woman who is going through a 'difficult' divorce after discovering her husband was a drugs dealer. More than 'difficult' the divorce turns out to be 'life threatening'. The tale winds through intrigue, threats and murders twisting and turning to the last

It is also a coaching manual for a better life as the woman seeks treatment in a variety of ways to avoid a nervous breakdown from the stress she comes under.

You can read it as a novel. Many will enjoy it just as that, and that is fine. You can always read it again at some later date as a coaching manual and get two books for the price of one.

Actually you will want to read it more than twice and enjoy it each time.

Prof Tam Llewellyn-Edwards
EFT Master

Chapter 1

I couldn't help but pick up this journal at the bookstore today. It feels only right to document my feelings at this time of my life. Actually, I never thought I'd have this "time of my life." When I married at 21, I thought it would be a fairy tale, forever kind of thing. Jack was working for his father's business on the docks, and I had just graduated from business school. We had known each other since high school, and when we got married, I was already three months pregnant with Cassie. Vows seemed so important to me then; actually, they still do. That's why it's so difficult to believe my vows don't mean anything right now. The man I married isn't the man who (sometimes) lies beside me at night. He's often away from me and the kids nowadays and is secretive and bad tempered when I question him about these absences. He's into some activity I can't deal with right now—I probably never will. My big decision now is whether to be straight with him and ask for a divorce or leave while he's on one of his "trips" and work through a lawyer. I'm really scared. I'm feeling really stressed right now; I need to talk to someone I can trust. I'll talk to Connie. She's been my best friend forever and I trust her opinion. What a mess my life has become.

I waved to Connie, who already had her latte in front of her and was seated in the far corner of the patio at one of our favorite places, the French Café, at the corner of 6th and Bainbridge. Connie was always on time; I could always count on her for that. I ordered a double espresso and sat down beside her.

"Sorry I'm late. The office had a special meeting today, and what would a special meeting be without their esteemed manager?" I told her as I plopped my purse down next to me. I rolled my eyes when I said "esteemed manager." I didn't feel like my job was all that important, even though I was head of the office. I glanced at my watch; it was 4 p.m.

"I'm glad the kids are at soccer practice for a while yet. I need to talk," I told her.

Connie laughed at how harried I was. "I hear that my Brett and your Ben are on the same soccer team. This should be an interesting year, considering how competitive the two of them are."

Connie flipped back her shoulder-length, dark brown hair that curled up slightly at the bottom. She was small, trim, very well dressed, and could be described as attractive, with a pert, small nose and clear, large brown eyes. She was wearing makeup today, but she looked beautiful even when she had just come from the gym and wore sweats and no makeup at all. Connie and I are opposites in looks. I am tall, blonde, blue-eyed, and consider my figure curvy.

I let out a big sigh and said, "It should prove to be an interesting year all around."

"You said you had something to talk with me about?" Connie asked, ready to give her full attention.

I looked around the coffee shop instinctively, expecting Jack or one of his goons to be right around the corner. I let out a sigh of frustration. "I have no idea where to begin, Connie."

"Start anywhere. I'll catch on," she said, putting her hand on mine to encourage me. Connie was always a good listener. She and I have shared a lot of time and a lot of secrets together and have relied on each other for a shoulder to cry on when either of us needed it. I was glad to have her to talk to.

I squeezed the slip of lemon rind into my espresso and stirred it languidly, my mind spinning. I took a sip before beginning. I felt clammy, and my blouse was sticking to my skin as I got ready to blurt out the truth about my life.

"Well, between you and me, my marriage is ending after 13 years."

There. I finally said it out loud. I had been planning this move for almost a month, and it felt like an explosion I just couldn't let out, for fear of Jack finding out about it. Sometimes he was kind, mostly toward the kids, but he had a really short fuse. I couldn't risk him getting wind of my plans; I didn't know how he'd react.

"I don't get it," Connie said, shaking her head. "I didn't see this coming. I thought you two were doing fine. What happened?"

"Connie, it's more complicated than just two people not liking each other anymore. It's a matter of life and death, as a matter of fact." How was I going to explain this to her—that my life and the lives of my children were probably hanging in the balance?

"Go on," she said slowly, tightly gripping her coffee cup.

That was when I just let everything go and told her what I knew. I told her about how Jack and I had drifted apart . . . that we were practically strangers living in the same house . . . how much he traveled on "business" and how he had stopped telling me about his work. I gave him his space, but then came the day I stopped by Jack's job at UPS, only to find out he didn't work there anymore. When I confronted him, I found out he hadn't worked there for several years. He told me he was an enforcer for a debt collection agency. He said he couldn't tell me about it because it was a dangerous occupation and he was worried I'd be scared of the consequences. I didn't believe him. Call it woman's intuition. So then I told Connie about hiring my own private investigator to try to find out the truth.

I told her my PI, James Pruitt, found out that Jack was one of the main men in a drug trafficking business that expanded from Philadelphia to who knew where. I also found out that the more Jim delved into it, the more concerned he became about handling the case. Jim kept going as long as it took him to find out what thugs my husband was acquainted with. Once we had the lowdown on Jack's drug cartel activity, Jim's assignment was complete, but he made his services available to me if I needed him sometime in the future. He suggested in the meantime that I keep my knowledge to myself. He gave me good advice about watching my back if I confronted Jack.

Of course, in my usual fashion, I did confront Jack with what I thought I knew. Now I wasn't sure I had done the right thing. But my being complicit into investigating Jack was out there, so I needed to be aware of my safety as well as the children's.

"Connie," I said, my voice low, "these are drug dealers—a dangerous bunch of people. How could Jack do this to us? What about the kids? What do I tell them? How will they react? Am I in danger? What'll happen to us?". . .

. . . Sondra has been busting my balls. We had the argument about my work. I always knew it was going to happen, but it had been a long time coming. Somehow she figured out I was up to no good. Found out I wasn't where I was supposed to be when I was supposed to be. Silly bitch hired an investigator and she found out. We had to tighten our security. She shouldn't have gotten that information so easily. She had been acting strange for a while. I got one or two of the boys to keep a tail on her; I needed to know what was going on. One of my guys saw her sitting with another woman at a coffee shop around 4:30 in the afternoon. What was she doing at a coffee shop during work hours? I'd never been able to get her to leave work early no matter how many times I complained that she spent more time worrying about her precious employees than she did about me. I knew from the description my guy gave me that it was Connie she had met with. Those two went back more years than we have been together. They became friends at some really young age, four or five, I think, and they've been best buddies ever since. I never had a lot to do with Connie really, but I knew her in high school. She's Sondra's friend, not mine, and that husband of hers, some smart hotshot lawyer with expensive suits, a big ego, and a big mouth, isn't the sort of guy I'd want to hang out with. Sondra and Connie are both smart ladies. Both of them are good looking and both kept their figures even though they had kids. I had a minor league fling with Connie early on in high school—nothing serious. When I figured out she was going to hold out on me, I let it slide. Nothing to aim for, I guess.

I hear she's gone kind of nuts lately. She works for some alternative health care clinic—the kind of place where sandals and purple ribbons in your hair are the dress code. For the men as well as the women. I always found that stuff real "woo woo," right up there with the Buddhists chanting on every street corner. All that meek inheriting the earth crap. Why don't they get it? It's guns, not roses that rule the world. People like me and my brother Sol, men who strike fear into the hearts of other men, are in control.

So why were Sond and Connie hitting the caffeine trail during office hours? I didn't ask. I knew she'd never give me a straight answer. "Oh, just girl talk" is all she'd say. Connie probably missed her period or something girly like that. I sure as hell knew that it wasn't Sondra; we haven't done anything in ages. I'd have to fix that or she'd be looking for a little something on the side . . . or maybe not. Sond was far too high and mighty to commit adultery. Still, it had been a while, so maybe next time I was home. . . .

. . . "Does he know how much you know?" Connie asked incredulously. "I mean . . . this will get dangerous if he feels threatened, so watch what you say around him."

I sipped my espresso as if I were talking about the weather when, in reality, I felt like I was falling apart. "I told him I knew he was up to no good and I begged him to stop. I promised I'd support the family for a while so he could find a legitimate job. He practically threw me across the room that night, he was so angry with me." The memory of my bruises was still fresh in my mind. I knew that Jack could be a violent man. After all, he had had a tough upbringing working down on the docks with his father. He was very rarely violent at home, though, and his physical response had shocked me, to say the least.

"That's when I knew he wasn't the man I married," I said. "The private detective said he's in one of Philadelphia's largest drug rings—and the most dangerous—with likely Tijuana connections to a cartel called Los Archos Hermanos." . . .

. . . When I was born, I was given the name Jacob Isaac Emmanuel Ackerman. After my bar mitzvah, I was happier to be known simply as Jack. A year or so after that, I met Sondra. We went to the same high school. So I seem to have known Sondra all my life. We started out by just fooling around like kids do. We would have the occasional date, but nothing steady. That's how it is during high school—suck a beer or two and hope you don't get caught, then learn about sex as first hand as you can. So me and Sondra didn't get serious till later, when she was in college and I was working for my father. I had had lots girls before Sondra, but she was a virgin. I guess I was lucky—all those girls but no diseases, only a couple of abortions that I know of, and—as far as I know—no brats.

Sondra was different. And that's why I hit on her—because she *was* different—a good looker with a brain. She had this way about her—she was a challenge for a guy like me who always got what he wanted when it came to girls. I was a jock with a reputation, and that reputation could only go one way if I laid Miss Benjamin. We hung out together for a while before I tried anything. I planned to seduce her down at the old man's yard. There was a cozy hut there that Sol and I, and the old man, used for laying our conquests. Sondra gave it up on about the sixth or seventh date—took me by surprise when she said yes. Needless to say I didn't wear a rubber.

She was incredible—so different from the other girls, and something I wanted over and over again. Before long she missed her period, just 21 and knocked up, carrying an Ackerman inside her. I offered to pay to get rid of it but she was high and mighty even then—didn't want any part of it, which of course I am glad of now. We were both Jewish, both free spirits but Sondra getting pregnant made us fall back upon our families. So we told our parents, and my father whopped me so hard I thought I was being beaten into oblivion. He made it clear that marriage was the only option. Our folks got together and worked it all out fast, so no lump would show at the wedding, and then the announcement of the near immediate pregnancy. I guess our families were old fashioned, hiding the truth like that and making sure we were married before the baby came. That's the way it was when our parents were young—all families did the same thing to stay respectable. It's different nowadays . . . but it wasn't for us.

That memory takes me back. Sondra had been a good woman, but I got bored with her. Divorce could be a way out; it all depended what she had figured out about my life now.

The kids were the reason I did all this in the first place. I didn't want them having to grow up the way I did—always fighting, stealing and looking out for the next crooked deal. When I think of the stuff my dad did for my brother Sol and me . . . it's a miracle we didn't serve time. Yet for all that he didn't die rich. And then the business collapsed, and the only thing me and Sol inherited was our tough skins. So I guess I always was a hard-nosed, selfish bastard. I have always looked out for me, and the only exception to that rule is my kids. I've only ever wanted what's best for them, and I'll do anything to make sure they have it.

When Pop's business got into trouble, me and Sol were relieved when UPS picked up the depot down on the docks and gave us both jobs. The ol' man had always groomed us to go into business with him, and that's what we did. When Sol got the offer to freelance, I guess it was only natural that he had me go in on the deal too. In the early days, we didn't know who we were dealing with and maybe that early we could have walked away. By the time we had moved the first shipment of dope for our Mexican bosses, that was it. We were in for life. But the money's terrific. It hardly seems worth getting out of bed if the day's not going to earn you 50 big ones.

I never showed the money off to Sondra; she had no idea of the kind of life I led when I was away from her. Parties, girls (or men, in Sol's case)—all there whenever you wanted it. I guess I should have got with Sondra every now and then—that wasn't too cool, leaving her frustrated like that. She always was a nice looking woman, but why have an old carcass when there is always nice fresh meat available?

Sol and I have always been close. If either one of us, or usually both of us, had been whipped by the ol' man, we only had each other for comfort. Our mom would never take our side, never defend us. We had a younger brother, Milton—he was Mom's favorite. She never let Pop near him. I was never close to him. I haven't seen him in years; he could be dead for all I know.

When Pop got older, he told us that he did what he did so that we would grow up right and know the tough realities of life. What he didn't know was that there was one thing he couldn't beat out of Sol, and that was his love of men. He came out as gay in his late teens. He tried it with girls, but they didn't hit the spot for him. I realized from his way, his manner, that it was wrong to assume gay men are soft. He was as hard as any straight man on the streets and on the docks. Cross him and he won't think twice about kicking your ass.

Sol is not a kind man. Sexually he's a predator. Once we started to make big bucks, he surrounded himself with male whores. Sol really likes younger men, especially Asians. His idea of a perfect vacation is to knock himself out for a month in Thailand surrounded by young Asian men. I've got no right to criticize, so I just keep my opinions to myself. I didn't care what kind of life Sol led, but I told him that if he paid too much attention to my Ben, I would kill him without so much as taking a breath. I'd heard how these guys like to "recruit" kids, and even though Sol swore that wasn't true, I wasn't about to take any chances—not with my kid.

I love fooling around too, but it's only women for me. I can't believe Sondra never put two and two together. Sometimes I was away for days, just getting some pussy and getting high or drunk. She believed me every time I told her I was going away on business. She never even figured out that I had changed jobs years ago. I had a cover story all ready, but I never even needed it. . . .

. . . "Oh my God. I can't believe it, Sondra. What are you going to do?" There were tears in Connie's eyes, and I couldn't help but start to shake from the enormity of what I was facing.

"I have to get out of there. It's too dangerous for the kids to be living in that environment."

I didn't know exactly what Jack was capable of. I wasn't sure I knew him at all now.

For the next hour, Connie and I schemed. It was just natural that my best friend and I put our heads together to find a solution to my problem. Somehow I knew she could examine my tough situation and find answers for me. She had always been balanced that way, and I respected her for it. I was reluctant to drag her into any danger, but I desperately needed help from someone I could trust completely. In the end, she agreed to find me an apartment—one where Jack couldn't find us—and I decided to hire a moving company that could get us out quickly, when Jack was away on one of his trips. I hated being so secretive, but I was certain that the people Jack worked for didn't like any witnesses.

The next time Jack was home for one of his rare dinners with the family, the mood was somber. Clearly, when it came to choosing between work and family, we came in second. In spite of the rift between us, though, we both tried to make things normal for the kids when we were all together. I had gotten home in time to make a decent dinner, and we looked like the normal American family.

"I almost scored two goals at practice today, Dad," Benjamin said gleefully. "And I nearly got into a fight with Billy Thorn, but the coach broke it up."

"Good job, Bennie," Jack said, playfully tousling Benjamin's shaggy hair. "What about little Cassie?" He turned to our daughter. "How did practice go today?"

"Coach tried me out at goalie today. I stopped six goals," Cassie said, gloating that she had done so much better than her brother. They were both sports-minded kids, and Jack and I had introduced them to a variety of team and individual sports starting when they were very young. Both had come down heavily in favor of soccer as their number one activity.

"Wow, Cassie!" Jack said, sitting down next to his daughter. "I always thought you'd do well as a goalie."

I put a casserole, rolls and a bowl of corn on the table as if ours was the most normal family in the world. In fact, it had been some time since we had shared dinner as a family. I got myself a beer. I didn't offer Jack one—just sat down to my meal. I pulled hard on the cold brew. This wasn't me; I rarely drank, but here I was just wishing I were someplace else. I was so unhappy.

Jack was laughing and joking with the kids most of the time, but at one point he addressed me. "What's up?" he asked.

I made eye contact briefly, then just looked down at my dinner and held onto my beer as if it were a lifeline. Maybe his being away from our home wasn't such a bad thing. When he was here, I felt his presence disabling me, if not psychically, then mentally and emotionally.

I was utterly miserable. In the last few weeks, my level of paranoia had increased dramatically. Every sound of a vehicle outside made me more tense. I kept thinking the drug dealers were

9

trying to make sure I was keeping the organization's big secret. I had never seen one of them personally, but instinct told me they were out there. Maybe I was being overly imaginative—even neurotic. What if there wasn't anybody watching my every move? Or maybe I was being self-delusional. Jack probably hadn't shared details of my investigation with his cohorts. Then again, I didn't really know either way. Jim had said to keep a watchful eye, so I would.

Jack's absences from both the family dinner and our bed were becoming more commonplace. I didn't mind the lack of sex lately; I knew I would feel violated and with no choice but to fake it—which, to be honest, I had been doing for years. Jack had never paid attention to what was going on beneath him, and I doubted I had ever truly had an orgasm with him in the last dozen years. The rift seemed to widen each time I thought about Jack—who he was and who he had become.

Maybe I was to blame. Perhaps it had been my fault that he had gotten himself involved with these people. Maybe I had pushed him out after the kids were born. But then I got to thinking that not all American men who felt neglected by their wives fell into a life of crime. . . .

. . . This act that I had to keep up in front of Sondra and the kids was beginning to wear me down. I loved my kids and always would, but I could have left Sondra behind at any time. Maybe I was scared of what her reaction would be when she found out what was really going on with my life. It had been a huge lie for a long time now. To be honest, I couldn't believe she hadn't gotten the whole picture yet.

She always was smart. Maybe I should have won her over earlier—maybe I still could. She's got to have a price—I could find a way to keep her happy and keep her mouth shut. Making her like me all over again would be good; get her a Mercedes and an AmEx platinum card, let her see the benefits of the money. She looks good in stylish clothes. I should have taken care of it. Sondra was my problem and I needed to work out a strategy. One thing I did know: If I couldn't get her to go along with this, there'd be no room for Sondra in my future. Still, she was the

10

mother of my children, so I figured I'd let things drift along for a while longer before I made long-term plans for me and the kids. . . .

. . . I've thought for a long time about when I really knew something was wrong with Jack and me. Most of it goes back to when Jack traded in his Buick for a BMW and didn't seem to have any car payments. I tested the waters by asking him to buy me a Mercedes. He told me he didn't have that kind of money—that the BMW was a company car that they let him drive as a reward for doing so well at his job. I didn't buy it. I was really suspicious and should have asked him right then what was going on. . . .

. . . Sondra put me under surveillance again, I was pretty sure. A guy was hanging around in a less than subtle way. I bet she had just opened the Yellow Pages and blabbed about my business to a bunch of agencies before picking one. Sondra always had to get quotes before hiring someone for a job—never less than six. It was her way of getting the right people and best value for the money. How many times had I heard her say "Get six quotes Jack"? So now people I didn't know had an inside track on my life. How stupid. If the wrong guy got wind of my stuff, he wouldn't think twice about bringing me down for the rewards the government pays out to get guys like me and the organizations we work for. Best way to deal with this was to send a message to all of them. They probably all know each other, talk to each other, share the risks—so I'd give them a risk to share. If we wasted this PI out in the open, they'd all get the message to stay away from Los Archos, and me in particular. . . .

. . . Finding out Jack's new status in life had been a chance event. My unannounced visit to his office, or to what I thought was his office, along with my suspicions had started everything rolling. That night at dinner, however, I was thankful my kids could see their father in a positive light; I didn't know how long I would be able to keep up that façade for them.

11

I'm worried about the kids playing soccer as they usually do. I am torn between wanting to protect them by keeping them out of public places or letting them play as if everything were normal. If my plan works out, within a month everything will be different. I need to decide if I should stay at my regular job and whether the children should be allowed to go to the same school. I'll speak to Jack through his lawyer and, in the meantime, if I'm lucky, he and his henchmen won't be able to find out where we live. I am so grateful that Connie is handling finding an apartment for me. I need a good divorce lawyer, that's for sure. Whoever I get needs to understand how dangerous this all is. After the divorce, I want to be sure that Jack can't harm me or the children because of what I have learned about his illegal activities. Just thinking about all of this is giving me daily headaches. I'm struggling to stay clear-minded at work, trying not to think about everything that could go wrong in all of this. I've never lived on my own before, and I don't know how to do it with two children who will depend on me for everything. Maybe I'll make an appointment with the doctor for something for these headaches. I've got too much to do to stay in bed. I've got to stay strong, no matter what happens. I have to believe I'll get through this.

Connie had three apartments for me to look at within a couple of days. The first was a second floor walkup in a large complex on Presidential Boulevard with an outdoor pool. I liked the fact that it seemed like a family-friendly environment and the kids would have other children to play with. The second choice was a two and a half bedroom apartment in an old Victorian on Powelton Avenue. It was quaint, but there was no guarantee there would be playmates nearby. The third apartment was just too small. The bedrooms were tiny, and I couldn't imagine fitting my living room furniture into the small space.

In the end, I asked Connie to rent the first apartment in her name. When things settled down, I would put the apartment and utilities in my own name. I didn't want to write Connie a check for the security deposit and first and last month's rent—that would leave a paper trail—so I offered her cash instead. I felt like I was taking part in some covert military operation.

Next came the scary part. Jack had a business trip coming up at the end of next week. That would mean he would leave home on Thursday evening and return on Sunday afternoon. So I had a three-day window to get us out of that house. And it was just a house to me—a pile of bricks rather than a home. I called a lot of moving companies before I found one that was available for the Friday. I also called Jim, the private detective who had carried out the investigation into Jack during July, to tell him where I was moving and check his availability.

"I'm glad you're getting out of there, Sondra," he said. "Everything I know about your husband's dealings tells me they're a dangerous bunch of guys. To be honest, if you had asked me for an opinion, I would have advised you to move right away. Now, I don't want to frighten you, but be really careful till this is done. If there's any more I can do . . . ." His voice trailed off.

I thought he was overreacting a bit, but I knew he meant well, so I said, all in one breath, "Actually, Jim, there may be something you can do. I'd like to hire you again for a week once I move in. I want you to stake out my new apartment to make sure Jack hasn't found it. I went through a lot to keep this apartment a secret." I gave him the new address, and he promised to start beginning Monday of the week after our move. I wanted him to be there longer than a week; I wondered how long I could afford to have him watch our apartment. Certainly it couldn't be indefinitely.

Things were happening so fast. I really wanted to take time off from work to get everything organized, but I didn't want anyone who may be watching to get suspicious. The kids were my main concern. How would they react? Would they want to stay with their dad? Would they resent me? Would they give me a hard time? I just had to hope that they would handle this well. They were just kids; I had to be aware of their emotional needs as well as my own. I prayed they would take my side and help me out once we got moved. Either way, it would be a lonely job.

I find that I have to force myself to smile whenever I talk with someone. I'm so stressed out that nothing seems to get rid of these headaches, and I toss and turn all night. I keep reminding myself to see the doctor, but I don't want him to think I'm a nutcase or something. It's a good thing that Jack's not around much. I don't want sex with him—it would be so difficult to fake nowadays—but he doesn't want me even when he is home. I wonder if my life will ever be normal again and if Jack and his crew will ever let us go. My lawyer, Aaron Sorenson, promised me the papers would be ready to deliver to Jack by the time he returned from his trip. He said he'd serve Jack with the papers himself on Sunday afternoon, just to make sure Jack got them. I don't know if I'm ready for this. I'm doubting my own strength, and a part of me feels like I'm losing my mind going through all of this. But Jim was clear that these aren't the type of people to mess with. He couldn't tell me what evidence he had, but he seemed to have no doubt that they'd kill if it suited them. I refuse to let me or my children be victims of Jack's stupidity.

I managed to squeeze in an appointment with my primary care doctor on Thursday of that week. I told him about my upcoming divorce and that I was moving out. We talked about my headaches and insomnia.

Dr. Wiley was always a nice man, but I never could shake the feeling that he had to get to an important meeting right after seeing me and that he was already late. I felt like he heard the words "headache" and "insomnia" and stopped listening right there.

"A lot of what you're going through, Sondra, will pass once the divorce is settled. If it doesn't, I may have to refer you to a psychiatrist buddy of mine. He's old school but a really good man. You'll like him, I'm sure," Dr. Wiley told me in a matter-of-fact way.

"A psychiatrist? A shrink?" I asked him doubtfully. "Do you think it's that bad?" The thought of going to see a shrink seemed a little extreme to me.

"You never know. Stress can lead to a lot of things that pills just can't cure," he answered almost condescendingly while writing up my notes. "In the meantime, here's a month's worth of Darvon for your headaches and a month's worth of Restoril for insomnia. You should be good to go for a while. Why don't you check back with me in a month or so?"

I weakly took the prescriptions from his hand and nodded. He was out the door before I could ask him any questions about my symptoms or the medications he had prescribed. I wasn't used to taking pills for anything but, if there were no other options, I guessed I'd have to give them a try.

Waiting in line to get my prescription filled was agony. Everyone in front of me appeared to have a tale to tell the pharmacy assistant. Or perhaps it was me who was the problem—there was little joy in me right now. I took a headache pill as soon as they were ready. My head was throbbing, and I couldn't think straight. I had a stack of paperwork to finish at work before picking the kids up at Marge's house. Marge was a wonderful, older woman who took in a lot of the after-school kids from Cassie's and Ben's school.

The Darvon I took for the headache made me feel a little woozy, and I didn't like driving that way, but traffic was light, and I got to work safely. I took the elevator to the third floor. The office was the same as usual. We were in the insurance business, selling insurance to large companies, and nothing much ever changed in this business. I bee-lined it to the sanctuary of my private office, stopping only once to answer one of my newer employee's questions.

Finally, still woozy but without much of a headache, I settled in behind my desk and started at the top of the heap of paperwork. As I reviewed and signed papers, I wondered how long I would be able to keep this job. I knew that Jack's goons would know where I worked. As I dwelt on that I realized what a fool I was. They'd just have to follow me to find my new home. Why had I believed I could stay in Philly and remain invisible? In my current paranoid state, no place seemed completely safe. I shuddered at the thought of finding another job or, worse yet, having no job at all. The new apartment lease was signed, so there was no going back. If I'd been a fool, I would have to live with it. I had to believe Jack wouldn't hurt me or the kids. Maybe the divorce would be best all around. It was time to separate. Time to move on.

15

I almost fell asleep at my desk, presumably because of the side effects of the headache pill. When my assistant, Shelly, knocked on the door, I jolted awake, sending papers flying in all directions. I couldn't believe I had nearly dozed off in the middle of the day.

Shelly was the perfect assistant for me. She was very efficient and made a point of organizing my work so I'd get the most done every time I sat down at the desk. She was always punctual, never had flaky days off, and never complained. I knew she valued her size 8 dress size and worked out regularly to keep trim. Her fitness was demonstrated not only by her well-toned body but her sharp mind also. "Sondra, it's time to pick the kids up at Marge's house. You had nodded off and I didn't want to bother you, but . . . "

"No problem, Shelly. I had this headache, and I just couldn't concentrate," I told her. It would take a while to get used to these pills, I thought.

"You've had a lot of those lately. Didn't you see the doctor?" she asked, obviously concerned. She leaned easily against the door of my office.

"Yeah, he says it's stress and he gave me some pills." I yawned as I spoke. "I think they're making me sleepy."

Shelly checked her watch. "Well, naptime is over. Time to be a mom."

I liked Shelly a lot, I decided, as I said goodbye to her for the day.

Tomorrow was the day they'd start cleaning out the house and moving us into another home. I'd have no choice but to tell the kids that Friday night. I figured we'd camp out in the apartment the first night until we got things organized the next day.

Ben and Cassie were as happy as ever when I picked them up from Marge's house. Marge told me she had given them both a turkey club and sodas, so they shouldn't be hungry right away. I swear she lavishes all of her profit on the goodies she gives the kids; she is so lovely to know.

"You take care, now. I'll see you both tomorrow," she called as we headed for my late-model Ford Taurus. As I got in the car, I wished Jack had gotten me that Mercedes I had asked for before our breakup.

Regardless of the fact the kids had just had a snack, I knew they would not be satisfied with less than a proper dinner. I whipped up some pork chops and potatoes but kept both in the warmer until

Jack came home. I hated having to keep up appearances, pretending that all of our lives wouldn't be turned upside down in the next 24 hours.

In truth, I didn't know what to say to the kids when the time came. They loved their father; I just hoped they understood the danger he had put them in by dealing in a profession that took no prisoners. I had a week and a day to come up with the words I needed to tell my children—that the man they called Dad was a crook and a gangster. I'd come up with something.

Nearly a week went by before we all saw Jack again. He'd stayed away as he had done so often. This time I was privileged with a call to let me know he wanted dinner and a bed that night. I seriously prayed he had no intention that we were going to have sex; my headache would at least serve a purpose for once if he did.

Dinner was uneventful, except that it pained me to hear Jack talk about his "work," knowing he was making it all up. He knew I knew he wasn't working at his old job down at the docks and that I knew what he was doing was illegal. Still, he kept up appearances for the kids—and probably just to drive me crazy.

"Abe and I are making the Delaware River run with some industrial supplies, so I guess I won't see you until late Sunday. Benjie, when you get older, you can take that run with me sometime. Maybe you'll join the business when you're older," he told his son, who was busy wiping the rest of his pork and gravy from his face with the back of his hand.

"What about me, Dad?" said Cassie. "Can I make the boat ride too?"

"Sure Cassie, no problem," Jack responded enthusiastically. . . .

. . . Looking back on that meal I can recall thinking afterwards, Goddammit, I just had to sit through a gut-busting dinner with Sondra looking down her nose at me. All I tried to do was what I felt was right for the kids and her too. Someone was going to supply the drugs these dopeheads wanted, so why not me? I was raised on the docks and there we were taught to look after family first, even if it meant breaking the law. What did the laws have to do with us if we were looking out for ourselves and our own? If you were unloading beef at 3:00 in the morning, why shouldn't some come your way? It's how it was.

Always was and always will be. Getting into the cartel was the best move Sol and me ever made once Pop's business went belly up and UPS picked up the pieces. Why shouldn't the two of us use our knowledge and years of experience to make more money than those college schmoes and city types? They wanted the stuff, and we could get it, so what was Sondra's problem with entrepreneurs like me? . . .

. . . As the meal came to an end, I said to the kids, "Okay, listen up—who's going to help me with the dishes in return for help with homework?" That always worked, and this time it distracted me from getting into a no-win argument with Jack. . . .

. . . Sol called me earlier in the day. He is not a subtle man; I could hear at least two other voices laughing in the room. Probably a ménage à trois in the bedroom. Not that I cared—I just didn't want to hear it. He wanted to know if I knew that we were being investigated by a PI employed by Sondra. Curious how he had heard; leaks on my home life I didn't need. Of course I told him I knew and I said I would take care of it—my way. There'd be no way out for this gumshoe. I smiled to myself at my use of the Bogie style name for a private investigator from the classic movies of the '40s.

These people didn't seem to understand how easy it was for us to reverse the process and tail the detective. We were a huge organization worth billions of dollars. With that kind of money, we could track or find anyone. This guy wouldn't stay hidden from us for long. When we found him, he could reverse his loyalties and work for us, for twice the fee, or die. Either way worked for me. . . .

. . . Both Ben and Cassie helped me clean up the kitchen so we could sit down at the table and do homework. Cassie struggled a little bit with math, and Ben was the worst speller I've ever seen. While Jack dozed before packing his duffel bag for his trip, the three of us finished the homework and shared a bowl of caramel fudge ice cream—a suitable reward, I thought. I wondered how many nights it would be just the three of us, struggling to make ends meet and sharing some ice cream together. I gritted my teeth, quietly seething that Jack was even conning his own kids, making those false promises about taking a trip downriver someday.

I decided to take one of the pills Dr. Wiley gave me for insomnia. While it helped me sleep fairly well, I felt like I was hungover in the morning. A couple of cups of coffee later, I was ready to head to work. Jack had left in the middle of the night without trying anything. I was ashamed, knowing as I now did, that he was off doing something related to his drug business. Maybe he had a whole other business as a front for the real business, in which he was now sailing down the Delaware River with a load of drugs rather than office supplies. Or was he? It had become impossible to separate reality and fiction as Jack spun me his web of lies.

I called in sick to work that Friday and greeted the moving company at my door later that morning. I needed a professional company to move the furniture I wanted to take with us and our personal items. Mostly, I just told them what to pack up and what to leave behind. They were fast and efficient. We were ready to move to the new apartment within three hours. I already had the keys; Connie was so good at getting all this set up for me and the kids, even all the utilities were connected. So it was time to go. Tears filled my eyes as I took a last look around at my marital home of 13 years. The irony of the 13 was not lost on me.

Once we got to the apartment, the men stood around, trying to figure out the best way to get everything upstairs. I noticed one of the movers tapping on his forehead—what I thought was a nervous tic. When he switched to the side of his eye, then below his eye, then below his nose, then tapped his chin, I found myself curious enough to sidle up and ask him, "Are you okay?"

"Oh," he said, as if he wasn't completely aware of what he was doing. "It's EFT. I learned it a few years ago. It helps me relax and see problems better. With all you've got to do after we're gone, you might want to try it!" He seemed amused at his own comments.

I was feeling edgy and was tempted to tell him not to tap himself on my time, as we had a job to do and precious little time to do it in. The guys started unloading the truck, and I stationed myself in the apartment, directing where the boxes and furniture should go. As I hadn't hired them to unpack, the rest of the job was left up to me.

I paid the crew in cash. When they were gone, I suddenly felt vulnerable in my own new home. I hadn't hired Jim to stake out the place until Monday. Rather than drown in my fears, I called Aaron Sorenson on my cell phone.

"You can deliver the papers Sunday night as we planned. I have a PI watching this place for the next week. Do you think I should get a land-line phone?" I asked him.

"I'd hold off on that, Sondra. They're so easy to trace. I've been talking with the DA's office and they're working with the Philadelphia police and the Feds in an attempt to get what they can on these guys. If they get wind that you're the one who turned them in, I don't want them to find you first. Stay out of public places as best you can, okay?"

Chills went up and down my spine as he spoke. "Sure thing, Aaron. Call my cell phone if the DA wants to talk to me or to Jim. He has more on paper against them than I do," I told him. "Say, thanks for delivering the papers Sunday night. That way I can guarantee he'll get them."

"Just stay safe, okay?" he warned. It seemed he had more to say but stopped himself. I knew he was worried about me.

Next I called the apartment office and requested they install an extra deadbolt lock. They gave me an appointment for later that day; I was relieved at how quickly they could take care of it. I unpacked until it was time to pick up the kids at Marge's house. I ran into Connie, who was picking up Brett at the same time.

"How's it going?" she whispered.

I tried my best to smile. "Well, I'm in the new place, so one thing taken care of, another 50 to go," I responded.

Connie and I agreed to meet at the boys' soccer game the following Monday. I piled the kids in the car and headed down 12th Street, making my way by Ridge instead of Vine to our new home as the wide, brightly lit street made it easier for me to keep watch around me. This did nothing for my latest headache, which was going full throttle now.

"Hey, Mom," Cassie said curiously, "aren't we driving away from our house? Are we going somewhere?"

I had steeled myself for that question. Now I had no choice but to say something to them. I pulled into the nearest parking spot and explained to the best of my ability why we had to live somewhere else for now. I had spent sleepless nights trying to figure out the best way to tell them without panicking them too much. In the end I tried to be as calm and as honest as possible about their father's dangerous and illegal drug business in words that they understood, without overdramatizing the events. It was such a hard thing to do. It gave me no joy to tell them that unless we moved to another home, we would be in grave danger.

By the time I finished, Cassie had tears running down her face and Benjamin was just staring at the floor of the car. Being the bearer of bad news is always tough. Being the bearer of bad news about your children's father to your children was even tougher. They were the hardest words I had ever spoken, and my resentment toward Jack for forcing this on me was immeasurable. It started to rain; I took that as a bad omen.

"Does that mean we won't be seeing Dad again?" Cassie sobbed, rubbing her cheeks with the sleeves of her jacket. "Won't he miss us?" Her long blonde hair was stuck to the remaining tears on her face. I could see that Ben was trying hard to be stoic. A moment ago he was a fun-loving 11-year-old. Now he was an 11-year-old with an unbearable truth to shoulder.

"Honey, I don't know what will happen. I just know your dad is playing a very dangerous game that could have gotten us all killed if we had stayed at the house. I know it's going to be hard for you, but right now we have to keep where we're living a secret, and we can't do anything stupid like talk to strangers or walk alone anywhere. Our apartment is secure, so we don't have anything to worry about there or at school. I'm working with the police to catch the bad guys who work with Dad." I hoped they didn't put two and two together and figure out their father would likely go to prison, too.

No such luck. Benjamin came out of his trance and grabbed me by the shoulder from the back seat. "You're not sending Dad to jail. No way." His voice had yet to break so his words, while serious, sounded strident. I could see tears in his eyes.

"Look, guys . . . " I paused. "There is no way I wanted to break this news to you this way—certainly not in the car. But I have had to move fast and take opportunities when they came up. Your dad being away this weekend was the best time to get out of the house. I understand you're upset, and I swear to you both now I will make it up to you just as soon as I can. In the meantime, I am asking you both to please help me. I need your love and support now more than ever. It's the three of us together."

I took this as my cue to start the car back up and get to the apartment complex. When we arrived, I tried to be cheerful. "See? Our new home is close to school and all your activities." Well, that fell flat. I wasn't going to win the Mother of the Year award at this rate.

Up in the apartment, the kids wandered around, sad and confused, mourning over every little displaced thing. Eventually we collectively decided where to put everything, but with very little enthusiasm. I told Cassie she needed to sleep with me until we got a three-bedroom apartment. Normally, she would have pulled a face at this, but this time she said nothing. There was nothing to say, really.

I tried to lighten the atmosphere a little by saying, "There's a pool and a play area in the center of the complex." I prayed the kids would find some new friends in our new home.

Benjamin perked up at the thought of a pool, but Cassie was still silent. Her tears dry, she now seemed to be seething at me for uprooting them from the only home they had ever known. Later, my headache, which never really went away, settled a little bit with one of Dr. Wiley's pills. I didn't like how woozy they made me feel, but I had decided to get used to it.

Connie surprised us by coming over that night with a pizza, which cheered everyone up. An extra pair of hands was just what was needed; the whole place took shape much quicker. By nightfall, the bedrooms and the living room looked fairly good; I just had the kitchen and the bathroom to organize the next day. The kids seemed more settled with Connie there, and they went to bed without incident.

Connie watched me pop another Darvon. "Are those for your headaches?" she asked.

I nodded as I gulped a bit of water to get the pill down. "Dr. Wiley gave me pills for my headache as well as for insomnia. I hate the side effects, but what choice do I have?"

"You know, the staff at the clinic can probably help you without prescribing pills," Connie said.

Connie worked as an office manager at an alternative health clinic on South 15th called Health Alternatives. It was philosophically millions of miles away from my opinions of healthcare and therefore was a subject we rarely talked about. Every once in a while, she dropped hints that the kids or I should go to her clinic, but as I shunned even regular health clinics most of the time,

I wasn't about to venture into the realm of "alternative" health. I could tell she was trying to be careful about the way she brought it up, knowing how I felt about alternative medicine. Connie and I were the best of friends, but when she talked about her clinic, I sometimes just couldn't handle it.

"Like how?" I said, more curious than exasperated this time around.

"Well . . ." she hesitated. She knew it was a touchy subject between us. "For example, we have a guy who does acupuncture for things like this."

I rolled my eyes. "No needles, please."

"Fine. What about one of our energy therapies? I think EFT— Emotional Freedom Technique—could be just right for you, because it's so easy to learn and use at home. It's based on the same principles as acupuncture, but instead of needles, they tap on several of the acupuncture points of your body to improve the flow of energy through the meridian channels. It's good for pain as well as for emotional distress."

EFT? Where had I just heard that? The moving man, I suddenly remembered. "No, thanks," I said, shaking my head. "This will get a lot better once the stress of Sunday is past. I think I'll hold out for a spontaneous cure."

"Listen, Sondra, you are blowing off something that can really help you right away. I know a lot about this—much more than you realize—so please just listen for two or three minutes. Please!"

I could see from the look on Connie's face that she was determined to tell me about this EFT no matter what, so I sighed, perhaps a little too loudly, and let her continue.

"The Emotional Freedom Technique, or EFT, is a method of tapping around certain points on your body. Basic EFT is so straightforward, Sondra! The tapping is simple for anyone to learn, and that's why you really should give it a try. Once you've learned the EFT tapping methods, you can usually complete a full round of them in less than one minute."

"Okay, you have my attention." Honestly, I wasn't really interested, but what else could I say? Connie was just being a very good friend.

"Okay, honey, just give me a minute or two more and you will have more of an idea of how it works. Then I'll drop the subject and we can talk about something else. I promise.

"So . . . the fingertips are the most important tool for EFT tapping. You find the acupressure meridian points on your body with your fingertips. As you tap into your energy system around the points on your body, you hold a thought of what's bothering you. For instance, the toxic thoughts you are having right now about Jack and all the crap surrounding him would be the thought you hold. Make sense so far?"

I knew Connie meant well, and I felt bad that I was wishing she would just shut up about EFT and tapping routines. I couldn't do that to my friend, though, so I listened in silence as Connie continued.

"Before you begin your EFT tapping, you need to recognize the negative thought you are feeling and replace it with a positive thought that we call an affirmation. Try to isolate the type of feeling you are having: guilt, anger or depression. As you tap, you repeat this affirmation. The combination of the thoughts and the tapping will train your mind, emotions and body to clear the negative issues and then use more positive thoughts and energies to achieve balance.

"EFT doesn't have to be perfect, so you don't need to worry that you are performing it correctly or incorrectly. It's very forgiving if you mistap or say your affirmation the wrong way around. Nothing can hurt you with this stuff. Even EFT newcomers can hit the spot right away. While tapping, you can even use music, which I know you love, to help the relaxation process kick in—that would be your choice. You could really benefit from this, today, this minute, with all that's going on in your life, and honey . . . " Connie leaned across and touched my hand gently, "it would take no time at all to make an appointment at our place to see one of our practitioners." Connie leaned back in her chair and said, "But then, it's your choice."

"This is all really interesting, Connie, and I know you are telling me all this to help me, but I am in such a mess I can't see how any of it can help. You never mentioned how it's helped you in the past."

"That's because you were never interested in other forms of healing except the conventional type, so I respected that. But I can tell you, Sondra, EFT has helped me more than you will ever know." At this, Connie lowered her head and began to speak quietly. "When I lost my mom a couple of years ago—remember how I was?"

I nodded sadly and remembered how, when her mother had been killed in a traffic accident, Connie had seemed to fall apart before my eyes. They had been close, and her sudden death had been a massive shock to Connie. Then, I remembered, she seemed to adjust to losing her mom much faster than I would have expected. Thinking back on it, I realized she had picked herself up pretty quickly.

"If it hadn't been for learning EFT, I just know I wouldn't have been able to deal with my grief and carry on with my life so readily. That's my personal experience, Sondra, but I can tell you that after working at the clinic all this time, I have seen that I'm not the only person that it's helped. Now, will you listen for a few more minutes without glazing over?"

I laughed and nodded. Connie resumed her demonstration and explanation and encouraged me to mirror what she was doing. I had to admit that I felt calmer after we had done several rounds of EFT together. But this was all still too new and unconventional for me. I was still skeptical.

"There is a good chance that one of our EFT professionals would be able to see you right away, if you want. Let me know; I can get you in anytime," Connie offered.

"Can you let me sleep on it?" I responded. "I'm still not convinced it's for me."

It was getting late; we said our goodnights and Connie headed for home. I felt bad for rejecting her offer, but I couldn't immediately accept it. All that tapping stuff . . . perhaps it did work, but then perhaps it was just the pills working their magic. I guess that did make me a skeptic.

I fell into bed next to Cassie. I wanted to journal but decided to save it for the morning.

Yesterday was the most difficult for me so far. Having to tell the kids they had to move from the only home they've ever known, and then taking them to their new home only minutes later, was tough—not only on them, but also on me—first having to tell them something so horrendous and then having to leave everything behind. How I found the words to tell them about Jack I just don't know. The words came tumbling out . . . and I watched the expressions on their trusting faces turn from interested to horrified. Jack has stolen their innocence, and I hate him for it. I have just survived my first 24 hours as a single mom. It's been thrust upon me, and I am boiling with rage. But I know I can do this. I have to do it, for all our sakes. The real test will come when Jack finds out. How angry will he get? How desperate will he be to find me? Something tells me now we should have left Philadelphia altogether, but it's all I know, and I'm hoping things will hold together until the police gather enough evidence to arrest Jack and his crew. I despise Jack now. I can't even feel love for him in that melancholy sort of way, where we grieve for the warm feelings we had when we felt life was happy and secure, when trust was implicit and a happy future was a foregone conclusion. All I feel now is betrayed. I have been taken for a trusting fool, and I'm so furious that Jack has put his family's lives on the line just to make an extra dollar. I was always taught it was never okay to break the law, even if doing so didn't hurt anyone. Jack will never understand why I did this, but I don't owe him an explanation. My obligations are to myself and my children now, and I refuse to stray from that. What Jack's doing is wrong, and I'll never be convinced otherwise.

The next day we found our new local market and bought groceries, then unpacked a bit more. By dusk, the apartment was looking in pretty good shape. We had an early dinner and then the three of us sat around and talked about what the future might hold. I also did my best to truthfully answer some very awkward questions from the kids. Cassie wondered aloud if her dad was sad about the change. I told her he didn't know yet.

"He's still on his trip, honey, and the lawyer won't serve him the papers until Sunday night," I explained.

"Will the men that Dad works for come to get us?" she asked.

I wished I knew the truth of that. Everything Jim had told me indicated they didn't like people knowing about their business. I only hoped they didn't guess at what I might know, which after all was only anecdotal from my PI.

"I don't know, honey. I have told your principal a few details, but not everything, and he understands that the school must not let your dad pick you up. You know Mr. Brady will not discuss any of this with anyone. I'll be at your soccer practice as often as possible. Just be sure to always be with someone when you go out. This goes for both of you. You have to be extra careful at the moment. I know, I know," I said holding up my hand to silence poor Cassie as she started to protest. "You have to trust me, honey, and do as I tell you. It will all be fine as long as we take care of each other. I'm going to arrange for Marge to pick you up from soccer practice if I can't get there in time. She doesn't know the whole story; I just told her your dad and I have split up. So you will always have someone with you. Now, don't forget, kids," I said, wrapping my arms around both of them, "if one of us feels down about all this, we have each other to talk to, and we have to do this to help us to feel better. Okay?"

Both kids nodded and Ben said, "Don't worry, Mom. I'll look after you and Cassie now." I smiled down at him. The poor kid had had to grow up so fast, and here he was promising to be our protector. I was choked up and couldn't reply.

"But why would Dad work in such a dangerous business?" Cassie blurted out. "Didn't he know it could hurt us too?" She was getting angry.

"I don't think your dad was thinking right when he got into this business. Nothing about it is right, and I would have thought he would have stayed away from all that," I told her. "Come on, let's change the subject. Why don't we play some games and cheer ourselves up?"

Although there was still a lot to do, the next morning, the first Sunday in our new apartment, we all elected to sleep in. I suggested it to the kids and it came as no surprise that they agreed wholeheartedly.

After lunch, the kids' attitude improved immensely when they saw the swimming pool. Despite the lateness of the year, it was still open, and I let them splash around for a few hours while I organized the kitchen. Ben even met a boy named Kyle, who lived

27

in another building in the complex, and they made plans to get together another day.

I knew Jack had gotten home and Aaron had served him with the divorce papers by the dozens of calls from him on my cell phone that afternoon and evening. When Aaron called, I quickly answered.

"Sondra?"

"Yes, it's me." I could feel myself getting nervous.

"I delivered the papers as he was getting out of the car," Aaron said. "He seemed pretty shocked and didn't say much. I'm guessing he'll have more to say once he has time to process the information."

"Thanks so much, Aaron. Now we wait until his lawyer contacts you, right?" For most of our married life Jack had done everything, even down to controlling the bank accounts and paying the bills. He never let me take care of anything that required even a semblance of responsibility. For the first few years of our marriage, Jack didn't even want me to work—he had me stay home and raise the kids like a dutiful wife. But once they were in school, I didn't have much to do around the house, so I decided to get a job—make the most of my college education. Around that time, Jack's family business was struggling, and we needed the money, so he didn't put up as much of a fight as I expected. And since we were growing apart, he didn't even seem to care that I had my own checking account and retirement account. Having access to my own money sure came in handy now, and I was grateful for it.

Now here I was talking to my lawyer. I was now a free, independently minded single woman. I had a lawyer. I had an apartment. I was a single mom. I was filled with a sense of purpose, of responsibility. Jack would rue the day he inadvertently empowered me.

"That's right. I expect to hear from someone within the week. I'll let you know. Stay strong, Sondra, and keep safe," Aaron said kindly. . . .

. . . I couldn't believe Sondra had me served with divorce papers. I never saw it coming. But then I really hadn't been paying much attention to my home life—well, certainly not since I met Carmen. She was so possessive and so carnal; she was at me every minute of the day. I would have been happy just taking advantage of the fact that she was the boss's sister—she could be really useful as a stepping stone in the business—but the fact that she was so hot for sex was a real plus.

Anyway, I couldn't afford to have my dirty laundry aired in public. And the Brothers would never allow it once they heard about it. So I guessed I'd better get a watch put on Sondra, then wait for a good moment to grab the kids and arrange an "accident" for her after that. I wished I didn't have to, though. I wished I could get her to see it my way instead. You know—"keep your friends close and your enemies closer" and all that. I thought I could get closer to her again, make love to her and get her to lower her guard, but it was too late for that, with her serving me those divorce papers and all. It was obvious she was pissed about the whole situation. Now I had got no choice—got to have that accident arranged. Too bad, but hey, she brought it on herself. . . .

. . . The cell phone started ringing again after I hung up with Aaron. I didn't answer it and instead got the kids' clothes ready for school the next day and sent them to bed. When they were in bed, the phone rang again. This time I picked it up.

"Hello?" I said softly.

Jack's voice was loud, and I heard the TV on in the background. I suspected he'd had a few drinks already, or worse, for all I knew, he'd helped himself to some of what he was dealing. "Sondra, what the hell are you pulling here?"

"I'm doing what's best for me and the children, Jack." I tried to keep my voice calm. "I know the kind of business you're in, and it's just wrong. It's too dangerous. I can't believe you've put us through that."

"I don't know what you're talking about. I've been in the same business for the last 10 years, you know that," he yelled, his voice slurring a bit. How I wished it were the truth.

"Jack, I've had you investigated. I know what kind of work you do, and I don't want to have anything to do with it."

He was silent, but I knew he was still there. With a rage I had never heard in him before, he spat out menacingly, "You cannot do this Sondra. You can't walk away—and sure as hell not with my kids."

"I have, and I will. You don't have the right to say what happens to your kids now that you've almost ruined their lives. You've lied to them. They're upset and confused about what you've done. You've let them down, Jack, and I will never forgive you."

"I want to see you," he said, his tone changing to a pathetic whine. "I miss you so much." It sounded as hollow as the platitude it was. I couldn't believe what I was hearing.

"You should have thought of that when you got into the drug business." I noticed he wasn't denying it, but he wasn't coming across with any information either. I didn't know if telling him what I knew was dangerous or not. Jack was a bad man, but he wouldn't hurt his family, I reasoned.

"Jack," I ventured, "what if you got out?"

"You just don't get out when you're at my level. They'd kill me first," he countered. "Babe, you just can't do this to me. I gotta be able to see the kids," he whined again.

I had heard enough of his lies. "I'm going to hang up now. If you want to see the kids, have your lawyer talk to mine." I hung up and turned off the phone.

On one hand, I feel like a strong, assertive woman; on the other, I am scared as hell. Jack's the source of all my misery and I'm so angry he put his family at risk. We had agreed to be married forever, he and I. How could everything have gone so terribly wrong? Part of me wants to get inside his brain—to see what lured him into the drug business. He was never into using drugs, so what happened? The kids don't need to know all the details of what their father has done yet; they wouldn't understand. And I don't want them to hate their father any more than they do right now. Still, he's ruined more than just his own life with his poor decisions. I, for one, am not going down with the ship!

The next week was so hectic my headaches were almost constant, and I was running out of Dr. Wylie's pills. In between work, picking up the kids from Marge's and talking with the FBI and the U.S. District Attorney's office, who were working in cooperation and claimed to be close to making a series of arrests around the drug operation Jack was working with, I was constantly on the lookout for cars or people that seemed out of place in my life, including Jack. I knew Jim was watching both the school and the apartment, but as a mother I was still nervous about everything.

On Thursday after work, I found my tires slashed. Just knowing they had found my car in the parking garage made my knees go weak and my heart race. I took some deep breaths to calm down, leaning against my car to make sure I remained standing. Once I felt I was back in control, I started to call 911, but hesitated. After all, the police could consider this just another case of vandalism—hardly a priority. Then I would need to explain what was going on in my life, and then there would be forms to fill out, then more time wasted—time I didn't have. So I just called a tow truck and took a taxi in time to pick up the kids.

"What's with the taxi, Mom?" Benjamin said as we left Marge's house.

"I just had some car trouble," I told him. "It should be fixed by tomorrow." There was no point in sharing my suspicions with him. . . .

. . . Sondra needed to be scared off. I had to let her know I was close. It was worth sending her a clear message that she can't fight me and the organization. We're too powerful. If the tires on her car got slashed, she would know for sure it was a warning from me. It had a certain menace to it. It sort of says, well it was your tires today; what could we slash tomorrow? Yeah, that would be clear enough even for Sondra to understand what would happen if she didn't behave the way she should. If I could get her back on track with one big fright that should do it. Find the weak spot and grind your heel into it. That's what slashing her tires would represent. Do as you are told, behave or it would be that pretty face next.

If she had just kept her nose out of where it didn't belong, none of this would have happened. I could have been like all the other guys in the business, with a wife at home with the kids and a mistress that you never own up to but everybody knows you've got. She could have had everything: money, cars, clothes and paradise vacations any time she wanted. All she had to do was bring up the kids

31

right, and then later maybe my son could have joined the firm. That was my mistake; maybe I should have outlined the plan a bit clearer. Let her see more of the money than I did. What else is life about? The money and what it can buy you. In my game, life's one big shopping mall where you can have it all. . . .

. . . When we arrived at the apartment building, I saw Jim waving me over to his car. I paid the driver and had the kids stand just outside the door of the building while I walked over to talk to him.

"Any news, Jim?"

"Did the school call you, Mrs. Ackerman?"

"No, they didn't, not at work or on my cell. Why?" I felt that familiar knot in my stomach as he continued.

"I was staking out the school for you. Your husband showed up. But they called the authorities, and he was escorted out of the building," he reported. "He didn't look like a very happy man."

"My tires were slashed today," I told him. "Sometime while I was at work. I'm guessing there's some kind of connection between the two occurrences."

"Sorry to hear that," he said, taking the time to write down the new information. "Probably not a random event."

"I don't think so."

"I'll check back with you if anything else happens," he told me. "I'm taking off for the night."

"Thanks a lot. You're doing great." I gave him a wave and headed into the building with the kids.

The next day was Friday, and Ben had a soccer game. Cassie's games were on Saturday morning. I took off from work a couple of hours early and met Connie in the stands at the soccer field. My car had been fixed and had been delivered to my office in good condition. The four new winter tires had relieved me of nearly three hundred dollars. I didn't realize protecting myself was going to be so expensive.

"I've missed you," Connie said. "I'm guessing you've been busy."

I filled her in on the week's events. "Jack didn't call me after that Sunday night, but he's been pushing the limits and trying to see the kids already." It felt good to vent my frustration about the whole mess.

"Are the kids safe?" Connie asked anxiously.

I shrugged. "They're as safe as I can make them. They go from one thing to the next throughout the day and they're never alone. They are taking all of this seriously, but they still miss Jack, even after everything he's done."

"That's normal," she commented. "It's going to be worse if he goes to prison."

"Don't remind me," I said quietly, bowing my head.

The teams came out to warm up and everyone cheered. The boys from both teams took turns kicking balls toward the goal and ran laps up and down the field. After that our boys' team did some sideways running, backwards skipping and calf warm ups. The coach certainly prepared them to win. Then the coach began a tapping routine with the team. I pointed it out to Connie.

"The coach teaches EFT to all his teams. It really helps the players focus. I guess Ben will learn it before you, considering how stubborn you're being," Connie remarked with a smile.

I swallowed my cynicism, particularly since I was desperate to find something that would help my headaches. "Well, if these headaches don't improve, I may take you up on your offer to see an EFT practitioner. I've been miserable."

"Anytime," Connie said, patting my hand. "While we're waiting for the game to start, can I tell you another EFT success story? Do you mind? I promise I'll keep it short."

"Of course I don't mind, Connie. As long as you don't proselytize, I'm all ears."

"No worries; I don't want to push it on you. I just want to keep reminding you that you're not alone," Connie said gently. "Anyway," she began brightly, in an effort to raise my spirits, I suppose, "I don't know if you know Moira McKinley—do you? I often run into her at the gym; we've gotten quite friendly."

I nodded. I knew Moira vaguely; her son was the same age as Ben and Brett.

Connie continued, "Well, Moira is really super fit—in fact, I'm quite envious of her, to be honest. But a little while ago, each time I talked with her, she kept complaining of generalized aches and pains and tiredness. We talked about other things, of course, but inevitably the talk would get around to how she had this unspecific pain or was just feeling 'blah' and she didn't know why. So this normally optimistic and energetic woman, who always seemed so healthy, just wasn't herself. It was really noticeable how different she was.

"I knew that Moira had recently started a new job. She'd been so excited about it. It was the type of work she was familiar with, but it was more of a senior position, and she was looking forward to the challenge. She's a perfectionist, and she wanted to do her very best at her new job. But her first assignment turned into something of a nightmare. She didn't expect to have such pressure put on her to come up with results so quickly. She was enjoying the job, but she wasn't familiar with the material she really needed to get a handle on. That upset her and made her worry. All she kept saying over and over again was, 'I'm just making a mess of it. I thought it would be easy, but it's really not.'

"So I told her about EFT and how it could help her and demonstrated the tapping routine to her."

Connie was looking at me, waiting for a reaction, I presumed. Secretly, and I suppose a bit unkindly, I figured that Moira must have thought Connie looked pretty weird sitting there tapping all over her head and body. I tried hard to listen to Connie as she went on with her story with her usual energetic enthusiasm, but I was finding it difficult to concentrate today. I felt so stressed and unhappy.

When Connie saw I was not going to comment she continued, "I tried to point out to Moira that her mind was set on these aches and pains being the problem, that as far as she was concerned they were the reason she was struggling to find new and helpful material for her project; they were preventing her from making a success of her new job; they were ruining her prospects! 'You are stressed,' I said to her, as if she needed to be told, but sometimes it does help to hear it said out loud. 'Break the problem into chunks you can deal with. You can always ask for help. . . . '

"All my advice seemed to be falling on deaf ears. Just like you, Sondra, Moira couldn't see how all that tapping was going to make her feel better," Connie said. "But I kept going with my tapping demonstration as I sat there with her. I think she thought I was nuts!"

"Nuts? I would think so, Connie. Be truthful, now—it's not as if this is an everyday thing you're doing. But go on. I think I can see where you're going with it."

"Okay. I just kept showing her the tapping, simple as that. There's nothing mysterious about it. I kept talking her through it, and gradually I felt like I was making just a little bit of a breakthrough. A really small one, but at least I'd gotten her attention." Connie smiled triumphantly at the memory.

"Sure, she was as skeptical as you are now, Sondra. But at least she was starting to take it a bit more seriously. So I said to her, 'I think that deep down you know the problem is that you're afraid of letting people down and not doing a good job. What I think you need to do is acknowledge that thought and realize that that's where the aches and pains started from.' But she just pooh-poohed me and said that once she got rid of the aches and pains, she'd be able to concentrate better on her job.

"I was so disappointed when she said that, Sondra. She looked worn out and I could tell she was getting irritated with me, but I was sure she picked up some of what I had shown her. I thought I'd better go home then and give her some space so she could either work some more or continue to panic about it. I phoned her the next day and she asked me to come by. I found her even more stressed. Instead of working on her project, she'd used her exhaustion as an excuse to take a three-hour nap. That was a whole afternoon of her already tight timeline for the project wasted. Before I could say anything, she said, 'Yes, I know, I know! I look terrible. I certainly feel terrible, so look—just show me this tapping routine again, will you? This time I promise I'll listen!'

"Of course I did, and when we were done, I left her with a hug and my positive thoughts and energy."

I almost rolled my eyes in exasperation. What the hell were 'positive thoughts and energy' anyway? My lovely Connie, she was always so fired up about things she really believed in, and she so believed in this stuff. Still . . . perhaps there was something to it after all. Oh, I don't know, I thought wearily, perhaps I should give it a try. What did I have to lose? Connie spoke again, pulling me out of my reverie.

"D'you know what, Sondra? The next week, she called me, and she was *much* brighter. She was almost shouting into the phone. 'I've done it! I've broken through the wall, and this project's not so hard after all!' She sounded so proud of herself! 'That's just great, Moira. What happened?' I asked her.

"She explained how she had taken a few minutes one evening to center and focus on the now of her situation and really see what was important. Then she tried some tapping. She said she came up with a great setup statement that really resonated with her. She told me that doing the rounds of tapping made her feel really calm, and this led her to feeling relaxed about the challenges of her new job. The project was still there, and it still needed to be completed, but she affirmed to herself that she was capable of doing it and that when she had finished each component, she would be happy and proud of the result. Then, every time she felt herself panic or get overwhelmed, she would perform the EFT tapping routine again. And guess what, Sondra? She finished her project. I was so happy for her. So how's that for a success story?"

Well, I had to agree with Connie. It was a pretty good story to tell someone like me who was still making up her mind about EFT.

The game got under way and ended up being an exciting one. Cassie, who had been attending her chess club meeting in the school, joined us shortly after the game started and we screamed our lungs out. Brett was clearly the star and made two goals. Benjamin had one assist. After the game, we took them all out for ice cream at the Italian Gelateria on South 13th to celebrate the win. We ordered ice creams and sodas all around for the kids, and Connie insisted that it was her treat. Connie decided to have some tiramisu, and I settled for a double espresso. Connie and the kids were all lighthearted and enjoying the moment, and I liked the fact that everything at least appeared ordinary. I, however, felt persecuted. I noted how these little shots of black coffee were becoming as important to me as Dr. Wiley's drugs.

It was near dusk when we pulled up to our apartment building. Ben was so wound up after the excitement of winning the game, he was almost bouncing off the walls of the car.

I glanced over to where Jim normally did his surveillance on the apartment and was surprised to see his car still there. I told the kids to stay in the car while I went to check out why he wasn't gone yet. It crossed my mind that maybe he was just waiting to make sure we got home safely; I figured that would be typical of him. . . .

. . . You can't believe the stupidity of some people. Frank offered this Pruitt guy, the private investigator, five big ones to feed Sondra phony information and then to lure her into a

36

trap. He said no. Frank messed him up real bad to get him to change his mind. All I can say is this guy must have been tortured by pros at some time in his life. Maybe he was a soldier who got captured, I don't know what, but he still said no. That left me in a bind; I'd have to kill him, but it'd be his own fault. What is it about heroes? Are they are just stupid, with all their causes and the like? There is only one person you should look out for, apart from your kids, and that's number one—yourself. It doesn't make any sense to get yourself killed for a woman who fished you out of the Yellow Pages. For Chrissakes, what was wrong with the man's mental capacity? I know Frank, and I know that when he beats you, you are going to be in a world of hurt. How come Pruitt didn't get the message? Frank left him half dead. Finishing him almost seemed like a humane act. . . .

. . . It was just light enough to see inside the vehicle. Instead of the empty seat I expected to see, there was a body slumped over toward the passenger side. Jim's dark curly hair was just visible up against the passenger side door—and I could see what looked like a smear of blood on the driver's side window.

I stepped back in horror and suppressed the urge to scream. This couldn't be happening, I thought. I wanted to open the door to see if he was still alive, but instead I pulled my cell phone out of my purse and dialed 911. I still don't remember what I told them.

I got back to the kids as fast as my shaking legs would carry me and hustled them into the apartment. I told them that something bad had happened to Mr. Pruitt. The kids raced upstairs, their eyes wide with panic. I ordered them to stay put and went back outside just as the first police car arrived.

I stood back while the officers opened the car door. I overheard one of them say that the victim was dead. Immediately they started to cordon off the area to restrict access to the vehicle. I realized I was watching police procedure in response to a murder unwind first hand. Another police car arrived and two more officers got out. I stepped forward and told them it was me who had made the emergency call.

They brought me closer, past the police tape. "How did you find the victim, ma'am?" one of the officers asked me, holding a metal clipboard and pen.

I explained that Jim was a private investigator I had hired and that he was making sure my estranged husband, who was heavy into drug trafficking, didn't find my apartment.

"How long have you known the victim?"

I told him I'd known Jim about three or four months, and I rambled on about how Jim had uncovered this drug trafficking "business" that my estranged husband was involved in.

"So you think someone from this drug trafficking group had something to do with the victim's death, ma'am?" the officer asked me.

I was so tired, scared and sad at that point that I just wanted to refer them to the narcotics unit, as the officers and detectives there knew the story. I pulled out Detective Dermot Murphy's card and handed it to him. "He's in charge of the case," I explained. "He'll want to know all about this." I hoped the officer was finishing up his questioning; my head was throbbing, and the familiar pressure was amassing behind my eyes.

"One more thing, ma'am," the officer said hesitantly. "Do you think you could manage to ID the victim before we move him to the morgue? I know this is hard. . . ."

"Sure," I sighed. I wondered how much deeper all of this would go before my life was normal again. "What do I have to do?"

"Step this way," he told me and led me by the elbow toward the passenger side of Jim's vehicle. He shone a flashlight on the side of the victim's face. There was no question it was Jim. I nodded and turned away, then vomited.

The officer who had been interviewing me promised he'd call Dermot Murphy as soon as he could and took down my address and cell phone number. "You'll be asked to make a formal statement. You okay with that?"

"Yes." I said.

"Okay. In the meantime, will you be safe, ma'am?" He looked at me compassionately. "We don't have the manpower to protect everyone, but we can have a cruiser go by more frequently if that would help."

"Thanks." I shook his hand, so weary now that I could have fallen asleep in the stairwell of the apartment. "I'll stay in contact if anything else happens." I should have told him about my tires, but that was nothing compared to what had happened to Jim.

The kids were agitated and full of questions when I got up to the apartment; I couldn't think of anything to tell them except for the truth. First, though, I needed a moment to myself. They kept up their questions through the bathroom door while I washed my face and rinsed my mouth out. Once I felt a bit better, I opened the door.

"Kids," I blurted out, "I told you this would be dangerous. Maybe we want to think about moving a long ways from here for a few months. I don't know when it will get better."

"We don't want to move, Mom," Benjamin said, his voice rising as he struggled to control his tears. He hugged me as though he were a tiny boy again and held on to me tightly. I could feel the heat of his body flattened against mine. Poor Ben, he was so frightened. He pulled away from me then, and stood in front of me. He said quietly, "I'm not scared of those horrible people, Mom. We promise we'll be careful."

Cassie was more introspective. She looked at me with sad eyes. My heart lurched when she asked, "Mom, did Dad kill that private investigator?"

I shook my head. "No, I'm sure he didn't do it himself. But he works with the people who probably did." I let out a deep breath and said, "That means Dad knows where we live, so you won't be able to play outside by yourselves anymore."

Cassie gave me a big hug. "We understand, Mom. You're just trying to do the right thing." Darling Cassie, trying to put a brave face on things to help me feel better. This was all so much for them to cope with.

"What if that kid, Kyle, wants to play with me? Can we play at each other's apartments?" Ben asked fervently. He had played with his new friend at the apartment complex on several occasions, and I didn't want him to lose that friendship.

"Of course, Ben. We'll work something out. Don't worry," I answered.

It took a while to get the kids to bed. They had had such a traumatic time, but what little fighters they were turning out to be.

The next day was Cassie's soccer game, and I hoped Connie could sit with me in the stands. I just didn't feel safe alone anymore.

I can't help but dwell on Jim and the people in his life he left behind. Surely they knew he worked

39

in a dangerous profession, but it's shocking to think that he was most likely killed because he was helping me. I don't feel safe going to his funeral, but I will send some flowers. When I made the decision to do the right thing and stop Jack and his thugs from drug trafficking, I never expected someone I hired—an acquaintance—would get killed over it. Everything seems so black and futile now. I can only hope that the police and the Feds move fast in getting these guys off the street. I just hope they're trying to send a message and that someone else isn't next on the list. I'm scared for my own safety, I'm scared for my children, and I'm scared for anyone who knows me. Damn Jack and his greed. I'm already over the fact that the man I thought I married isn't the guy I know now. I wonder how long he's been lying to me and for how long I have been so foolish as to believe in him. I do know I'm not hiring another private investigator. I couldn't stand the thought of having another person killed trying to protect me and my family.

I felt my stomach churn. I took a gulp of water. I was too afraid to take a sleeping pill but felt the overwhelming need to close my eyes and get some rest. As I lay my head on my pillow, rivulets of tears slipped from the corners of my eyes.

Chapter 2

The weather had cooled down quite a bit over the past few days, and Connie and Brett were bundled up in fleece jackets. Connie climbed the stands to where I was sitting with Benjamin. Ben had wanted to play with Brett on some playground equipment next to the field, but I wouldn't let him out of my sight. He started to fuss until he saw the serious look in my eye.

I half watched the game while I filled Connie in on the events of the previous night. What a lot of news I had to impart. First I told her how I found my car's tires slashed and how vulnerable that had made me feel. Then I told her about the murder of Jim Pruitt. I started crying as the words left my lips, remembering the sight of Jim's body slumped in the car.

"You mean, the guy you hired to keep you safe was killed in cold blood in front of your apartment building?" Connie blurted out, aghast at the news. "How did he die?"

"They didn't say. I saw some blood splattered on the driver's side window and around the dashboard. It was getting dark, so I'm not sure I could see everything; I think he had a hole in the top of his head. It was just awful and so barbaric," I told her. "Then the police asked me to identify the body. You cannot know how traumatizing it is to have to do that, especially for someone you had just talked to. The officer who called it in requested an APB on Jack; they're pretty sure he's the prime suspect."

"Oh my God! Sounds like he was probably shot," she murmured. "Are you sure it was Jack or the guys he works with who did it?" Connie asked. She was still clearly shocked by what I had told her.

"That's what the police think, and I think they're right. I mean, Jim was at my apartment on surveillance when he was killed. What am I supposed to think? That it was a random event?" I wiped the tears from my cheek with a tissue.

Connie shook her head in amazement. "I think you should pack up and move to another state—go into the witness protection program or something. It's obvious you can't stay in Philly."

"Connie," I said, "this will all be over soon. The cops will arrest everyone involved in the ring, and they'll be behind bars. I can handle a few more weeks." I didn't know if I was reassuring her or myself by that time.

"Let's just hope that's all it takes," Connie added. "You'd think they'd give a case like this some priority."

Cassie did well in her game. She blocked several goals and their team won by a single point. I gathered her up shortly after the game ended and the five of us walked to the parking lot together.

"You know if you need anything, just call," Connie told me.

"I appreciate that," I answered, giving her a tight hug laced with uncertainty.

I headed home with my kids. . . .

. . . I was truly pissed off when I went into our home. Well, of course it was clear it wasn't actually our home anymore, as over half the furniture was gone. That included the bed from our bedroom. Maybe she took it as a memory of happy days—who knew with Sondra? One thing was certain: I needed to find her, and fast. Sondra is Philly born and bred, so I figured it didn't occur to her to move anywhere else. She didn't know what kind of organization I worked in, that with our resources, finding her would be easy if she stayed in town.

As soon as Frank was available I had him watch the kids' school and follow them to their new place. It was too easy. I had her new address within two days. It was just so like Sondra to believe she could disappear and stay in Philly at the same time.

I gave Frank the job of keeping track of her. He was a smooth guinea, and I took him up on his offer to help me out with Sondra. I told him if he could seduce her along the way, all the better, because if it came to a showdown in the courts, what better way to trash a woman's rep than to show her to be a bed-hopping whore? Sondra was not about to get the better of me.

Frank moved fast; within a day he got an apartment in the same building. Everyone has a price, and the complex manager's price was one big one. With a thousand bucks lining his pocket, that fresh-faced kid sure didn't ask any questions. He accepted the references without a second glance.

Frank was scheming; he had a large pool of guys on hand to make use of. Frank knew this was his priority job until I said otherwise. All I had to do was leave him to it. . . .

. . . The apartment that I walked into was nothing like the one I had left a couple of hours before. In spite of all the security in the apartment complex, someone had gotten in and ransacked the place. Bookshelves were overturned. Papers were everywhere, including my financial records. Ben and Cassie stood motionless in the doorway. I called the police before I let the kids touch anything. Hitting 911 on the phone keypad was happening with an unwanted and sickening regularity right now. Would it ever stop?

While we waited for the officers to arrive, I dialed Jack's cell phone but got his voicemail. By the time I got through listening to his voice giving the outgoing message, I was mad as hell.

"You and your goons will leave me and my family alone! We have nothing to do with the police or your business, so just make them go away, Jack, or you'll never see the kids again," I shouted, then snapped the phone shut.

Ben, careful not to touch anything, just wandered around in a daze. Cassie sat down on the only chair left upright, in the kitchen, and was desperately trying not to cry. Finally, the police rang the doorbell and I buzzed them up.

These were different officers from the night before. One was a rookie with a short buzzcut, and the other was tall and had red hair and a short red moustache.

I explained the complex issues associated with the break-in to the two officers, including the murder of the previous night and the collaboration with Detective Murphy. Both had heard about the murder. They looked around, paying special attention to the areas that had sustained the greatest damage, which were basically my papers.

"Did you keep any important information related to the drug operation here?" the younger cop asked me.

43

"No, nothing," I affirmed.

"Anything taken that you can tell?" the same cop asked.

"Not that I can tell," I told him. "Can I start cleaning this up?"

"Not just yet. We'll need to have a forensics team go over the place before you can come back in. I'm sure you understand. . . ." he reeled off with ease. "Did Detective Murphy give you any idea of when this will all be over with?"

"Not really. He's gathering information from his sources, I guess," I said. "I hope it ends soon."

"It's possible we could talk to the Feds about hiding your family until this is over with, but it really should be your decision," the officer explained.

"I told the other officer yesterday that I think we'll hold out a little longer," I said firmly.

The officers were quickly joined by a forensics team; they dusted for prints, studied the damage and took pictures and a page or two of notes. Once they were gone, the kids and I started to clean up the mess. One kitchen chair was irrevocably broken, but it didn't look like anything was missing, including my journal, which was tucked underneath my mattress. I couldn't shake the feeling that the intruders were, in fact, looking for something but as I kept no data on the drug ring at home, they likely went away empty-handed. By the time I was done putting the apartment back together, my seething anger had worked itself out and I was just plain tired.

We ordered pizza that night and watched an old Disney movie on TV. The kids were tired after all the cleaning they had done, so I sent them to bed early and just lay on the couch, wondering what calamity was going to happen next. Once again tears welled up; I was tense like I had never been before in my life.

I knew that my anxiety was running high when I caught myself checking the deadbolt for a fourth time before I went to bed. It seemed these thugs could get away with anything they wanted to, and I felt helpless and scared. I'd never been depressed before, but that night marked a low point for me—one that I wasn't able to shake in the coming days. My life was in a shambles. I was on autopilot now, always on the lookout for the "bad guys" without really knowing who they were. I actually started entertaining the idea of seeing a psychiatrist. I promised myself that if I didn't feel any better in a week, I'd make an appointment to see a shrink. I certainly couldn't function much longer the way things were going.

The next week was relatively uneventful. Detective Murphy stopped by my office on Tuesday to give me an update on the investigation. While things were going too slowly for my taste, at least he took the time to update me every once in a while, and I appreciated it.

"It sounds like these guys are really putting the squeeze on you. It's too bad about Pruitt," he said, sitting on the edge of the chair across from my desk. Detective Murphy always wore plain clothing but had a dark gray trench coat on that screamed "detective."

"I know you can't guarantee these things, but how long will it be until you arrest these guys?" I felt I was owed the courtesy of being somewhat in the loop, even though I was just a layperson.

He rubbed his chin as if doing calculations in his head. "See, we've got some people on deep cover and they haven't come up for air for a while to give us all the pertinent information. As soon as they surface, we'll get the warrants ready."

"What if they don't turn up?" I asked heatedly. "What if they're dead, too?"

"They're not dead; that much I do know, ma'am. They're just doing their job. We just need to be patient," he said kindly.

"I think it's too late for Jim Pruitt to be patient," I retorted.

"I'm really sorry, ma'am," he said. "We'll do the best we can. If things get heated, we can always resort to the witness protection program."

"I'll let you know when I'm that desperate," I said as I showed him out.

With no more solid information than I had before talking with Detective Murphy, my spirits sank even further. That day, like every other day that week, I operated in a trance, doing only what I had to do and avoiding anything that took too much effort. I was still wracked with headaches, and my work volume was steadily going down. Fortunately, as the manager, I could push off much of the work onto some of my subordinates, and no one was complaining yet.

Shelly, my assistant, was a real doll. She made sure only the important things crossed my desk, and every afternoon she'd go to the nearby coffee shop and bring something back to brighten my mood. While I sincerely appreciated her efforts, I felt like "dead man walking" for most of every day.

By Friday, I broke down and finally called Dr. Wiley for the name and number of the psychiatrist he had mentioned. I called the psychiatrist's office and made an appointment. He worked in the clinic I went to for all my medical care. I didn't know him personally, but I didn't care by that point. Any port in a storm would help me now, I reasoned. Connie tried one more time to get me to do EFT, but I told her I wasn't ready to take on anything I didn't understand yet.

The psychiatrist had an opening the following Tuesday. By that time I felt like a complete wreck. I was watching my kids like a paranoid mother bird, I was suffering from nearly intractable headaches and I was seeing "assassins" on every streetcorner. My sleep patterns were disturbed despite the sleeping pills Dr. Wylie gave me, and I was so depressed that every step was an effort.

Dr. Salem Richardson's office was tucked in a quiet corner of the large building, and I almost walked right by it because of the medical items stored on either side of his door in the wide hallway.

There was no secretary, just a beige and brown waiting room with a dark brown love seat, two table lamps and a couple of sturdy chairs. A water cooler and some paper cups sat in one corner of the room. I drank some water, threw away the cup and sat down on the love seat, expecting I just needed to wait.

I checked my watch; I was right on time. I had never seen a psychiatrist before, and the part of me that wasn't desperate for some help was simply curious about the experience. A few minutes after I checked my watch, Dr. Richardson stepped out and waved me over.

"Sorry to be late. Come inside. You're Sondra Ackerman?" Dr. Richardson was short, with a little paunch. He wore a well-worn brown tweed jacket and baggy pants. Graying at the temples and in need of a good haircut, he had to be no more than 50 years old, although I didn't consider myself a good judge of that kind of thing.

He ushered me into his inner office. Dr. Richardson had a huge oak desk and a black leather chair turned away from the desk so as to face a dark brown couch, which matched the love seat in the waiting room, and a comfortable chair next to it. There were windows behind the desk, but he had thick, beige striped curtains covering them. The only light in the room came from the lamps on either side of the couch.

The doctor motioned for me to have a seat. "I'm sorry, I forgot to have you fill out the forms while you were out there. Perhaps you could take a moment when we're finished?"

I nodded as he passed the forms to me.

Dr. Richardson sat down in his leather chair. "I didn't get a sense of why you're here when you made the appointment, so you'll have to start at the beginning." He had an easy way of talking; I could see why he was in this business.

I sighed and looked at the floor for a few seconds. Where to begin? "Well, I guess I should start by saying I'm going through a divorce." That sounded stupid, but I had to start somewhere, I guessed. I wondered how many times patients started a new session with exactly the same words.

"An amicable one, or are there troubles with the separation?" he asked calmly.

"It's . . . uh . . . complicated. It's definitely not amicable. Far from it, in fact," I told him.

"Let's start by talking about your divorce and we'll go from there," he said. This required a massive leap of faith on my part, to tell my story to a man I knew nothing about and who hadn't even told me what path the therapy was going to take. He seemed nice, though, and I'm sure that he meant well. He looked up from his notepad expectantly, and his kindness shone through at that moment. Something told me we were going to get along all right.

I didn't know exactly what to tell him about Jack, so essentially I told him the truth— how I had become suspicious about him and had hired a private detective to look into his activities a few months ago. I told him that the private detective was now dead, thanks to me.

"My husband is near the top of a group of people who traffic in drugs up and down the coast. He has a fake company that operates near the Delaware River," I finally blurted out. "I couldn't take the pressure of his illegal activities, so I arranged to hide in an apartment on the other side of the city and filed for divorce."

"That's a bold move. Did you contact the police narcotics unit?" he asked me, with the same dispassionate voice he had been using so far. I wondered if he had training in talking that way—as though everything you were saying was important but had the same value as everything else you said.

47

I nodded. "I started getting what I think are stress headaches right around the time we moved, and my sleep went into the gutter. My doctor gave me some pills, but they're not really working."

"Any other symptoms?" he asked me smoothly. I watched him make a few notes, probably about the medication I was taking.

That's when I gave him the details about Jim Pruitt's murder, and my tires being slashed, and my apartment getting trashed. "I've been getting more depressed with each passing day. I live in constant fear that these people will do something to my children, and it seems like everything I need to do takes an overwhelming effort." As I talked, I imagined a small snowball rolling downhill, starting slowly at first, and then picking up enormous speed and growing in size with each word I uttered.

"Tell me about your depression," he requested, scribbling something on his notepad.

I thought for a second and realized he might not think this was really depression at all. "Well, I'm not sure that's what it is, but . . . it started about two weeks ago. I feel tired all the time, and like I can't get up the nerve to do anything. I'm constantly feeling guilty about what this is doing to my kids and about what happened to Jim. I mean . . . if it weren't for me, he'd be alive right now."

"Any suicidal thoughts?" he asked.

"No, I'm afraid I'm going to die. My nerves are shot, and it's more like I can't go on anymore," I rambled, not knowing what he really wanted. I had never tried to explain myself to a psychiatrist before; I was flying by the seat of my pants.

"How about self harm?" His pen was poised.

I shook my head. "No. Nothing like that."

Dr. Richardson scribbled for a few more minutes while I sat there stupidly, trying not to see what he was writing down. Finally, he set his pen down. "Well, Mrs. Ackerman, I think you have a great many reasons to feel depressed, anxious and completely out of sorts. Your life is very well in danger and any logical person would feel exactly the way you feel."

I stared at him. "Does that mean you can't help me?" Just my luck; even a psychiatrist can't help me, I thought.

"Not with any pills, although medication for anxiety would probably be a good idea," he admitted. "I'd suggest you keep working with the police and come back to talk to me once a week until this is over with. Just talking about your issues will help bring about a resolution of them. You'll feel better, I promise."

I hadn't planned on seeing a shrink on a regular basis, and I wasn't exactly sure it was going to help. Maybe he was right, I reasoned. What did I know, anyway? "Uh . . . I can come back next week," I said, not knowing what else to say.

He wrestled with his calendar before peering at it intensely. "How about a week from today at the same time?"

"That sounds good," I said, making a mental note of the date and time. Something told me this wasn't going to be much help, but my insurance covered several sessions a year, so I thought I'd give it a try. What did I have to lose?

"We still have a few minutes," he noted. "I'd like to know what you're doing to stay safe."

I told him about the extra patrols around my apartment, the deadbolt lock and the fact that my children were never alone, even at sporting events and while playing.

"What about times you're personally alone?" he prompted me.

I looked away. "Well . . . uh . . . I'm not alone much, and I just don't think my husband's group would do me in. I think all of these things were done so far to scare me. They know I don't know much of anything anyway."

"Well, I'm still concerned," he said, trying to make eye contact with me again. "Can you make sure you're with other people as much as possible?"

I nodded. "I'll do my best." I felt like I was a 3-year-old with an overprotective father.

In the next few minutes, the doctor gave me a prescription for some Xanax for my anxiety. "Take one or two every eight hours as needed," he said.

After I had tucked the prescription away, Dr. Richardson ushered me to the door, and I found my way out of the vast building. I didn't remember until later that I forgot to fill out his forms. I knew he was right about the risk of my being alone, since these goons didn't seem to be afraid of killing off whoever was in their way. I promised myself to be more careful.

That evening, Connie showed up at the kids' soccer practice. We could see Cassie's field from where we were sitting and were in a good position to watch both Brett and Benjamin practicing.

"How did the appointment with the psychiatrist go?" Connie asked me, pulling her lawn chair up next to mine. It was a cool fall night and the kids were having a great time.

I shrugged. "He's a nice man. He gave me a prescription for some more pills to keep my anxiety down. I think I'll get it filled, but I doubt I'll take any."

"I'll say it one more time," Connie said in a motherly tone. "EFT at my clinic would be much better for you. You've been through so much."

"Consider it heard," I said, brushing it off. "EFT—I never even heard of anyone using it before—well, except for a moving man and the stories you've told me. I'll keep thinking about it, but I'll stick with my traditional medicine for now, thank you."

"I can get you an appointment anytime you want," Connie said simply, her eyes on the soccer field.

"I'll remember that," I told her. I appreciated her caring attitude toward me, however displaced it was.

We took the kids out for ice cream after practice, then I gathered my two and headed for home, stopping on the way to pick up a few things at the grocery store. As I pushed the cart up and down the aisles, I thought how buying groceries was such a normal, everyday event. I wondered how it was that I was doing this right now, sauntering past the shelves, looking like any other mom. I even picked some items I probably didn't need, just to feel normal in this moment. I even managed a happy smile for the checkout girl. I put the items in three separate bags for the three of us to take up to the apartment . . . the apartment where normal ends whenever I turn the key.

When we got to the top of the stairs, I saw a man kneeling at another apartment door, using a screwdriver to apparently repair the lock. He turned and stood up as we approached. He seemed to be about thirtysomething, and tall, around 5' 11".

"So, I finally get to meet my new neighbors," he said, smiling at the three of us and showing a set of beautiful white teeth. He had nice looks and an easy smile, I thought.

He extended his hand, and I shifted my groceries to my left hand to shake his. "Hi, I'm Sondra Ackerman. These are my children, Ben and Cassie." He was wearing an expensive aftershave; I liked it.

"Hello," he said to the children. "It's nice to meet you. I'm Dwight Osborne. I've lived here for a little over a year. I knew someone new had moved in, but I needed to wait patiently in order to finally meet you."

Dwight was all smiles and was clearly the kind of guy who liked to talk. "Would you like to come over for coffee?" He really needed the company, I guessed.

"Uh . . . maybe one cup, if it's okay with the kids. I have to put these groceries away first," I fumbled. He's going to think I'm an idiot, I thought.

I quickly put the groceries away and got the kids playing video games in the living room. I told them to be sure to lock the deadbolt behind me; I stayed in the hallway until I heard the loud "click."

Cautiously, I knocked on Dwight's door, and he answered it, this time with an apron on. "I just made some cookies. Maybe you could bring back some for the kids?"

His apartment was immaculate and done in a red and black motif. All of his end tables and his entertainment center were done in black lacquer; colorful red pillows topped his black suede couch. He walked around to the kitchen and called, "How do you like your coffee?"

"Black is fine," I told him. The entire apartment smelled like fresh-baked cookies, giving it a comfortable feeling. I relaxed immediately as I walked around.

"Have a seat here at the table," he said, setting a large mug of coffee and a plate of cookies down on the dining room table. He went back for his own cup and sat down next to me. I caught a whiff of that aftershave again; I liked a man who took pride in his appearance.

"So, how long have you been divorced?" he asked, as if in passing, while stirring his coffee.

"Is it that obvious?" I laughed.

"I was just guessing," he said, with a twinkle in his eye. "Mom, two kids and no dad—it's a dead giveaway."

"Actually, I'm not divorced yet. Maybe not for several months. It's a complicated divorce," I told him, not wanting to give too much away.

"That's too bad. When I was divorced, I was young and had only been married a year or so. It was fairly painless," he said, grabbing a cookie and taking a bite.

51

"So, what do you do for a living, Dwight?" I asked him.

"Well, right now I sell insurance. I'm going to night school to get my MBA," he said. "What about you?" He pushed the plate of cookies in my direction.

I laughed. "It's funny you should ask. My company—I'm division manager—sells business insurance. I don't sell much myself; I mostly keep up with the employees and do a lot of paperwork."

"Sounds very businesslike. Do you like your job?" He seemed so interested in what I had to say. I seriously wasn't used to that in a grown man who wasn't also a psychiatrist.

I picked up a cookie and took a bite before speaking. "Well, I'd really like to own my own business—something fun, like retail— but I think I'll wait until this divorce mess is over with before checking out my options."

"Speaking of checking out your options . . ." he said, grinning from ear to ear. He was just a little chubby, in a cute sort of way, and sported a thick head of curly black hair and a trim moustache. "I bought way too many ribs to grill tomorrow night. Would you and your children like to join me?"

I couldn't exactly say I didn't have any plans, so I just nodded. "I can make a salad and some brownies," I offered. I was glad I'd just bought some groceries.

"Great. I'll make a big bowl of spiced corn, too. I hope the kids like ribs," he said. I could tell he was pleased to have a little bit of company.

The following evening, the four of us met at the picnic tables near the grill the apartment had available for anyone to use. I laid out a tablecloth and the kids put the brownies and the salad on the top to keep the tablecloth from blowing off.

Even with the moderate breeze, it was a surprisingly warm night for fall. From the patio we could hear the very soft whooshing of traffic noise. I watched Dwight slather the ribs with barbecue sauce on the grill. I suddenly felt safe and protected with a man nearby.

"Did you go to cooking school?" I asked him jokingly. He really did seem to know how to handle food, I thought.

"Well, actually, I did take a lot of community education classes on cooking. I once thought I'd go to cooking school one day," he told me, looking introspective.

"There's always time for change," I reminded him. "Who says you can't go for your MBA some other time if you really want to be a chef?"

He smiled. "I wish," he said wistfully. "Anybody ready for ribs?" he called out. I had obviously hit on a touchy subject.

The meal was terrific, and we stayed outside until well past dusk. When it got to be too dark to see much, we gathered the remains of our food and took it upstairs to our respective apartments.

"Well, Sondra," Dwight said as we climbed the stairs. "I'm glad we met. Perhaps we'll have supper together again."

I smiled. "I'd like that very much," I said, then winced. I hadn't meant my answer to sound like a come on, just a polite acceptance of the possibility, but I was afraid that it sounded like "Come and get me." Still, I had to admit that at only 34, I am a healthy woman and like a nice man when I meet one.

After saying goodbye to Dwight, I called Connie and told her about him.

"He sounds like a nice guy," she said, "but Sondra, be careful. You just left Jack. And you don't want to do anything that may upset the balance of the divorce, which is all in your favor right now. Are you going to see him again?"

"Well, considering he lives next door to me, I think that's a sure bet," I replied. "I think he's a nice guy."

"Well . . . be careful," she said again. "Your emotions are very fragile at the moment." She paused. "He sounds almost too good to be true."

It was just so like Connie to be looking out for me.

Just when I thought there were no good people in the world, I run into one right at my front door. He seems like the most unique of all men—so unlike Jack and so interested in me as a person. I think he really likes the kids, too. As I'm not the kind of woman to jump into the arms of the first man I meet, I'll take it slowly—which I'll have to do, because of the divorce. Well, slowly or not, I think I'll enjoy every minute of it. He's a decent man and I really think that, if nothing else, he and I will become close friends. That's more than I had yesterday. I need to count my blessings, no matter how tough things get.

My anxiety about exactly when all of this with Jack and his thugs would be over was heightening by the day. I heard bits and pieces of what was going on with Jack through my lawyer, who informed me on Monday that Jack and his lawyer were ready to meet with us face to face on Wednesday. A divorce moved ever closer. Would I live to see the papers signed? But I figured if they wanted to kill me, they knew where to find me.

I headed for Aaron Sorenson's office on Wednesday, nervous about seeing Jack. I didn't anticipate an easy divorce. I took a couple of deep breaths as I walked into Aaron's plush office. Pictures of his family, taken at home and on family trips, hung on the walls and adorned the credenzas. They made me feel very comfortable about putting my trust in him.

I met with Aaron for a few minutes before Jack and his attorney arrived. Aaron had been referred to me by a friend of Connie's husband, and I thought he had turned out to be a gem so far.

"The complicated thing," I explained to him as we sat at a large mahogany table in a conference room, "is that Jack will most likely be arrested by the Feds for drug trafficking in the next few months. So how do we pretend that it's not going to happen? We need to waste as much time as possible finalizing this divorce, as I'm guessing he'll have no rights to see the children whatsoever after he's incarcerated."

Aaron made a note on his yellow legal pad. "I can stretch this out for several months. Today, we'll talk about what you want to keep and what you're willing to give away in the divorce settlement."

"Well, I have an apartment, and I took all of the furniture out of the house that I wanted. He can have the house, his car and what's left inside the house. I want sole legal custody of the kids. For now, we can give him supervised visitation," I added.

"Did you have any stocks, annuities or other forms of money?" he asked.

"I have a retirement account, and Ben and Cassie are the beneficiaries. I think Jack has some stocks or mutual funds," I remembered, "but he can keep them."

"What about things like boats or motor homes?" he asked me.

"No, we had nothing like that. It's actually pretty simple, unless he wants some of the furniture or wants joint custody," I told him. "I'm standing firm on the sole custody issue."

At that moment, a petite, dark-haired secretary in a smart navy suit knocked on the partially open conference room door. "Mr. Ackerman and his lawyer, a Mr. Felix Appleton, are here. Should I show them in?"

Aaron said, "Not yet . . . can you give us a minute? I just need to finish up with Mrs. Ackerman."

As the secretary left the room, Aaron turned to me and said, "Sondra, I appreciate you want to get out of this quickly and with as little hassle as possible, but take my word, you need to go for half of everything he's got, plus financial support for the children."

"Well, okay," I said. "I guess you've done this many more times than I have. You know my issues, but I'll leave it to you to work out the best possible arrangement for me and the children."

"Okay, Sondra. You can trust me to do what's best for you," Aaron replied, then leaned toward the intercom to tell the secretary to let Jack and his lawyer in.

I felt good that we were doing this at my attorney's office rather than Jack's.

Jack came in, dressed casually in jeans and a long-sleeved button-down plaid shirt. He sat down in one of the chairs at the far end of the table. He didn't even bother to shake Aaron's hand. A moment later, a morbidly obese, balding, middle-aged man with heavy jowls entered the room and plopped down on the chair at the end of the table.

Aaron stood up and walked over to the pair. "Hi. I'm Aaron Sorenson. You must be Felix Appleton and Jack Ackerman." He shook their hands.

"Would you like today's discussion to be on the record today, or should we just take notes?" Aaron asked. "I can have a digital recorder sent in if you're interested."

"Good offer," Mr. Appleton said jovially. "Could we have the meeting on the record?"

Aaron stepped out and came back, followed immediately by his secretary who set up a digital recorder between the two parties. Lines were drawn by this simple act. A no holds barred battle was about to commence. Who could have known that day that lives would hang by a thread until one or other was vanquished?

Aaron spoke the date and the names of those in attendance into the recorder. "We're here to discuss division of property in the divorce settlement," Aaron said, a little louder than he had to. "My client has stated her wishes and we can put them on the record."

"Go ahead," said Mr. Appleton. "We have our list as well."

Aaron listed the things we had discussed earlier, but very much couched along the lines of 50 percent of everything plus support for the children, and then waited for the other attorney's response.

Felix Appleton shuffled some papers. "On behalf of my client, we can't agree to that type of settlement. However, Mr. Ackerman does agree to keep the home and the items that are currently in the home. He also agrees to keep his money market fund and stocks, while Mrs. Ackerman keeps her retirement fund. Mr. Ackerman, however, would like to establish some immediate visitation of the children and wants to have at least partial custody of the children, say on weekends."

I stiffened when he said that. First of all, Jack worked a lot of weekends. Second, there was no way I was going to give my husband immediate visitation of Ben and Cassie without supervision. I wasn't so much worried about the future, because I was convinced Jack's future involved being in a penitentiary, but right now I wanted the kids close to me at all times.

"Jack," I said simply, "there are things about your work and your lifestyle that I think are prohibitive to your being able to safely take care of children right now. If you would like to get a judge to order me to hand the children over to you for anything other than supervised visitation, I think I would have something to say to that judge."

Jack coughed a little and gave me a look I didn't ever want to see again. "Uh . . . I think we can hold off on that issue until the final proceedings. I think a judge will grant me weekends at least, unless you can definitively prove your allegations."

"Don't tempt me, Jack," I said bitterly, my bile rising.

"So, we'll put the issue of a settlement and the children on hold until we go before the judge," Aaron said. "The rest of the issues, that there should be a divorce, seem to be in agreement with both parties for the present. In the meantime, we'll get a date and fill out the documents on both our parts."

"Do you want to get a date before the court or should I?" Appleton asked while stuffing papers into his briefcase.

"I can do that," Aaron said, looking at me and giving me the slightest smile. I knew I could trust him to push the divorce proceedings as far in the future as possible. I suddenly saw that the extended claim that Aaron had suggested would definitely serve me well for seeing Jack behind bars before a court hearing could be set.
. . .

. . . It'd been a long day. Sondra really stood up to me at her lawyer's. I had to pull back. I'll give her credit, she had balls. I thought it would be easy enough to walk all over her. Maybe she felt I was a poor father and she had the right to be with the kids and I didn't. But I'm their dad—that counts for something. It has to. Still, that small battle she won was just part of a bigger fight. The firm sent me that greaseball of a lawyer, but I guess he must be good at what he does. The guy representing Sondra sure was a smooth operator; how the hell did she find him so quick? Serving me on a Sunday afternoon must have cost Sond some big bucks, so either she has more stashed away than I gave her credit for, or she drained her well dry to pay him. I can use that during our divorce hearings. If she's run out of money she can't realistically support two kids. I'll mention that to my guy the next time I see him. This is far from over. . . .

. . . After the meeting, Aaron told me he'd let me know when the court date would be. If Jack wasn't behind bars by then, we'd have to have some proof of his illegal activities in order to convince the judge to give me sole custody. I thanked him and left the office, feeling like the meeting went as well as it could have. All I needed to do now was get home in one piece; I felt like a moving target as I made my way to the car.

The next night, Dwight asked me over to watch a movie while the kids were watching their own shows at our apartment next door. I was nervous, but I let him snuggle a little bit with me as we sat on the black suede couch. I couldn't help but notice how muscular his arms were. Despite being a little overweight, he was clearly a strong man. The movie was good and there were times we could talk a bit. I decided to take the plunge and tell him about Jack.

"Remember when I told you about my divorce?" I asked him. He had nachos and cheese for us to eat and he was in the middle of eating a cheese-laden chip but was able to nod.

"The reason I'm getting a divorce is that my ex-husband is involved in some illegal activity. I didn't know about it at first, but when I discovered it, I decided to leave him." I waited to see if there was a negative reaction from him but I saw only passive interest.

"Remember when the cops were all over this place a few weeks ago—twice, in fact?" I figured he probably kept an eye on the activities that happened around the apartment buildings.

"Yes, I do. I never did find out what was going on, though," he said, grabbing another chip.

"Well, the second time they were here was because my apartment was ransacked. They didn't take anything, but I think they were looking for some proof I had of my husband's activities."

"Did they find anything?" he asked.

"No. I don't have any personal papers about what my husband does—at least, I don't keep anything with my personal items," I told him.

"And the first time the police were here?" he asked.

"That was horrible. A man I had hired to stake out my apartment—to make sure no one from my husband's . . . organization . . . was hanging around—was killed—shot to death— outside of the apartment, in his car. We're pretty certain that it was my husband's group that did it, but right now there's no proof." I was wondering if I was starting to ramble too much, but Dwight only hugged me closer.

"That's horrible," he said. "Why don't they get these guys?"

"The detective in charge told me that the autopsy showed he had been beaten half to death before being shot at close range. That poor man."

"You poor thing, Sondra. But you can't blame yourself. I assume the man was a pro, so he would have known the risks of his profession. So are they close to closing the case?"

"They tell me it's not time yet. They haven't told me exactly when it will be time. I'm just waiting around until something happens." I appreciated his caring attitude. I wouldn't have been surprised if he had run away screaming that my life was too chaotic for him to deal with.

"So it sounds like you're not much in the loop about those kinds of things," he commented.

I grabbed a couple of nachos. "I wish, but I'm not that lucky. They don't tell me much."

I felt better being honest with Dwight. He was such a kind and caring man, and it was nice to have someone other than Connie to talk to about what was happening. When the movie was over, I let him kiss me on the cheek before I went back to my apartment.

Dwight hitting on me put me on strange ground. How should I respond? I had been with Jack forever. I was a normal woman with a healthy libido, and I can't say I wasn't intrigued by this physical attraction, let alone from a man who enjoyed listening to me and who was fun to connect with. But with two kids and my life in chaos, I was going to go slowly, that was for sure.

The following morning, after I dropped the kids off at school, I arrived at work to find the office in shambles, police taking reports, and my employees standing around, wondering what to do. Shelly was wringing her hands, and she visibly relaxed when she caught sight of me.

I took a deep breath and walked up to the officer who appeared to be in charge. "I'm Sondra Ackerman, the manager. Can you tell me what happened?"

The tall, lanky officer looked me up and down as if to assess whether I was telling the truth or not. I must have passed inspection, because he said, "Well, ma'am, it appears that someone broke into the office and rifled through all the file drawers and desks. Some of the staff members have already said they didn't think anything was taken from their areas; they tell me your office took the biggest hit. I was wondering if you could have a look as soon as forensics is out of there."

With memories of my ransacked apartment, and knowing exactly who committed this crime, I stepped into my private office. I took in the sight of my normally tidy office. The place was a disaster. Drawers were opened, and files were scattered all over the floor. My desk was practically cleaned out; the only things left on the desk were a pencil and a blank notebook. Everything else was thrown on the floor. I gazed across my office and out onto the familiar Philadelphia skyline; for a moment or two, I was lost in my darker thoughts as to what was happening to me.

"Mrs. Ackerman," ventured the officer, "are you okay?"

"Oh, yes, thanks," I answered, not feeling okay in the least. "Just shaken up a bit, that's all."

After I got over my initial shock, and as soon as I was allowed, I looked wearily through the files. I felt almost a resignation to the fact that these despicable people were determined to frighten the hell out of me. What in the world had happened to my marriage—how could it have gone so wrong? Had my guardian angels deserted me and left me to be devoured by the wolves of Hades?

I shook off my thoughts and stood up. Nothing seemed to be missing, as far as I could tell right now. I hadn't kept any files related to Jack's activities in my office. Jim Pruitt had all of that, and he had already turned it over to the federal authorities and the local police. As I picked up the contents of my desk and organized what things I could, it occurred to me that Jack's "organization" must not know the Feds had anything on them. Jack would probably be surprised to know I had already gone to the police. It would most definitely surprise Jack that it was me who got this investigation started. I think he believed I'd never rat him out. And despite what those thugs were doing to my life, I had no regrets—fears, but not regrets.

I had nearly finished straightening up my office when the same lanky officer appeared in the doorway. "Anything missing?"

I shook my head, but beckoned him to enter. "Shut the door," I requested. "I think I know who was behind all of this 'breaking and entering." I waited for a moment to see if he knew what I was talking about. He didn't seem to know anything, so I continued, "My estranged husband is involved in a drug trafficking ring, and they seem to think I have something on them that would put them away. Everything I have is already with the Feds and the local police. I don't think they know that, however, and I think they're breaking into my work and my home, hoping to find something. They ransacked my apartment as well, a few weeks ago." I had told this story so many times now that I was able to keep it to a few short sentences.

The officer haphazardly scribbled some notes. "Do you think that's why your own office was targeted the most?"

"Yes, I do. The rest of the destruction may have been just to cover up what they were really trying to do," I suggested.

"Let me pass this by my superiors. I'll be back in a minute," he said, opening the door and stepping out.

I continued to tidy my office until it looked at least livable. I knew Shelly was probably out there wondering if she could come in yet, but I wasn't ready for company. I felt bad for my coworkers who were probably doing the same thing in their own offices, unaware that it was probably all my fault that this had happened. I finally sat down at my desk when the officer returned.

"I spoke with Detective Murphy, and he corroborated your story. He wants to talk with you as soon as possible," the officer relayed. "You'll need to give us a statement. If it helps, we can do that here instead of you coming downtown. You okay with that, Mrs. Ackerman?"

"Thank you, yes, I am," I said, wondering at the same time what Detective Murphy wanted from me. I was getting frustrated with the man and his office for not arresting these guys by now. I fumbled through my purse and found his card. My desk phone didn't work after being thrown on the floor, so I dialed his number on my cell phone.

"Detective Murphy."

"Hi. This is Sondra Ackerman. I understand you heard about what happened at my office today. I was told you wanted to speak with me."

"Yes, Mrs. Ackerman. Thanks for calling. I hate to bother you after what just happened, but I have a favor to ask you," he said, sounding hesitant.

"Go ahead," I prompted him.

"I was wondering if we could get you to wear a wire around your ex-husband—get him to say something incriminating. We have a fair amount of data to put the organization away for good, but I want to make sure your husband definitely gets put away for a long time." He stopped, waiting for my response.

My nerves were on edge just thinking of it. I hadn't been anticipating meeting Jack alone ever again in my life. How could I find an opportunity to talk with him where he would be candid with me? Should I use the fact that he wants to see the children against him? I supposed we could meet at a park somewhere, have a picnic and I could see if he would admit to anything. But would the kids want to see him now? Still, if he wasn't put away . . . the thought really scared me.

"I guess I could come up with something. He wants to see the children, and as long as they are happy to see him—they've recently experienced a lot of bad stuff connected to their dad, obviously—I could arrange for us to have a picnic in the park, and maybe I could get him to say something incriminating," I suggested.

"You realize we'd have plainclothesmen nearby in case anything sounds dangerous at all. They'd be able to hear everything you and he are saying in real time," he told me. "They'd do everything in their power to protect you."

I felt a little better knowing we wouldn't actually be alone. "I need to call him and set up a weekend day to have a picnic. Then what do you want me to do?"

"We'll meet you at one of our local offices or in a van outside your apartment and fit you with the wire. When you get to the meeting place, it will be up and running," he told me.

I told him I'd let him know once I'd scheduled the meeting, then just collapsed in my chair. I was afraid, but I knew that I was being irrational. Jack wouldn't hurt me, and there was a good chance he'd talk to me if he thought we were alone. He was such a braggart, who knew what he'd say?

I talked with the kids on the way home about the idea of having a picnic with their father on Saturday. Ben immediately whooped with delight, but Cassie was somber. I could hear them in the back of the car whispering to each other. To my relief, after a few minutes they agreed to run with the idea. It would have been more than I could bear to tell either of them about the wire and the Feds being in on the picnic; it was a relief when I decided not to. They had to act naturally and not say a single word that would give the whole thing away; therefore, I just couldn't tell them about the plot. I wasn't worried about Cassie so much, but Ben was only 11, and I really didn't know if he would be able to go along with it without giving something away. All I told them was that we would be going to the park and that I needed them to go play on the playground equipment after we ate so that their father and I could talk alone about our divorce plans.

They understood, and both agreed to give Jack and me time to spend alone. "You won't go anywhere we can't see you though, will you, Mom?" Cassie asked anxiously.

"No, Cassie, you will be able to see us both the whole time. Don't worry, honey," I told her.

Later, I closed the door to the bedroom and called Jack on my cell phone. The phone rang a couple of times before he picked it up. "Hello?"

"Jack, it's me." Just talking to him on the phone irritated me. "The kids have been talking about seeing you. I want them to stay in touch with you if that's what they want, but I am not prepared to have you come to my home—and I am certainly not coming to yours. So I thought we could meet in Hadley Park on Saturday. I'll bring a picnic lunch. All you need to do is turn up." I didn't think I breathed once during that recitation.

"Uh . . . I guess so." He sounded surprised and a little taken aback to hear from me. "I miss the little buggers. I'll bet they're both doing well in soccer," he said. I guessed he probably knew exactly how they were doing in soccer, down to the slightest detail.

I ignored the small talk. "So we can meet you on Saturday at 12:00, by the playground equipment at the park," I told him. I wasn't bothered if the time suited him or not. It was me that was calling the shots.

"That sounds fine. I can't wait to see them. If anything comes up, can I still reach you on the same cell number?"

I didn't answer his question; I just hung up. Now was not the time for friendly goodbyes. I reminded myself to call Detective Murphy the next morning to tell him when they should come by and fit me with the wire. I was acting so nonchalantly about this, but inside I was a nervous wreck. . . .

. . . Sondra wanted to meet at the park with the kids. It was a great idea and I would go. Would she be in league with the Feds? Would she try to entrap me by wearing a wire? I really didn't think Sondra had the cojones to bug our conversation. Besides, I was missing the kids so much I had to go. I would just tell her that she had to accept that this was my job now, and that if she came back home, she could have her share of the millions I had stashed. We were responsible for most of the Acapulco Gold that hit Philly and the upper East Coast, and there was plenty of cash. If I went on a spending spree that lasted the rest of my life, I'd have a hard time spending what I had already, let alone what I was going to get in the future.

My guess was I would climb the ranks even though I was not in the family; I knew the Brothers could see what a good job I had done increasing distribution. So if I gave Sondra a chance to come back home when we talked on Saturday, told her about the money, she'd get back in line—even if she tried to stick to her moral high ground routine. It's always about the money. Nobody was incorruptible, not even Sondra. . . .

. . . When I saw Dr. Richardson on Friday, I talked about what was going to happen the next day. For the first time, I opened up about how frightening all of this has been. He listened carefully and, instead of taking copious notes, just sat back and listened to me. I really appreciated that.

"I just can't get any real sleep," I lamented. "Every time I close my eyes, I think they're going to storm the place or take my children from me. I mean . . . these aren't people to mess with."

"I agree with you," he said soothingly. "You're a very brave woman."

"It scares the hell out of me to meet with Jack wearing a wire, but if it means he'll have a greater chance of going to jail, I will go through with it," I said with conviction.

"How is the Xanax working for you?" he asked me, picking up his pen.

I blushed. "Actually, the first time I took one, I felt so woozy that I haven't taken another one since. I'm guessing I'll just have to cope with this nervousness."

"I could prescribe something milder," he offered.

I shook my head. "That's okay. I've coped so far; I guess I'll be able to hold it together in the future." But I wasn't so sure. The anxiety was affecting my ability to concentrate whether I was at work, driving or at home. I didn't say anything to him because I just didn't think another pill would make that big of a difference. My mind went back to Connie's EFT suggestion. I kept blowing her off, but in truth I was kind of curious. I decided I would ask her more about it the next time we got together.

We talked a little bit about the break-in at my office. "I know it was Jack's cohorts who did that," I said bitterly. "I didn't dare say anything about it at work, but I felt so guilty that they went through everyone else's desks at the office too."

"People like that don't care who they victimize," he said, leaning back in his chair. . . .

. . . I found out Sondra was spilling her guts to a shrink now. Well, I was hardly surprised; she had been on the edge since the second kid came along. There was a name for that . . . Carmen would know what it was. So—a shrink, that could be a problem. I knew they had all this confidentiality crap, but I also thought they had to inform on serious crime. I thought maybe I should find out from someone who knew about this kind of stuff. If Sondra was seeing a shrink, I just knew she'd talk about stuff that was upsetting her. That's what you do when you lay on a couch—yackety-yak, spill your guts. Since I was the one stressing her out, I knew it was me she'd be blabbing about. It would be a good idea to go get her record out of there and waste the shrink; that way the situation would be taken care of once and for all. . . .

. . . Our time was up, and I made another appointment for the following week. He was a nice enough psychiatrist, and I liked the fact that I could tell him things, but I wasn't sure I was making any serious progress—whatever that looked like.

My schedule was so hectic that week that I only had time Thursday night to spend with Dwight. This time he had a big spaghetti dinner for all four of us, then I sent the kids back to our apartment to do their homework. I told them that they could watch TV or play video games after they finished. I made sure they locked the deadbolt behind me, as usual.

Dwight was very affectionate that night. We kissed deeply a few times and his hands started roaming over my legs and stomach. "I'm starting to care about you very much, Sondra," he whispered to me.

I didn't know what to say. I liked Dwight, but I felt I needed to know him better. I mumbled something like, "I care about you, too," and then changed the subject. It didn't help that we were watching a love story on TV. I think the movie was giving him too many ideas. Still, he was a nice man, and he was someone uninvolved with the drama in my life. And I found him easy to talk to. The undemanding cuddles helped, also; it felt nice to be wrapped in a man's arms. But I was just hoping he stayed undemanding for now.

I didn't mention my upcoming meeting with Jack, as I didn't want to give Dwight the impression that I had mixed feelings about my estranged husband. Instead, we talked about the office break-in and other topics.

"The spaghetti was excellent. I still think you should go to cooking school," I teased him. He really was an excellent chef.

"Actually, I've looked into a few night programs. I could work during the day and take night classes at a local cooking school. I could put my MBA on hold. I'd get my degree in two or three years," he told me. "I really think that being a chef is my passion, and I'm definitely sick of selling insurance. And I have you to thank for the idea." He kissed me again, and I didn't resist.

"Well, I'm on your side," I said, after the lingering kiss. "I think everyone should follow their passion. I may still have my retail store some day. I don't think I'll get much money in the divorce, but I'll probably get something in child support." Actually, if Jack was in jail by the time we got divorced, I couldn't expect much in the way of child support. Secretly, however, I hoped I'd get some kind of reward for alerting the authorities on the trafficking operation, but I wasn't holding my breath.

"I hope you get your dream, too," he said, sneaking in another kiss.

The movie came to a close, and I finally said my goodbyes, which concluded with a long, smoldering kiss at the door. I could feel his passion, and I realized I needed to rein this in before it went any further. I hoped the rest of my week would be uneventful until Saturday.

I never thought I'd be in the business of espionage. All of this seems totally unreal to me, and I'm trying not to think of the danger involved. I need to believe that Jack wouldn't hurt me outright—especially not in a public place. And I'm praying that he says something incriminating. Jack has always been so cocky that I think, if he believes no one but me is listening, he will brag about his involvement in the drug trafficking business. If nothing else, he'll brag about the money he's getting. I suspect he has hidden bank accounts, maybe even overseas. This is money I'm sure I'll never see. Whatever happened to the man I married? Maybe it was the boredom of his other job or the enticement of getting rich that lured him into a life of crime. The trouble is, the longer I am away from Jack, the more I think about the faults in our marriage. I was always so in love with him, despite his quick temper, that I couldn't see anything wrong with our relationship. But now that I've distanced myself from him I can see the real Jack. I suspect his brother is in on all of this, too, but I won't know until all the arrests are made. I'm afraid of wearing a wire, but I need to be brave and do my best to see that Jack is put in jail and the kids can feel safe and happy again. And so he will never hurt me again.

Chapter 3

I got a call from the Feds in the morning, instructing me to meet them downstairs to be fitted with the wire. Sure enough, at 10:00, there was the ubiquitous white van in the parking lot. I had gotten up early to make our picnic lunch. I made sure it was reminiscent of the picnics we used to have—fried chicken, coleslaw, and potato salad—to pluck at Jack's heartstrings and make him more likely to relax. The coordinating agents from the Bureau had pointed out that it was important everything looked normal . . . as if this could ever be normal. So my cooler contained massive portions of normal. I threw in some sodas, as well as some cookies for the kids, along with plates and silverware.

The agents tried out the miniscule microphone, first on my bra, then on the shirt I was wearing under my sweater. They finally decided to keep the wire on my shirt so they could hear the conversation clearly. It was so tiny, I was fairly convinced that no one could see it as long as I kept my sweater on. It was late October, and I didn't think I'd ever need to take it off during the day.

"Now, let's talk about how you're going to talk to Jack," one agent suggested.

"Uh . . . I thought I'd just ask him why he did it and let him know I know a lot about the operation already because of the private investigator I hired," I told him. I felt like a fool. What did I know about covert operations or espionage of this caliber?

The agent surprised me by saying, "That's great. Always give the assumption that you already have information on what you're talking about. If you ask too many questions, he'll get suspicious."

"I have thought a lot about what I'm going to say, and I think he'll be receptive," I explained. If there was one thing I really knew a lot about, it was Jack. I knew how to push his buttons to get him eating out of my hand. . . .

. . . Meeting at the park got me thinking. My kids loved playing soccer. Cassie was really good at it, and Ben . . . well, Ben tried hard, but he just didn't have natural talent. Even at 11 you could see he wasn't going to make it as a soccer star. Still, soccer had become their top activity, and I bet they'd want to kick the ball around some at the park. It might be worth a shot to snatch the kids from there. Those soccer fields are usually crowded, though . . . but the parking lots have their isolated areas. Sondra couldn't keep her eyes on them all the time, so if I got some of my crew to come along, we could split them up, get the kids to one place and Sondra to another. . . . It might be worth taking a look at. All kinds of weirdos hang around the places kids play, so that could be the decoy. Maybe we could just get a real weirdo to approach Sondra and pester her. Give him a C-note or broken legs—it would be his choice—distract her, then grab the kids when they're far away from her. After all, I'm their father, so surely I got rights. I'd have to think about it some more. . . .

. . . "Okay. We'll be listening to your conversation the entire time. Once you have the information, cut it short and get out of there. We'll have everything on tape and will meet you back here to remove the wire," the officer said.

At exactly 11:45 a.m., we loaded up the car and headed toward Hadley Park. We got there at noon and parked near the playground equipment. As I lugged the cooler toward a nearby picnic table, the kids noticed Jack standing by the slides. Ben ran over to him; Cassie lagged behind. We were over the first hurdle: Jack was here. I wasn't really sure he'd show.

"Dad!" Benjamin called out. "We're here!" He gave his dad a big hug, and Jack tousled his shaggy brown hair. Jack never did understand that Ben hated that.

Cassie was more aloof. She let her dad give her a hug but wasn't as excited about seeing him as Ben was. Jack and I didn't bother with pleasantries. I chose a picnic table about 30 yards from the playground. That seemed about the right distance to avoid any extraneous noise when Jack and I really began to talk.

After a few minutes, Jack and the kids moved over to where I was laying out the tablecloth and getting the food out of the cooler.

"Care for some fried chicken, coleslaw and potato salad?" I tried to be as bright as possible for the kids' sake, in spite of the tension between us. My gut was full of knots and I wasn't sure I'd even be able to get any of the food down.

"Sounds good. I've lost a few pounds since you left," he said eagerly. He grabbed a chicken leg and began munching on it.

He did look thinner, but I didn't know if he just wasn't eating right or if he was actually using the drugs he was trafficking. His shirttails were hanging out, and his jeans were dirty and baggy. I wondered if he did any laundry for himself. Was he seeing anyone else? He certainly was dressed down for visiting with me.

While we ate, the kids chatted about school and their respective soccer teams nearly the whole time. After they finished eating a fair amount of food, they each grabbed a couple of cookies and asked to play on the swings. I started to quake inside at the thought of finally being alone with Jack, but I kept my voice calm as I said yes.

Jack had at least three pieces of chicken and double helpings of both coleslaw and potato salad. "I miss your cooking, Sondra." He seemed sad as he said that. "In fact, Sondra, I miss you." For one moment in time he sounded genuine. I said nothing. Then, in a flash, the cocky Jack returned. "You are looking terrific. Are you working out now?"

Yeah, right, I thought angrily. The "fear diet" had taken me down a dress size, and I didn't welcome the comment or the attention. I could feel the bile rise within me; I hated him at that moment.

"Well, you'd still be having decent meals—and me—if you hadn't made up your mind to do something illegal," I retorted, carefully watching his eyes. "Tell me, Jack, are you with anybody else now?" The show was on, and I hoped someone was listening.

He didn't answer my question and instead asked, "How did you find out about my business?" He took a cookie from the plate, avoiding eye contact.

"I became suspicious about your long and suddenly erratic hours and hired a private detective. I didn't know what was going on with you. As it turns out, you guys aren't that secretive about what you do, and I found out about the whole thing. Why did you go that route, Jack?" I implored him, acting like I wished we were back together.

"The old business was gradually going under. Sol heard about the Brothers—Los Archos Hermanos—and, since it wasn't much different from my old job except for the cargo, I went with it," he explained. "And, by the way, we've really beefed up our security since then."

So I was right about Sol being involved, I thought. "I mean . . . you would be gone for three days at a time, Jack. What was I supposed to think?"

"Yeah, I know. We go down the Intercoastal Highway to pick up the product in South Carolina. Then we have to bring it back to Philadelphia for distribution," he explained.

"I know there's a big drug problem in Philadelphia, but surely it doesn't all stay here." I was trying to get him to talk further.

He hesitated a bit before he answered. "No. A lot of the coke goes to New Jersey and some to New York City. Most of the pot stays here, though." He took the last piece of chicken and didn't seem suspicious in the least about our conversation. I started to relax a little.

"So, apart from being the birth place of freedom, Philly is a mellow town," I commented, trying hard to keep the sarcasm from my voice. "You don't use that stuff, do you?"

"Well . . . you know . . . I have tried it, but I'm not that into it. Most of us don't use what we transport. We get our high on the money that comes in," he teased back. "It really isn't a bad way to earn a living, Sondra. I really shouldn't be telling you this stuff, but now that you know, why don't we enjoy the benefits together?"

"You know I couldn't tolerate that kind of lifestyle. The kids deserve better," I said, beginning to pack up the cooler and collect the garbage. I figured the Feds had heard enough. "Kids, come and talk to your father for a while!" I called out. I'd had enough and just wanted to leave. Ben and Cassie came running almost immediately.

"Wow! You two sure are growing!" he told them, tousling Ben's hair yet again. Ben grimaced.

"Maybe that's why they made me goalie last week. I'm tall and I can block really well," Ben answered.

Cassie, deep in the midst of puberty, had actually grown some, but she wasn't about to call attention to her body. Her figure was rounding out nicely, but she made sure she covered it up with her baggiest clothes. I couldn't help but notice Jack didn't ask her about her soccer playing abilities.

I threw away the garbage and stood next to the cooler while they finished talking. "Maybe we'll do this again sometime," I lied. "The kids need to keep you up to date on their lives."

Jack stood up and turned to the kids. "Yeah, this was fun." He said to me rather than the kids, "Give me a call sometime. I'd definitely like to see the kids around the holidays."

I hoped Jack would be behind bars by then. I just nodded.

The kids said goodbye to their father, and I walked back to the car with the kids without a second glance his way. During our picnic, I had looked around occasionally when Jack wasn't paying attention, trying to see any federal agents, but I never did catch sight of one. They did their job well.

Within 15 minutes, we were back at home. I took the kids upstairs and told them to stay in the apartment while I got the cooler out of the car—and have my wire removed. I hoped Dwight was busy and wouldn't notice the big white van in the parking lot. While the agent busied himself with removing my wire, I started to feel a little weak in the knees as my adrenaline level dropped. I am not a big drinker, but if somebody had offered me large bourbon straight up at that moment, I would have readily gulped it down. . . .

. . . The picnic got me thinking. It seemed that I've had three lives. First there was my work life, tough and hard as life on the docks always had been. Earning well but stealing more—it was a tradition. You'd steal something because you could, and even if you didn't want it, there were always plenty of buyers in retail and on the streets. Then there was my married life with Sond and Cassie, who was born six months into our marriage, then Ben a couple of years later, after we decided to try for a boy. Then there was my third life: girls. Plenty of girls. It's as if some girls saw a guy's being married as a challenge. Years before that, me and Sol had built that wooden shed in one of the warehouses—just a storage shed with a mattress and a locked box with some bourbon and paper cups. We kept a lock on the outside in case any of our employees got nosy, and a slide bolt on the inside kept our wanted visitors in. I used to bring girls there occasionally—hell, that was where I got Sondra to give it up—but now I really gave it a workout. Sol and I tried to stick to a schedule, but most of the time it didn't really

72

work. The old man wanted some, too, so we used to have to keep our distance and our mouths shut when he took a woman there. He used to pay for his, mostly, but me and Sol just kept getting a whole bunch of willing partners. At least two of the girls I laid got abortions, which of course I had to pay for. But I didn't really care—I refused to wear a rubber. I'd rather pay for an abortion, and even risk getting some disease, than wear one of those uncomfortable things. Besides, it was always a thrill to fill a girl. But damn, the number of calls I had over the years of women agonizing about being late. I always told them the same thing, though: Tough—you got what you wanted, so live with the consequences and don't bother me. If they pushed it, I paid for an abortion, but only two ever did. So maybe I am responsible for more abortions than I know about, and maybe I got more kids than I know of. All the time this was going on—in fact, it's never gone away even to this day— Sondra never seemed to know. Or maybe back then she knew enough to keep her nose out of my business.

So with a house, a wife, a beautiful daughter, and an endless flow of mistresses, I always seemed to need more money than I had coming in. The more girls I had, the more I would steal. The more I stole, the more I was able to stash away. And it was that stash that funded my share of the franchise with Los Archos. So I figure I've got the girls to thank for more than the sex: If I wasn't so interested in partying with them, I wouldn't have needed so much money, but as it was, I stole enough to be able to buy into the drug game. You know, when you get right down to it, I'm just a bad man. . . .

. . . "You did a great job, Mrs. Ackerman," the agent said as he placed the microphone in a protective case. "I think we got enough information to haul him in when the time comes. We didn't know about the South Carolina piece, although our undercover people haven't been able to contact us for a while. We've just had to let them do their thing."

He shook my hand. "We'll let you know when we're getting close to rounding up the whole bunch. It shouldn't be any more than a month. At least, that's what the higher ups are telling us."

I said goodbye to him and tried not to show my disappointment about finding out I'd have to wait another month before all of this would be over with. It was frustrating to just have to wait, and I didn't want anything else to happen in the meantime.

I grabbed the cooler from the trunk and lugged it up the stairs. The apartment still didn't quite feel like home, and somehow the kids and I were more comfortable spending time away from the place. I told them we could go to a movie the next day; I wondered if Connie and Brett could go with us. I decided to give her a call on the new land line I had just had hooked up.

"Hi, Connie," I said cheerfully. I always felt better connecting with my best friend. "I was wondering if you and Brett would like to join us for a movie tomorrow. We're going to the Bridge Cinema near Rittenhouse Square Park, do you know the one?"

"Yes, I know it," said Connie, "and I would love to go to the movies with you guys. I'm sure Brett would, too. Let's take the kids for lunch at the Pizzeria on Walnut Street before the movie—it's really close by."

"Okay, sounds great to me," I told her. "I have a couple of questions to ask you about EFT as well. Are you up for it?"

"No problem. I'm glad you're thinking of it. How about meeting at the restaurant at noon?"

"Sure. We'll see you then."

We all seemed to arrive at the pizzeria on the stroke of 12. It was a wonderfully casual place with a long bar and lots of tables. The kitchen was out in the open, so you could see them preparing your pizza. Seeing the disks of dough curling up into the air was the great theatrical element of a good family-friendly pizzeria. The service was very quick, which I guess is why a lot of people had their children with them. The kids picked out the movie they wanted to see from the six screens available; we had more than an hour before it started. We ordered a medium margherita pizza, a large "the works" pizza that was the house specialty, and two family-size salads, one with bleu cheese and the other with light Italian dressing. I started to wonder if I had ordered too much, because my stomach was in knots, and I couldn't see myself having any more than a little salad and yet another double espresso, a drink that was fast becoming my crutch in life.

The place was bustling and full of noise. While we waited for our pizzas, the kids grabbed some quarters and headed for the video games. I stayed with Connie at our table and asked her about EFT.

"What does it stand for, again?" I asked her.

"It stands for 'Emotional Freedom Technique,' " she answered. "It's based on ancient Eastern medical meridian therapy—like acupuncture. No needles are involved; the practitioner uses tapping points along what is known as the meridians to help heal physical and emotional problems that you are holding thoughts about. It's so gentle. We've used it at our clinic for more than 15 years, and our clients really swear by it."

"Hmm," I said, waffling between wanting to give it a try and thinking I would be wasting my money. "The reason I'm asking is that I've been seeing the psychiatrist for the anxiety, insomnia and headaches I've had, and all we do is talk or he gives me a prescription. The prescriptions all have had side effects, and I'm not much better. I keep thinking there is more I could be doing about this."

"With EFT, there are no side effects. Basically, you just get better," she told me.

Our meal arrived, and I called the kids back to the table. "How long does it take to get better?" I asked.

"That depends," Connie said, "on what you have and how serious it is. When I had EFT done after my mother died, it worked after three sessions, although I remember feeling much better right from the first session." She paused in helping the kids get the hot slices onto their plates to gaze at me intently. "I really think you ought to give it a try."

"Well, I'll think about it. I should see the psychiatrist a couple of more times, then I'll give you a call," I said. I liked Dr. Richardson and didn't want to give up on him. Maybe I'd ask him about EFT when I next saw him.

Connie laughed. "I'll wait for your call."

The meal was good, and we finished up with plenty of time to cross the square and get our tickets for the movie, as well as popcorn, which the kids insisted on; it was as if they'd never stuffed themselves with pizza only minutes before. It was your typical feel-good kid's movie, which was the perfect way to get my mind off things for an hour and a half.

I'm still reeling over my meeting with Jack. He was as cocky as I expected, and he really spilled his guts to me about his activities. Now I know that no-good Sol is involved as well. Talking to him made me even more convinced I did the right thing by leaving him. He never would have quit the business, he made that clear. I'm more sure than ever that he has money hidden somewhere. I wonder how I could get hold of the account information. If I am still legally his wife, I could take out some of that money to take care of the kids. I feel a little guilty about it, but since I'm not likely to see any child support, I may have a chance at recouping some of the money owed to the kids. After he's arrested, he won't allow me to touch any of the money and the Feds may not know how to get to it. I think I'll sleep on it and decide whether or not I should go for his cash. What a crazy life I now lead.

Chapter 4

I felt an immediate sense of guilt when I woke up the next morning. I couldn't believe that I was actually thinking about taking some of Jack's ill-gotten gains. I dropped the kids off at school and went to work, ruminating on the issue as I drove. I knew Jack's amassed fortune was illegal, and I also knew helping myself to some of it was just as illegal. There was no question that if I could manage to find out where he was keeping the money, I should tell the Feds, and it would be seized as evidence in the case against him. Yes, that's what I should do, I thought.

Then memories of recent events came into my head, one by one: Jack staying away for days at a time . . . my discovery that he'd been lying to me about his job . . . his putting me and the kids in danger by working with dangerous thugs . . . Jim Pruitt's death . . . and all the harassment. And I knew exactly what I was going to do: get a little reward for all the misery that had entered my life, thanks to Jack and his "business."

When the slightest notion that I, too, could be implicated in the case if I touched even a penny of Jack's money crossed my mind, I pushed it out quickly. I was going to do this—for me, and for the kids. If Jack was going to spend years behind bars, we were going to need something to live on, and Ben and Cassie deserved some happiness after all this.

I felt a little sick to my stomach—before all this happened, I never would have even entertained the idea of doing something illegal, even by association. And I was furious with Jack all over again, because he changed my life, and not for the better. I was now aware that not everything in the world was absolutely good or absolutely bad; there were many gray areas. And taking some of his money definitely was in the gray area of moral ambiguity. But I was willing to risk it for my kids.

I knew that Jack would be dumb enough to keep all his banking information in his study back at the house. The next thing I had to decide was when to go through his things and find the accounts. I doubted he had changed the locks on the house; I only needed to find a time when he was on one of his many three- to four-day "jobs."

To make sure I didn't lose my nerve, I decided to do it right away—that night, after the kids went to bed. The children never woke up at night, but to be sure, I planned to make them a special treat at bedtime. The only difference from the usual cups of hot chocolate I made them was that this time there would be a bit of Restoril in each one. It would only be a small amount—I just couldn't risk their waking up and finding me gone. And if they did that, they'd likely call my cell phone, which I had on me at all times. It was not going to be my finest mommy moment, but it had to be done.

I took time during my break that day to do look online for banks in the Cayman Islands. I found one, NCB (Cayman) Limited, and gave them a call from my cell phone. It was long distance, and I didn't want to do this on the company dime.

"I'd like to open a bank account," I said.

The customer service representative asked me for my name, my address (which I so wanted to falsify but did not know how), and how much I wanted to deposit. The minimum was $10,000. I had much more than that in my retirement account, and it was worth the penalty of early withdrawal to have some of it wired to this account in the Caymans. I told them I'd be wiring the money in an hour or so. They gave me the account number, and I told them the password I wanted to use to access the account. Just as Jack's account was likely just a number and a password, so was my new account. All I needed to do to complete the opening of my very own offshore account was to have a notary see my passport and send a notarized copy to them.

I then called the company that managed my retirement account and requested the money to be wired to my new bank account. I expected the customer service representative to ask me a bunch of questions, but he seemed comfortable with what I was asking and only reminded me that there would be a withdrawal penalty. I did, so he said he'd wire the money. Wow, I thought. I couldn't believe it was that easy to get an overseas bank account.

I went to a nearby notary at lunchtime. She was very forthcoming and knew exactly what was needed to finalize my offshore bank account. It was all done in 30 minutes.

The rest of the day was uneventful, but I couldn't calm my nerves. What if Jack didn't keep the information where I thought he would? What if I got caught? It was all so scary and so unlike me. Still, the kids deserved every cent I could get out of Jack before the divorce. I wasn't about to get divorced and be penniless at the same time. Now I figured there was a way not to be.

I picked the kids up at Marge's house and took them out for subs. When we got back to the apartment, they did their homework and played video games until bedtime. Ben complained he hardly ever saw Kyle anymore, so I promised he could invite him over the next day.

At bedtime, I casually offered Ben and Cassie some hot chocolate with marshmallows. That was a big hit, in more ways than one. Both of them were fast asleep within minutes. Now all I had to do was rob my old home, but not until I got a little rest myself, if I could.

I set my alarm for 3:00 a.m., but I was too nervous to sleep. I got out of bed just before the alarm sounded and put on my darkest clothes. I felt like some kind of low-life thief. Cassie was sound asleep in the bed we shared, and Ben was out cold in the other bedroom. Grabbing my keys and my purse, I carefully snuck out the door.

The streets were nearly empty, but I was still nervous. I turned down my old street and looked for Jack's car. We lived in a row house with a garage underneath, but the garage was always full of stuff, so we had always parked on the street.

Just in case Jack had cleared out the garage and now parked his car in it, I grabbed the flashlight I had in my purse and peeked through the windows. Nothing had changed; no car was parked inside. I had a moment of panic that Jack may have gotten a new car, but then I remembered getting a glimpse of the car he had driven for years at the park the other day. There were no lights on in the house. I looked up and down the road—there were no people and no cars. What else should I have suspected at this hour?

My key still worked. I punched in the security code, praying it hadn't been changed. No, Jack wouldn't have thought of that. The green light blinked reassuringly. Once I was inside with the door shut behind me, I felt it was okay to turn on a couple of lights. Just to be on the safe side, I slipped up the stairs to confirm that Jack wasn't at home. I had taken our bed, and the master bedroom was still empty; he hadn't gotten around to buying a new one. I checked the guest room. It looked like Jack had been sleeping there—the bed was a mess, but fortunately he wasn't sleeping in it. I couldn't help but check around the bed to see if another woman had been there recently. Nothing obvious. I headed back downstairs.

Jack's study was on the first floor, next to the dining room. I had always felt I needed a study as much as he did, but he always insisted on having that room to himself. It was a mess—not unusual for Jack. I didn't see anything that looked like bank papers on the desk, so I opened the file drawer on the right-hand side of the desk. Jack never marked any of his files, so I had to go through several unimportant ones before I came to the information I needed.

On a yellow sheet of notebook paper, he had written the names of two banks—ones that I recognized from my Web search. In fact, one of the banks was a subsidiary of the one I had chosen. The numbers of the bank accounts were there, and so were the passwords. How could it be so easy? Jack was so cocky that it never occurred to him that having the bank numbers and the passwords together was really a stupid thing to do. But, in truth, that's what I was counting on.

I felt nervous as hell despite being in my own home. I suddenly heard the sound of a large car cruising slowly by the house. I stood perfectly still, yet trembling uncontrollably inside. I made my way to the window and peered down at the street below. To my immense relief, I saw it was a large Ford Explorer with the Philadelphia police logo on the side. I exhaled violently, so tightly had I been holding my breath.

Crisis averted. Still, my heart was thumping noisily in my chest as I stood, frozen, in that spot, imagining footsteps and noises in the house. I had to take control, do something to get myself to move. I focused on the task at hand and carefully copied down the numbers so vital to my future well-being and that of the kids. I mentally made sure I had put everything back exactly where it had been, then turned off all the lights. Setting the alarm, I slipped out the front door and bolted to my car. It was 3:40 a.m.; I had gotten in and out fairly quickly, I thought.

My nerves were better after I was safely on my way home. I decided to wait until morning before transferring the funds, even though I figured they offered some kind of 24-hour service.

I really didn't sleep much after I got home, so I was groggy when it was time to wake the kids. It took some effort to rouse them that morning, and I felt guilty all over again for doping my kids. But I guessed it was a small price to pay for the information I had gotten during the night.

After dropping the kids off at school, I headed directly to the office. I did some work for a while and, when it was time for a coffee break, I carefully shut my office door and took out the numbers I had written down the night before. I chose the account that was in the same banking system as my own account.

I used my cell phone again, because I thought that would be safer; I didn't want this call to show up on any company telephone records. "I'd like to transfer some money from my account to another in this bank," I told the person on the other end of the line, trying to keep my voice from shaking.

"How much would you like to transfer, ma'am?" the woman said in such a matter of fact way it was almost scary. I was quivering from head to toe with the anticipation of discovery.

I gave her the bank account number and the password and asked what the balance was.

"On that account, the balance is two million, four hundred thousand, three hundred and thirty-three dollars U.S.," she told me.

I nearly fainted. Jack has two million dollars in just one account? How much did he have in the other account? "I'll take two million out of the account and put it into this account." I gave her the account number and password, and then waited.

"The transfer is complete, ma'am," she said. "Is there anything else I can do for you?"

"No, that's all, thank you," I said, definitely feeling shaky by this time. I hung up the phone and put my head in my hands. Jack must be into some really serious shit, I thought, for him to have that kind of money. And now some of that money was technically mine. I couldn't believe I had just done that. . . .

. . . That house I shared with Carmen was an amazing property. When we bought in Lancaster I could not have known that my relationship with Carmen was going to take on such a sense of permanency. I really thought she just viewed me as a fling—one I was not in a position to say no to. Still, it all worked out well. We have this fine six-bedroom house and all the money we need to run the place in a style that I was sure was the envy of some of the old money that lived around us. I brought up the issue of Carmen being mom to my kids, and she surprised me by saying she was okay with it, although I figured she'd want to send them to boarding school. As she always screamed the place down during sex, that was probably a good plan.

If Sondra knew all of this existed, she'd freak. She worked her butt off running that insurance office and then did the mommy thing at home. If I'd only had the courage to bring her in on the deal, she never would have had to work again. But deep down I knew she'd never be able to be the wife of a drug racketeer, which was what I was. Plus she probably never would have put up with the arrangements most of the guys in the business had—two homes, one with a wife, and one for the little something on the side. Why couldn't she just be like other wives and do what she was supposed to? Why did she have to be so high and mighty on the morals front? I had tried slapping her around, but it never worked. . . .

. . . I called the other bank just to find out the balance of the second account. There was more than three million dollars in that account. I just sat there after that call, wondering what to do. I had essentially stolen from my estranged husband, and now I had in my own bank account a sum of money the likes of which I had never seen before in my life. And Jack had even more in the other bank account.

I felt the guilt creeping up on me again. I decided to tell the Feds about the account I hadn't touched, but I wasn't going to say anything about the account I had taken the money from. I rationalized that the money I took belonged to my kids so they could have a nice life, grow up in a nice neighborhood. I deserved a cut of what Jack had earned as well and, if I got away with it, I was going to put the money to good use.

Now I got to thinking that if the Feds raided our old home and they found Jack's bank information as easily as I had, I was in trouble. The trail of the money to my account would be obvious. But if there was only one set of account details to be found, I might be safe. And Jack couldn't even protest—I was sure he and his goombas wouldn't squeal on themselves. That left me just one option: I had to go back and destroy the details of the account I had just lifted the money from.

"Detective Murphy speaking," the voice said. I hadn't even realized I had called him but, sure enough, my cell phone was in my hand. I guessed I was starting to really lose it.

"Uh . . . excuse me for bothering you, Detective. This is Sondra Ackerman. I have some information you might be interested in." I told him about the second bank account, including how much money was in it. I said I believed he got the money through his illegal activities.

"Ah, we were looking for information like this. How did you find out about the account?" he asked me.

I told him a half truth. "Well, since we're still married, and that's still my house, I don't think I did anything illegal, coming across the account number and password," I explained.

"No, I don't think you did," he said. "This is great news. Now we've connected him to a large amount of money he couldn't possibly have made legally."

If he only knew, I thought.

After I hung up, I felt a little less guilty about taking some of Jack's money. The Feds would be taking the rest of it, I was sure, but my kids and I would have a nice little nest egg for us to live on when all of this was over with. All I had to do now was to repeat my mission and revisit my old home, I decided to do it tonight. . . .

. . . The Brothers called a meeting. I loved those trips to Los Archos. I had a much better relationship with the Brothers since I got together with Carmen. But I knew that one false move on my part meant I would see a massive change in the Brothers' friendly attitude, so I knew I had to stay with Carmen no matter what. Lucky she was so hot and exciting—it wasn't exactly a chore. She sure could be exhausting, though. She said she wore me out so I wouldn't have any energy left for other women—and she was right. Her gain was Sondra's loss, that was for sure.

When we got to Los Archos, I was going to bring up the idea of my advancing in the chain of command. I was not asking for Sol, just for myself. The Brothers wanted to start up in Canada, and they were going to choose one of us regional guys to front the operation. It wouldn't be easy—a turf war, no doubt, but we were tougher than most other cartels. We were feared, and we wielded a lot of power. There were 12 of us regional directors, and only one would get Canada. The money would be huge. Carmen wouldn't be allowed to be at the meeting, but she had already influenced her brothers. Being with Carmen had given me the inside track. I had her bringing up my name to them all the time. And I was sure if I showed a commitment to her, marriage and kids and all that, they would have to treat me like family.

Man, Canada could be a dream come true for me. I would have more money and influence than the president himself. It's hilarious how these crazy politicians think they run the country. Nothing happens without the say so of an organization like ours. We rule with iron fists. The drugs, whores and people trafficking, that's the life on the streets people understand. The cops can't touch us—and they wouldn't want to. They all got families, and they know how far we can go.

So even though I had Carmen, to stay tight with the Brothers and advance my career I had to stay on my toes. I couldn't let Sondra ruin things for me. The Brothers knew everything that was going on with their people, so I was sure they knew about the divorce. That meant I'd better figure out a plan to deal with the situation. So the sooner Sondra was out of the way permanently, the sooner I could get closer to Carmen and Canada. . . .

. . . I was on time, maybe even a few minutes early, for my appointment with Dr. Richardson that afternoon. I sat in the waiting room for nearly half an hour, but he didn't come out to call for me. I checked the appointment card he had given me the week before. It was the right time and date.

Finally, I knocked on the door of his inner office. No response. I knocked again and then tried the handle. The door swung open. Dr. Richardson's big leather chair was facing the desk. I almost missed him sitting there, but then I saw his arm on the armrest.

"Dr. Richardson?" I asked tentatively. No answer.

I rushed to his side. Blood covered the top of his desk and the front of his rumpled suit and shirt. His neck was cleanly sliced across the middle.

I panicked, but still had the presence of mind not to touch anything. I used my cell phone to dial 911, shaking with fear and disbelief. I looked around the room. His filing cabinet was open and several files were scattered on the floor. He usually kept that filing cabinet closed, and I knew he wouldn't have thrown those files on the floor.

Building security personnel were the first to arrive, but when I told them Dr. Richardson had been murdered, they backed off and waited for the police. They kept guard by the door. Within a few minutes, the place was swarming with police. They, too, determined what I already knew—that Dr. Richardson was murdered. One of the officers called for a homicide detective while another officer took a statement from me.

The short, chubby officer who interviewed me surprised me by how suspicious he was. He made me feel like I had murdered Dr. Richardson, although I figured it was a fair assumption, considering the circumstances. Suspected murderer—something else to add to my ever-growing list of personal degradations.

"So you're a patient of his?" the officer asked me after writing down my name, address and cell phone number.

I showed him my appointment card, the date and time written in Dr. Richardson's hand. I told him I had waited half an hour before opening the door to check on him.

"How long have you been seeing the doctor?" he asked.

"Just about four weeks or so," I explained. I watched as he scribbled that information down.

"Have you ever been hospitalized for violent tendencies?" He just looked at me blankly.

I looked at him like he was nuts. "Of course not. I was just seeing the doctor for some stress I'd been having."

Fortunately, the homicide detective showed up fairly soon, and I worked my way over to him through the throng of police officers packed in such a small area. "Sir," I said, trying to get his attention. "I was the one who found the body, and I may be able to shed some light on what this is all about."

I hadn't said it to the first officer, but I was pretty sure that I may have been responsible for Dr. Richardson's death, just by being his patient. The thought made me sick. If my file was missing, I would know for sure.

The detective drew me aside, and once again I told my story about Jack's activities and explained that I was on the side of the FBI, helping them take the organization down. I talked about the death of Jim Pruitt. Finally, I told him that if my records were missing, it was more likely than not that Dr. Richardson was killed to get rid of my file.

The detective told me to wait in the waiting room. As I sat there, I wondered how much I had told Dr. Richardson in our sessions and what he had written down about what I'd said. If he had recorded everything, I had put him in serious danger. Damn, damn, damn! I hadn't thought of that when I agreed to see a psychiatrist.

The homicide detective stepped out of the office. "Ma'am, there's no evidence of your chart on his desk or in his files. You may be right in what you're saying. This was obviously a professional job."

"Can I call Detective Murphy? He's in charge of the case," I told him, rifling through my purse to find his card. I should have had Murphy's number memorized by this time. I finally found it and pulled it out.

"Why don't I give him a call, ma'am," he suggested. "That way we can coordinate our investigations."

"Is there anything else you need from me?" I asked.

"You'll have to come downtown and make a statement. As the person scheduled to meet him around the time he was killed, we have to treat you as a suspect, if only temporarily. I am sure you understand. And I'm not in a hurry to interview you—I don't believe you're the murderer—but please call me within the next two days to make an appointment to see me."

He was both fair and firm in his requests.

"I'll get in touch with you if we have questions we need answers to right away or if, by some chance, we find your chart," he said.

As I walked out of the office for the last time, I started shaking uncontrollably again. I leaned against the wall and tears ran down my face. Responsible for the deaths of two men. . . . When would it end? Was Dr. Richardson's murder in response to my taking the money from Jack's bank account, or would it have happened anyway, because I told Dr. Richardson some sensitive information?

On my way to the car, I called Connie. "Can you meet with me for dinner or for a cup of coffee? I'm freaking out."

"I can get off a half hour early and we can go to the coffee shop on the corner by my office. How does that sound?" she asked, sounding concerned.

"I can make it," I said.

I called Marge and told her I'd be 15 minutes late. She completely understood and I thanked her for that.

Instead of going back to work, I wandered around the small shops near where I would meet Connie. To keep my mind off Dr. Richardson's murder, I focused on the two million dollars and the fact that the money could mean I'd have my dream of opening a small retail shop, perhaps in this very area. I thought about what I'd sell in my own little shop and whether it would be successful or not. I was starting to doubt myself before I even got started, and that was not like me at all. My glass had always been half full—but not now, it seemed. The old me wouldn't have given a second thought to whether anything I tried would succeed—and that was how I should be thinking now. Besides, with two million dollars, I could always try something else if the shop went belly up.

I got to the coffee shop a few minutes early, ordered a latte, and had sat down by the time Connie rushed in, dressed in a stylish shirtdress and shawl. She ordered her drink and sat down.

"You sounded terrible on the phone. What's up?" she asked.

I told her about Dr. Richardson's death and about my belief that I somehow was the cause of it. I could barely hold back my tears as I told her about the horror I had seen.

"Oh my God, you must be terrified," she said. "Did the police talk to you?"

"They did, and they looked for my chart," I answered. "It wasn't there. It must have been stolen by whoever murdered him. I've got to go downtown to make a statement—technically, I'm a suspect, would you believe?"

"Now you really do need to have a treatment at our clinic. Please, Sondra, make an appointment and give it a try."

"Don't you get it, Connie? I'm afraid to see anyone at all, now—I'd probably just get them killed," I said, exasperated.

"You're right to be concerned. Maybe I can get you a home visit to my place—that way they can't find out," she said.

"These people seem to know everything."

I told her that I was worried about her and pretty much anyone in my life right now. The kids were relatively protected, but I didn't know what kinds of resources these people had. If they could get to Dr. Richardson, I believed they could do just about anything.

"These are bad people, Connie, and Jack is one of them. He's never been that good to me, but I've just been too weak to do anything about it or tell anyone about it. For years, almost since we got married, Jack has had a string of one-night stands and mistresses. I always pretended not to know, just to keep the peace and the harmony of a family home. I figured if I bugged him about it, it would drive Jack away, and I was worried about what would happen to me and the kids. I didn't want him to abandon me. I needed Jack, so I just looked the other way. But when you do a man's laundry and smell another woman's perfume or see a smear of her lipstick, you get hurt so deeply."

"Sondra, honey," Connie said, "you've allowed yourself to become enraged with negative energy. Jealousy brings negative energy into our being, and so do other negative emotional states—guilt, anger, hatred and feeling unloved. Even by simply accepting this situation, your energy has become depleted. You should come to our clinic and see an energy healer or, better still, an energy psychologist. Constant headaches are often caused when we become overloaded with negative energy and emotions. You have to put the past to rest. If you don't move on, Jack will be holding sway over you forever. If you continue to dwell on Jack's infidelity, you will stay a shadow of the old you. Honey, you need to be able to offer love to your kids, but first you need to love yourself. Sondra, you can start a healing process right now. Our energy healers can help you and, honestly, you'll see the results quickly, probably in the first session. What do you say?"

"It's so easy for you to spit this stuff out—you believe in it," I retorted. "My idea of getting better is popping a Xanax and downing a double espresso. But you know, finally talking about Jack's other life has made me feel lighter. I've never told anyone—not my sister, nobody. I just kept the hurt inside, I guess because of the shame. I felt like it was all my fault. Maybe he didn't find me attractive anymore, especially after I had children, even though I really worked hard to stay in good shape. And the further shame is I have never had the courage to confront Jack about his sordid double life. Now I just feel so wretched. I'm sick of crying."

Connie reached into her bag and handed me a tissue. "I know you've placed your faith in pills, but off the top of my head I can think of at least half a dozen toxic reactions you will get taking that anti-anxiety med," se said, starting to count off each symptom off on her fingers. "Dizziness, drowsiness, coordination problems, blurry vision. Um, what else? Headaches—as if you need more of those—and dry mouth, nausea, a rash . . . and those are just the few I can remember. Plus I'll bet you're not eating right. You have to admit that finding a way to get better without side effects makes sense. And you know Jack's behavior affects Cassie and Ben. Their energy systems will pick up on the bad vibrations in the home. They may not understand now, but in time they will. So it's not just you, Sondra; your healing will heal them, too."

"Thanks," I mumbled, dabbing my eyes with yet another Kleenex. She was right about my appetite; I barely had one and yet felt nauseous constantly. So what should I do now? After listening to Connie it was easy to feel that Xanax wouldn't help. "My stomach is absolutely knotted up."

"Sure it's knotted up!" Connie said. "It's your solar plexus. That is where your energy system dumps your unease. You need an energy healer or an EFT practitioner who can empathize and help you, and the sooner the better. Let me call the clinic now, please, for your own good." Connie reached for her cell phone, but I put out a hand to stop her.

"No thanks, Connie," I said. "Not just now. But you have helped me get closer to it. I can see that maybe I am carrying negative baggage because of my past actions. Or would inactions be nearer the truth? I promise, sweetie, I will make an appointment soon. Really."

"All right, then, but be sure you do," said Connie, returning her cell to her purse. "You okay?"

"Yes, I am okay, really. I need your love and support, Connie, I truly do."

"And you've got it. Gimme a hug."

I made an effort to change the subject, determined not to give further thought to the murders and tragedies, nor my friend's remedies.

"You remember my talking about Dwight, my neighbor?" I asked her. "I think he has a thing for me."

"Sondra, no—now is not the time," Connie murmured. "Don't you think it's a little bit early for a romance?"

"Believe me, I'm taking it as slowly as I can," I assured her.

"Are you sure he's safe to talk to?" she asked, suddenly suspicious. "You never know these days."

I thought for a moment. "I think he's safe; after all, he was living there before me, so he can't have followed me. But I haven't really told him anything confidential anyway."

"Best keep it that way," replied Connie.

"You know, considering everything you just said about positive and negative energies, wouldn't being with a man who cares about me help my positive energy?"

"Sure, that's true: If he loves you, that will uplift you. But be careful, Sondra. You've got too much going on right now, and you're not even divorced yet."

Speaking of confidential, I had told no one about my surreptitious acquisition of two million dollars. The coffee shop was nearly empty, and I was fairly sure no one could hear me. Even so, I dropped my voice down to a whisper.

"I did something I'm almost embarrassed to talk about," I began. "I found the numbers and passwords to Jack's overseas accounts, and I opened my own account. Now I've got two million dollars in a secret overseas account of my own."

"You did what?" Connie whispered back, her eyes huge. "I can't believe it!" . . .

. . . Our organization was used to keeping tabs on the people who worked for us. No racketeer likes to be stolen from, so it was second nature to have newbies and even old hands like me under surveillance. So I had Sondra's car tagged with a top-of-the-line GPS so we could keep track of where she went, and when. Tapping her phones was easy—Frank just palmed the apartment manager a C-note to borrow the passkey for an hour or two. What a hotshot that guy was. Now his plan was simple—get Sondra out of her apartment as often as possible, and get her to leave the kids alone. It'd tear her up for the rest of her life, assuming she lived, if her kids got stolen while she got laid. I loved it. And if anyone could do it, it was Frank. . . .

. . . "I broke into my old home and stole the numbers," I said, almost not believing the whole thing myself.

"Oh my God—good for you!" she whispered. "You deserve that money. Besides, you and Jack are still married—you have a right to what he's got!"

We actually managed to laugh at that. It felt good.

"If no one catches me, I'll be financially independent for the rest of my life. I can't imagine what kind of freedom that will bring me. I'll be able to open up that retail shop downtown, just like I've always dreamed," I said.

"Who would catch you? Jack can't very well say anything to anyone. Can you imagine him calling the cops and reporting the money stolen?" she asked.

"He might not even find out about the missing money for a long time," I said, not completely convinced of that fact myself. I glossed over the tiny fact that I had to make one more trip back to my old home to secure my actions. "Besides, how can he complain? He has three and a half million dollars left—that I know of. And he may have other offshore accounts. I found two sets of numbers; what if there were account numbers I didn't find? If I'd gone through all his files, I might have found evidence of even more money. I shrugged. "I'm not going to think about it anymore. Two million will be just fine."

"I think that's fantastic. I promise not to say anything—not even to Gavin." Gavin was Connie's husband. "It will be our secret. And don't tell anyone but me. You never know who might be listening in."

That made me think about the possibility that there might be bugs in my home or office. I felt stupid not thinking of it before. I had made a point of making the calls to the banks on my cell phone, but I made them from my office, which could be bugged—as could my apartment. They could have planted bugs when they broke into both places. . . .

On my way to Marge's house, I gave Detective Murphy a call. Fortunately, he was still in his office.

Thinking I was calling about Dr. Richardson's murder, he said, "I think the homicide had a great deal to do with the drug cartel. Your chart never turned up; I'm guessing the murderer took it with him. I'm getting very worried about your welfare."

"Thanks, but it's a little late now," I told him. "I have another question for you."

"Go ahead," he said.

"Can we have my apartment, car and office swept for bugs? And I want to make sure that calls I make on the cell phone are okay," I said.

"I was going to suggest that. I'll have a crew over to your house in a few hours if that's all right. They can check your office first thing tomorrow."

"That's fine."

"Okay, the officer who will be checking your apartment will give you a password when he buzzes your intercom. That will be 'Jack Daniels.' Got that?"

"Thank you so much. I really appreciate it."

I felt a lot better, but the whole idea of needing secret passwords to make sure visitors were legitimate bothered me, even though I knew it was a safety precaution. What next, though? And why couldn't they make any arrests before someone else got murdered?

I picked up the kids and swung by the sub shop we often frequented. I was cooking less and less these days; I was too stressed out.

We had just finished our sandwiches when the doorbell buzzed.

"Jack Daniels," a voice said, followed by silence.

Four officers came up to the apartment with a load of equipment. The lead officer, John, asked me how many phones I had in the house. I told them about the land line with two phones.

"What about cell phones?" I asked him.

"Cell phones can be picked up, but it's an erratic system that involves trying to tune into a specific wavelength. It's hard to track a specific phone unless the phone itself is bugged," he said. "If you've had it with you all the time, that wouldn't be likely, but I can check it if you want."

I handed it to him and he opened up the back. "It looks clean," he said. He put the phone back together. "It might be your best bet to use only your cell phone in the future. Keep it on you at all times."

"I will," I promised him.

Then I sat watching TV with the kids, trying not to get in their way, while they conducted their sweep. They looked everywhere and whispered to each other. When they were done, John came to me with a handful of tiny black things, some of which had wires snipped off of them.

"I'm pretty sure we got them all. We found that both phones were bugged, and there was a bug in the bedroom, the kitchen, and here in the living room. I don't know how long these have been there, but if you talked openly about your situation, they've been able to get a lot of information on you," John said, putting the bugs in a paper bag and scribbling something across it. "Where are your car keys?"

I followed him down to the car. They found a GPS tracking system but no bug inside the car. I almost cried. The GPS would already have shown that I went to our old house the other night, but Jack and his crew wouldn't necessarily know what I did there. At least my next trip across town wouldn't be monitored, I thought.

"So, tomorrow?" He looked at me expectantly. "A couple of guys and I will go through your office. I have the address. We will call your cell before we come down."

"I'll be there," I told him, happy that I had regained my privacy, and especially glad that no one would know about my next trip to my old house.

Once the police officers left and it neared the kids' bedtime, I once again offered them some hot chocolate with my special ingredient. Once they were asleep, I tried to get some rest myself before going out.

> *I feel infected somehow—as if I'm contagious, and everyone I touch catches the disease and dies. Only it isn't an act of God that takes these victims; it's a man, and I was his wife. I wonder how far up he is in the organization and why they are making such a point to destroy any evidence I might have. I can't possibly be the only one—there's got to be someone else who has even more dirt on them. Did they think that Jim Pruitt collected a great deal of information when he worked for me? All I cared about was that it was an illegal activity. I never asked for details. Jack himself told me more about what was going on than Jim ever did. And why kill Dr. Richardson? I hardly told him anything. I'm still afraid for my own life and for the lives of my*

children. Sometimes I think that there is some residual love Jack has for me, and that the love he has for his children is what is keeping us alive. He's killed all around me—enough to make me nervous about telling anyone anything—but he hasn't come after me. Much as I need to talk to someone, I'll protect Dwight and say nothing more about Jack's activities. He doesn't deserve to die. I think I'll also hide this diary in a very safe place. I've been lucky they haven't found it so far. If I have a handle on these guys at all, they'll be back with more bugs to make sure I'm behaving.

I closed my journal, tucked it inside a heating vent behind my bed, and finally fell asleep with my alarm once again set for 3:00 a.m.

Chapter 5

Dwight caught up with me as we were leaving the apartment the next morning. Ben was still half asleep and Cassie was struggling to put on her heavy backpack. It was getting colder out, and they both had their winter coats on.

"You have a party last night and forget to invite me?" he asked. He was dressed in gray sweats and was taking the garbage out to the dumpster. "I couldn't help noticing the commotion," he said apologetically.

"No commotion," I said as brightly as I could, sticking to my commitment to keep him in the dark so he'd be safe. "Some officers stopped by to ask me some questions, but I didn't have any idea what they were talking about. How are you?"

"Lonely," he said, smiling. "Would you like to come over to watch a movie tonight? I'll rent a few today if you'd like. Oh, and I'd like to make dinner for everyone."

I couldn't pass up that offer. "Sure thing. Whatcha serving?"

"Hmm," he said, cocking his head to one side. "I haven't decided yet, but it will be kid-friendly."

We all walked down the stairs together and parted at the car. I was happy he held off on his affection in front of the children. I took the kids to school and headed to work to see what the police would find in my office.

There were three officers there when I arrived. Fortunately, it didn't take as long to sweep my office as it did to go through the house. In the end, however, they did find a bug in the phone. The rest appeared clean.

For some reason, I was angrier about this than I was about my home being bugged. I worked with clients and employees who didn't deserve to have their business made public to these thugs. I wondered, as I had at home, what I had said over the phone that would have been important to them.

I thought back to Jack's ill-gotten gains, and any lingering guilt I had about taking some of it disappeared. With the deaths of two innocent people and the hell my family was going through, I felt I deserved that money. Maybe I would give some of the money to the families of Dr. Richardson and Jim Pruitt. They suffered so much more than I did.

Thinking of their families reminded me to send flowers to Dr. Richardson's funeral. I found out through the clinic where to send the flowers and sent a small arrangement with a card that said simply "Sondra."

The rest of my day went quickly. I raced through a bunch of contracts and held a company-wide meeting, and before I knew it, it was 4:00 already. I hurried to get my children from Marge's house. Marge was always understanding if I was late, but I hated to put too much pressure on her. In my own illogical way, too, I worried about her welfare. I ceased to doubt what these people were capable of.

"How are things going?" Marge asked me as the kids got their things together and put on their coats.

I gave her the briefest outline of what was going on between me and Jack. She listened intently, her expression barely changing. "Actually, we're hanging in there," I said. "I don't know when all of this will be over, but the police have sort of promised me it will be within the month. I don't know how much longer I can wait."

Marge put her arm around my waist and said, "I will be praying for you and your family. I really believe things will turn out fine in the end."

The kids joined us before I started crying, and we said our goodbyes. As I got ready to leave, I touched my cell phone in my pocket like a talisman. I never left home without my phone ready to use at a moment's notice; I had put a speed dial to 911 on the 9 of my keypad. This tiny gadget was a lifesaver but, if I understood Connie right from one of our chats, it was also an anchor for negative emotion. Every time I picked up my cell now, I was anticipating having to use it to save our lives.

I reminded the kids on the way home that we were eating at Dwight's, which was a big hit with both of them.

"Dwight's cooking up one of his masterpieces today," I said in a sing-song voice as we pulled into the parking lot. "I can't wait."

We went into our apartment first and waited for Dwight to come knocking, which he did soon enough. "Are you ready for lasagna, French bread and homemade apple pie?" He was grinning from ear to ear when the kids popped up from their video game and cheered.

"When do you have the time?" I asked him.

"I got home at 2:00 today. Everything was made fresh for my favorite family." He smiled as he spoke. "And dinner, my dears, is on."

We followed Dwight to his place, where we ate lasagna until we could hardly eat any more, and then Dwight served his homemade apple pie, complete with vanilla ice cream for the kids.

"I'd be huge if I ate like this every day, Dwight," I laughed. "You are truly a really good cook."

"Remind me to show you the culinary school information I got recently. I can't wait to get started," he told me.

As the kids were full and anxious to watch television, I ushered them over to our apartment and discussed their homework obligations with them before going back over to Dwight's for a movie or two. It was only about 6:30. The kids had plenty of time to do their homework before watching their favorite programs. I made sure they were locked in and walked back to Dwight's apartment.

He had rented a couple of recently released movies, and I selected one that was sort of a thriller. I was tired of anything "thrilling," as I was exposed to it so often in my life these days, but I thought Dwight would like it better than the other one. . . .

. . . Frank had a text message all set up on his cell to transmit the moment Sondra went into the apartment opposite her place. Frank still had the key to the dump from when he trashed the place, but I didn't want to try to get it from him. He had set up the perfect opportunity, and I had to go for it. Jimmying a lock is no big deal anyway. The prize of getting my kids back with me and Sondra permanently out of the way was one hell of a draw. If we got our timing right, her neighbor could well be screwing her while I was making off with the kids. If it went to court, if she lived that long, her infidelity would justify my actions, that was for sure.

So now all I had to do was to settle back and wait for the text message to get the plan under way.

Carmen was going to play mom, but she didn't have much that looked like mommy-type clothing, so I sent her to Franklin Mills to get some practical outfits. No cleavage and nothing too short. I told her to buy the kids a gift or two and hand 'em over as if she really meant it. . . .

. . . As the movie started, Dwight showed me the information about the Philadelphia Institute of Culinary Arts' night program. It looked pretty extensive and included sessions that lasted all day on Saturdays. Dwight planned to start in the winter, he said, and he was excited about becoming a chef.

"Finally, I'll be in a profession that moves me. Like tonight, for example; I loved cooking for all of you. I put my all into making those dishes, and I look forward to having my own restaurant someday. You'll be my first customers, okay?"

"You don't have to convince me," I said, resting my hands upon my full stomach. "You already know a lot about cooking, and these classes will only help you boost your skills. I'm sure the kids would agree with me when I say we will be your testers, for every dish."

"I'll miss our movie nights, though," he said, snuggling next to me on the couch. "This has been fun."

I didn't realize encouraging Dwight to go to cooking school would cost me our evenings together. I decided to think about that later. We settled into watching the movie, which wasn't as violent as I thought it would be. Dwight had opened a bottle of Californian red. I have never been a big drinker, so a couple of glasses into the bottle I was feeling quite mellow. Even my headache was gone. Dwight was being a real smoothie, cuddling up and necking. He seemed very determined, and I wasn't fighting him off. But I wasn't used to this, and before things got overheated, I decided to take a bit of a break, even though I was tingling in all the right places. By good fortune the movie ended, and it was time for me to put the kids to bed. Dwight tried to convince me to stay, or at least come back once the kids were in bed, to watch the other movie.

"Maybe," I said, wondering if he really meant we'd watch the other movie . . . or something else. "Let me get the kids to bed first."

I grabbed my keys and left Dwight's apartment. Going back to Dwight's tonight had a sense of promise waiting to be experienced. As the door swung open, I could hear the familiar sound of the video game, but when I got into the living room, I saw the game was on standby and the same music was just playing over and over.

The kids had their homework scattered everywhere, and I was irritated that they hadn't cleaned up their stuff yet.

"Ben? Cassie?" I called toward the bedrooms. There was no response. Trying not to panic, I rushed from room to room but found nothing. I even checked all the closets. They weren't there. "Kids, don't tease me," I ordered. I raced back out to the living room and kitchen. All the windows were closed and locked. My kids were gone. They had just vanished from inside a locked apartment.

My first phone call was to Ben's friend Kyle's apartment. "Are my kids over there?" I asked Kyle's mother, trying to hide my growing panic. Her "no" hit me like a sledgehammer. Almost in a trance, I grabbed my cell phone to dial 911. I hurried over to Dwight's apartment. When the operator came on the line, I said in a rush, "Hello? I'd like to report a kidnapping. My God! Someone just stole my kids!" I could feel my life unraveling as I said the words out loud.

I was shaking as Dwight met me at the door. He overheard what I said to the 911 operator and he looked horrified. He pulled me into his apartment and held me close to him. My shaking body settled down, but by then, I was so upset and angry that nothing would actually help calm the rush of feelings I was experiencing.

"I should stay in my apartment. The police will come there first," I told him.

"Do you want me to stay with you?" I could see the pain in his eyes as he looked at me.

I shook my head. "No. They'll just ask questions about why you're there. They'll be here any minute." I quickly sent a text message to Connie: NEED TO TALK PLEASE WAIT UP FOR MY CALL SONDRA. I was in unknown territory. I was the mother of kidnapped children. The only person in the world right now that I could seek comfort from was Connie.

I went back into my apartment and Dwight returned to his. I leaned back against the wall and the now familiar clamminess spread across my body. This was not a time to be out of control. Instinctively I drew in three or four deep breaths. My hysteria lessened, and a sense of calm came over me. I saw the flashing lights outside the apartment, then there was a knock on my door. Two officers stood there, and one—I recognized him as one of the officers I had spoken to the night of Jim Pruitt's murder—said,

"Downstairs door lock is broken. We let ourselves in." Before too long, it seemed the entire Philadelphia force was in my apartment.

I spoke as fast as I could with the officers. I felt like I told my story a hundred times that night. "We ate dinner at the apartment next door. I stayed behind to watch a movie and they were locked into this apartment. When I came back at almost 9:00, I found the video game on and the books strewn about like they had been doing their homework, but the kids had disappeared."

"Can anyone corroborate your statement, ma'am?" said one of the officers I had not met before.

"Yes, the man in apartment 214—Mr. Osborne. I was with him. I just know my husband is behind all of this!" I shrieked, unaware that the level of my voice had been continually rising.

"Yeah, we know what he and his cohorts are capable of already," the officer who I recognized nodded. "Did you check with any of their friends?"

I nodded furiously. "They have only one friend in the area, and his mother said they haven't seem them. What are we going to do?"

As I spoke to the first two officers, three others were looking around—peeking in closets, checking the locks on the doors and windows.

One of the officers called me over to the front door. "Do you see that tool mark there? It looks like someone unlocked your door from the outside without having to use a key."

My heart sank and I just stood there dumbly, looking at him as though he'd tell me something more along the lines of what I wanted to hear.

Another officer tapped me on the shoulder. "Ma'am; do you have any good, clear, current pictures of the kids? Given the circumstances, I'd like to send out an AMBER alert. That will go nationwide."

I vaguely knew what an AMBER alert was, but all I could think was that they were for other people's children, not mine. I nodded and went over to my desk in the corner of the living room where I kept the extra school pictures of the kids. I gave the officer both packages of photos, including some eight-by-tens. "Now, Mrs. Ackerman, before we get going with AMBER, we are required to completely search the apartment, just in case the kids are playing games. Please don't be upset by this; it's procedure. We need to look everywhere like checking closets, piles of laundry, in and under beds, inside large appliances, things of that sort—wherever a child could fit, in case he or she is hiding." The officers all pulled on latex gloves and set about their task. The search revealed nothing; my kids were gone.

One of the officers told me they were sending a couple of squad cars over to Jack's house, and that they were already in contact with the FBI. "Do you think this is a kidnapping for ransom situation?" he asked.

I thought of the two million dollars that I would now gladly give back in exchange for my kids. "I don't really know," I said, my voice aching with despair. "Who knows with these people?"

About that time, one of the officers left the apartment and came back with a contraption he said would be able to trace any phone calls that were made to my apartment. I wondered how they would be able to trace calls to my cell phone but didn't ask him right away.

My apartment was abuzz with activity. There were walkie-talkies crackling and cell phones going off all over the place. The cacophony made me feel lost and confused. My headache had returned with a vengeance; I wondered if I could find my headache pills in all the chaos.

I looked at my watch. It wasn't that late yet, so I called Connie on my cell phone. That's when I burst into tears. "Connie! Jack, that heartless bastard—he's gone and done it this time Goddamn it. He's stolen the kids right out from under me!"

"What! Oh my God, Sondra. I'm coming over right now. Give me five minutes."

"No, please don't," I replied. "There's nothing you can do here, and there are police all over the place. But . . . I might have to bunk at your place—if not tonight, then maybe tomorrow," I told her. "I just can't be here—not until they're found." I refused to believe in any other outcome but that they'd be found soon.

"Okay. You know anytime you need a place to stay, you're welcome here," she said. "Are you absolutely sure you don't need me over there?"

I looked around at the officers swarming over the place. "Connie, it's a zoo here. If I need you, I promise I will call. Just keep praying for us." I sat down on the armrest of the couch as I spoke; my knees felt weak.

"I will, honey. Call me when you can," she said.

I hung up the phone and turned to the officer who appeared to be in charge, who had been waiting for me to finish my conversation.

"Mrs. Ackerman, we're going to have to ask you to come down to the precinct to make a statement."

"Why? Isn't obvious who did this? My rotten-to-the-core husband—I told you already," I raged.

He said calmly, "I truly appreciate your view, Mrs. Ackerman, but we have to interview all suspects. Until we have conducted that interview and ruled you out, then, I'm sorry, but you remain one of our prime suspects. So can we say 10:00 tomorrow morning? Here's my card with the address and my contact number. Please don't skip this interview, Mrs. Ackerman. If you don't come, you'll just slow down the investigation. I can feel you firmly believe your husband is the perpetrator, but police procedure has to be followed. If you want, we could go downtown now—your choice."

"Sonafabitch, I can't believe this!" This all barely seemed rational. "You think I'm making all this up? Fine—let's go now. I'm not up to driving, though. You'll have to take me there."

"That's fine. If this works out, you can be back here within the hour. And we'll have to interview the man you claim to have been with. What's his name again? Osborne? We will have to run both your names through the national database for previous felonies and misdemeanors. Have you ever been in trouble with the law before, Mrs. Ackerman? Or has your friend?"

"Let me get my coat," I said, standing up. "You can ask me all you want at the station. Will I need a lawyer?"

An officer was talking to Dwight at his door. I called goodnight as I passed. He called over to say he had elected to make his statement the next morning. I didn't blame him for that; how could it help the investigation if he sat at the police precinct half the night? When I looked back at him as I descended the stairs, he blew me a kiss.

The Fifth Precinct building was both imposing and oppressive at the same time. I was led into the building through a rear entrance and taken to an interview room. The room was almost a TV cop show cliché, with a two-way mirror and a table with a recording device on it. I answered their questions for an hour. I had my fingerprints taken, as well as with my photo. I could see all of it had to be done: I could just as easy have staged the whole event to steal my children from my estranged husband instead of the other way around. Now the local police were on my side. After about two hours I was allowed to go home. Two officers gave me a ride and a female officer escorted me upstairs. I thanked her for her kindness, and then she was gone.

I was tempted to knock on Dwight's door. The thought of the loving comfort that may have awaited me was indeed inspiring me to cross over the hall, but then I checked myself. If the police came looking for me and I was once again in the apartment of another man, a man who was not my husband, then further suspicion could fall on me.

Instead, I turned to a detective who seemed to be in charge. The only officer there without a uniform, he instead was wearing a dark blue sweater and blue pants and had a badge around his neck. He was tall with gray hair and a matching moustache. He exuded a feeling of authority; I guessed he'd been an officer for a long time. The craggy lines etched across his face made him appear that he'd earned his badge. "So what now?" I asked him, not knowing what else to say.

He shook my hand. "I'm Detective Littleton. I'm working on the Pruitt case as well. It's obvious the two cases are related."

I liked him immediately; his voice gave all the indicators of being shaped by Philip Morris and Kentucky sour mash.

"Before I ask you any questions, Mrs. Ackerman, I must say we will be offering you counseling with one of our experienced family counselors. You take my advice—don't refuse the offer. The counseling will help you through the psychological difficulties this type of incident puts a parent through."

"Thanks." I thought of Connie's stuff and wondered if it would help me more than this standard type of counseling.

"We've got a good chance of getting your kids back if your husband is involved. He won't hurt the kids. We'll put a 24-hour tail on him as soon as we can. We've already confirmed he's not at his place of residence. We're on the lookout for his car. We've just completed a full sweep of your apartment for evidence, including prints. We'd like to get your prints now to eliminate the ones we've found, especially around the door frame."

"I was just printed downtown when I gave my statement."

"That's all right, then. Now that we have your prints in our database, we can rule them out."

I looked over at the dining room table, which now had a bunch of electronic equipment on it. "What's all that for?"

Detective Littleton walked me over to it. "This is the equipment we use to record and trace calls coming into your home. It's state of the art. We can set it up so you can be anywhere, and we can still trace and record the call."

"Is it hooked up already?" I asked. An officer wearing headphones was seated at the table with my phone attached to the apparatus on one side of him.

"Yes, ma'am," he said. "When the phone rings, pick up the phone and just speak normally. Try to keep them on the phone as long as you can. The officer will do all the work."

In spite of the high-tech help, I just wilted. That meant an officer would be with me as long as I was in this apartment, which was okay for my protection, but I just lost my privacy—and there was nothing I could do about it. It was how it had to be. But if it helped get my kids back, I was willing to do anything.

Slowly, the army of police officers and forensic investigators filtered out of the apartment, leaving me with Detective Littleton and the officer running the tracing equipment, who told me to call him Dave. Dave said another officer would take over in the morning, and that various officers would monitor the phone around the clock. He suggested I get some rest. I thought he was kidding.

Detective Littleton took the time to ask me what I knew about my husband and his drug trafficking. As it turned out, he knew much of what the police and the Feds knew already, and I really didn't have much more to offer. I asked him about Detective Murphy and if he had heard about the kidnapping.

"Yes, I spoke with him tonight," Littleton told me. "He's been apprised of the situation."

I wondered if the kidnapping would become a federal case, but I thought that would happen only if the kids were transported across state lines. Every time I thought about what my kids were going through at that moment, I was just sick to my stomach. A part of me hoped Jack was intimately involved in all of this, because then they would be treated with some kind of decency. Where was Jack, anyway?

At about midnight, I said goodbye to Detective Littleton, and he once again mentioned counseling and that it could be set up immediately. I thanked him, but declined the offer. He nodded in an understanding way as he left. I settled down on the couch, just a few feet away from Officer Dave. I dozed off and on, getting up once to get a pillow and blanket. The phone never rang, but Dave was alert, reading a book, every time I peeked to see what he was up to.

Just after the sun rose over the Philadelphia skyline, there was a knock on the door that made me jump up from the couch. It was Officer Martin coming on duty for the next shift. I said goodbye to Officer Dave and got up to make a large pot of coffee. I figured these guys must live off the stuff, like I did.

Officer Martin took a cup of coffee. As I sipped mine I thought about checking on Dwight, but it was still too early. I waited a couple of hours before calling the school and Marge. I told the school secretary the kids would be out for a couple of days, but she had already seen the AMBER alert on television and knew the whole story. So did Marge.

"I'm praying as much as I can for those two babies," said Marge. "I just know they'll be found safe. I won't keep you now. You must have lots of calls to make. God bless."

I thanked her and promised I'd tell her any information as it came my way.

Aaron Sorenson was next on my list of people to contact. I was glad I had a cell phone to use so that my home line would be kept open.

Aaron was in, and he took my call right away. "I already heard. The alert is on every news channel. I'm sure they'll find them," he reassured me. I was impressed with the AMBER alert system, and I felt sure it would be effective in the return of my children.

Something had been bothering me all night long, and I knew Aaron could help. "I have a question, though," I said. "He's their father. Can they get him for kidnapping if he's their father and the divorce hasn't gone through?" I was so afraid he could just take them from me and not be punished for what he did.

"Well, we have it on record that he isn't allowed visitation, and it sounds like someone broke into the apartment and actually stole them. I think that's a far cry from just taking custody."

My relief was palpable. I couldn't live with myself if Jack could have just gotten away with this whole thing. Again I prayed that my children were being well taken care of. I thanked Aaron and told him I'd be in touch. . . .

. . . Well, that was easy enough. Once I broke into the foyer and then got the apartment door open, the kids were just right there in front of me. Neither one of them looked upset or unhappy to see me, and my heart started racing just seeing them again. I told them Sondra had an aneurysm at Dwight's and was at the hospital, and they just followed me out to the car. Seems I arrived too early for Dwight to ride Sondra—or did she leave too early? Either way, they didn't get it on, I found out.

So now I needed Carmen to make the grade as a mommy. This wouldn't be easy. Ben was 11 and Cassie 13, and a 27 year-old free spirit like Carmen wasn't about to settle down and cook three squares a day for them. There had to come a point, say when we're in the Caribbean, that they're going to have to accept that she's looking after them instead of their real mommy. Maybe I should tell the kids Sondra's dead. That kind of a statement is final, and if they accepted that along with the fact that the four of us were now a family, they should get over missing Sondra pretty quick. Of course, there was the very real possibility that Sondra would be dead soon anyway, so then it would be the truth. Once everything calmed down, we could send the two of them away to school—separate schools would be better. It would toughen them up. And when the time was right, Ben could come into the firm and Cassie could marry one of the nephews. Los Archos wouldn't let women be managers; the Brothers had very traditional views on the roles of women. As far as they were concerned, women stayed home and took care of their husbands and had babies. I wasn't going to try to get them to adjust their belief system. Cassie would do as she was told. She might need some discipline early, to get her to behave better. I should check into religious schools, find one with nuns. That ought to do it. After five years of nuns, she'd be more subservient than she was now. Sondra had given them both too much free reign. My fault—I guess I ought to have been around more. Anyway, Cassie could marry at 18. I would tell the Brothers so they could select one of their many nephews for her. This would be another steppingstone for me; marrying Cassie off in five years

106

would give me a boost in the organization. As for Ben, a military academy would be the best option. That should give him some backbone, which he needs. I should have primed the Brothers sooner about having him join us. He could come in at 16 as an apprentice, and he'd be a millionaire by the time he was 20. I would make sure of that. . . .

. . . It was late enough in the morning that Connie would be at work. I wondered if she had her cell phone on but, just to be on the safe side, I called her direct number. She picked up immediately. It was so good to hear her voice after everything I'd just been through; it gave my spirit a boost. "It's me," I told her.

"Sondra, I've been worried sick about you. The kids are all over the news, and Brett was crying today when he heard. Are you coming to stay tonight?"

I didn't mind hanging out with the officers who were monitoring my phone, but being at home without the kids was really starting to scare me. "Maybe I will stay with you tonight; I can come over after you get off work," I said. I explained the system the police had of monitoring my phone and told her I could have the phone transferred to her house if that was okay with her.

"Of course. You can stay in the guest room downstairs, and we won't let anyone use the phone while you're there," she assured me. "How about if you come over at 6:00? I'll have dinner ready by then, or at least well on the way. I'll keep it simple; I'll wait until you get there to finish."

I had barely ended the call when my cell phone rang again. I recognized Jack's cell phone on the caller ID. Damn. They wouldn't be able to trace this call. I quickly told Officer Martin that my husband was on the cell phone and he put down his book, waiting intently.

"Jack?" I could hardly contain myself. "What have you done with my children, you fucking bastard!" I guess I couldn't contain myself after all.

"Whoa, hold up—I'm clean here. Yeah, the cops just stopped my car. I was coming home from work. I haven't been watching the news so I didn't know anything about it. What happened, for God's sake?" He seemed panicked; however, Jack was a very good actor, as I now knew only too well. This was really starting to scare me. I told him about the abduction and my belief that he had something to do with it.

"Me?" he said. "I had no idea and, no, I don't know anyone who would have done this. Maybe I should ask you what *you've* been up to lately."

He sounded like he was accusing me of being unfaithful or something, but I wasn't buying it. "You know very well I haven't been up to anything," I cried. "It's that fucking group you work for. They took my children, didn't they?"

"Just stop it, Sondra! Enough already. No one I know took our children. I would never let that happen," he insisted.

I could feel the panic welling up inside me again. "Then who took them? Who broke into my apartment? I figure the only person interested in kidnapping them, Jack, is you," I shouted into the phone. I could feel the life drain out of me as I talked to him.

"I don't know, Sondra. I told the police I would cooperate as much as possible. I guess we just have to trust that someone will call and ask for a ransom. I'll pay whatever they ask for," he said.

I'll bet you would, I thought bitterly. . . .

. . . The call from Los Archos came through early evening my time, which would be midafternoon there in Tijuana. The bosses did not want Sondra loose on the streets. Two hit men, cousins of theirs who were damn deadly, were being sent up to take care of the situation. Pablo and Nesto had never failed to complete a contract. This was my mess and the Brothers would insist on using them and me paying. That would be a million dollar hit. Those two didn't offer any "buy one, get one free" deal like at Wal-Mart. I had to stand my ground about my kids and was very firm that they remain alive and well. I could look after them with Carmen. I was relieved when they agreed to that. And that meant Carmen couldn't complain, when her brothers said okay on that score. All I had to do was stay cool and then lull Sond in such a way as to make her drop her guard.

This was becoming a snowball rolling down a very steep hill. The push to eliminate Sondra now seemed to have a will of its own and was fast becoming a matter I couldn't control. Not that I wanted to. I guessed if she made me mad, my temper would take over and I would do it. An accident I could deal with also. Getting her down on her knees in front of me and pulling the trigger . . . I couldn't do that. In truth, despite all the ramblings in my head, I would rather have someone else take her out. Even if I had to pay. So let these deadly cousins come up here and waste her. So long as Ben and Cassie were out of the way when it went down, I was cool.

Sondra had never had much to do with her sister and mother, but if she gave me a hard time, I'd tell her straight that they were both in danger. Sondra was so friggin' noble, she wouldn't let them get hurt. She was a "take me not them" sort of woman. I would use that against her—no question. One short call to her cell—that's all it would take to pull her into a trap for the two cousins to take care of her.

When I think about it, I have to admit I've been cruel to Sondra ever since Ben was born. That was still the time when we had regular sex together. For my personal pleasure and to make her subservient, I used to force her to do sex in ways that she found unnatural. The more she would plead for normal lovemaking the more I enjoyed turning her over or having her kneel in front of me. She could never scream, because the kids were in the next room, so she just had to take it, like it or not. I always called the shots—she wanted something one way, but I was more aggressive and powerful than she was. And things haven't changed. I'll keep on getting my way. . . .

. . . Jack and I agreed to stay in touch; I promised to call as soon as I heard anything. He gave me another, new cell phone number, and I wondered if drug barons all needed more than one cell phone. The thought momentarily enraged me.

"Damn," I said out loud. "He called me on the cell phone."

Officer Martin, however, seemed more positive about the call. "This is perfect," he said, jumping up and walking over to the living room where I had been sitting on the couch. "First of all, we put a bug in your phone last night, so the whole thing was recorded. I was listening in on your conversation as you were talking. I think he's lying, but he's smooth."

"You're kidding!" I was so relieved. I hadn't even noticed they had gotten into my cell phone that night; things were so chaotic, they could have put a bug in my ear and I wouldn't have noticed.

"And second," he went on, and I could see the twinkle in his eye, "we have his cell phone number. We have software that can triangulate the location of any cell phone, provided it is turned on, so we can follow him without always having to *follow* him. Get it?"

I thought I did, and I was amazed at the things they could do now. "So you think he was lying about not knowing anything?"

"Ma'am, he's still our top suspect, whether or not he actually did the kidnapping. There will be people following his car and tracking his phone at all times."

I called Connie and told her I'd be over at 6:00 to stay the night. I talked to Martin about transferring the land line and trace to the telephone number at Connie's house. He assured me they could do that and that my cell phone would be continually monitored via the bug. "I think we have a good chance now of getting your children back," he reassured me.

I wrote a note to Dwight saying I'd be away from the apartment for a few days and taped it to his door. Then I packed a few things and chatted with Officer Martin until it was time to go to Connie's house. Officer Martin assured me that the police and the FBI would be in constant contact with me.

Around 5:30, as I left the apartment with Officer Martin still manning the phones, I heard a door open behind me. It was Dwight; he still looked as pained as he did the night before.

"I got your note," he said. "I take it they haven't found anything."

I shook my head and allowed him to give me a hug. "No, they haven't. It's a waiting game now. I need to wait until the police or the FBI comes up with something. I just have to trust the process. In the meantime, I can't stay at my apartment without the kids; I'm going to a friend's house for a few days."

"Well, stay in touch, okay? That is, unless you want to sleep over here," he said. "I can sleep on the couch." I thanked him for his kindness, but declined the offer—although I must admit it was tempting. He walked me out to the car, gave me a peck on the cheek and said, "I'll be praying for you." He watched as I drove away from the apartment complex. I hoped he didn't feel guilty about the fact that I'd been with him when it happened. I was the guilty party—the bad parent, so to speak. I was still kicking myself for what had happened the previous night. I should have known that even a locked door wouldn't stop them.

Connie's house was warm and relatively peaceful, but just seeing Brett gave me pangs of longing for my own children. Gavin hadn't gotten home from his law office yet. Connie was making a meatloaf. She apologized, as she had gotten home later than expected. The ground sirloin looked good, and I saw the horseradish on the countertop, so I knew we could expect a kick to our taste buds.

"Can I help?" I asked her after I had dropped my duffel bag in their guest room. "By the way, if the caller ID says my number on it, I'm supposed to pick it up."

"Okay. Brett never answers the phone, so it's just me and Gavin who need to know," she said, crunching up some crackers for the meatloaf. "So let's make it easy on ourselves just grab a bag of any kind of vegetables from the freezer; we can microwave them."

"Sure," I said, grateful for any distraction at the moment. I dug out some mixed vegetables and put them in a bowl to microwave.

By that time, Gavin had come home and we chatted in the kitchen for a while. I told him about the telephone setup just about the time the telephone actually rang.

"The caller ID has your number on it," Connie said, handing me the cordless phone. My knees went limp as I took it from her.

It was my sister Laura from Cincinnati. She had just gotten home from work and had turned on the news. "What's going on?" she asked with fear in her voice.

I told her about the events of the last 24 hours and that I believed Jack had something to do with it. "I have to believe it's going to be okay," I said, putting on my bravest front. "The police and the Feds are doing everything they can." Inside, my heart was aching for my children, and I was praying desperately that nothing bad was happening to them. I discouraged her from telling our mother, who had the common form of dementia, mild Alzheimer's disease, and was in a nursing home near where Laura lived. I explained to my sister that I didn't want to have to deal with Mom phoning every five minutes, which I had read recently in *Women's World* could happen with an Alzheimer's sufferer, so it was best she wasn't told.

Laura promised to say nothing to our mother and asked me to stay in touch. Dad had died about five years ago and it was just me

111

and Laura in the immediate family, besides Mom. Laura offered to contact our various cousins, aunts and uncles, both to update them and to tell them not to call. Harvey, an old family friend we had grown up with, had already called Laura several times and was very insistent to be given my number. Laura very sensibly had figured out the "keep the phone line clear" protocol and told Harvey I would call him when the time was right. He had asked Laura to pass on his offer of help, saying if there was anything he could do, he would. The three of us went way back, and it was good to know he cared; in fact, it was especially comforting. I took the number from her.

It had been good to hear Laura's voice again. It had been a while. We had not kept in touch as often as we should have. It was probably because Mom had lived with her. Mom had always been very critical of me, and I had long since made a decision to have little or nothing to do with her. The outcome of that was, with the extended bouts of silence between Mom and me, Laura and I had drifted apart.

I got off the phone just in time for an evening cocktail while the meatloaf was baking. I didn't drink much, but I agreed to a glass of red wine. We sat in the large living room. My head was pounding again, and I remembered that my medication had run out and I had forgotten to refill it. I hoped the wine would help. In what seemed no time at all Gavin was refilling my glass. I hardly recalled having drunk the first glass.

Connie, noticing my pain, moved closer to me. "Have you given any thought to using one of our drug-free therapies yet? I really do think it will help you."

I was so miserable. I missed and feared for my kids something terrible, I felt incredibly guilty for leaving them alone for even five minutes, I despised that low-life husband of mine, my head was pounding—I was even upset about leaving Dwight behind this evening. I wondered about the statement he made to the police. I hoped he wasn't feeling bad about himself and the fact we were together at the time of the kidnapping.

With all of these thoughts swirling around in my aching head, I realized my pills were practically useless even when I had a decent supply, and my psychiatrist had been murdered right out from under me. Maybe I should try something different, I thought.

"Actually, it doesn't sound half bad right now. I don't know how long it will take before the kids come back, and I really do need some relief," I told her, rubbing my temples furiously.

"How about you come to work with me tomorrow morning?" Connie suggested. "I can get you in first thing in the morning. Just keep an open mind."

"I don't need a lot of help in that regard," I remarked wryly. "I'll try just about anything at this point. Really, I had been thinking about trying EFT for a while—and now with the kids missing . . . it's like it had to get this bad to actually get me to go. Being victimized really crystallizes your decisions, you know?"

"Okay, it's set then. We'll leave at 8:00 tomorrow," she told me.

I called Officer Martin, who was just done with his shift, to tell him that I would be out of Connie's home for a few hours the next morning. He said he'd have the phones switched over to my cell phone before he left that night. That way, any call going to the house from then on would go to the cell phone directly. I wondered why he hadn't thought of that in the first place, but I didn't say anything.

Dinner was quiet. Gavin and Connie did their absolute best to lift my spirits. So as not to upset Brett, who had a real soft spot in his heart for Ben and Cassie, we avoided discussing the kids' kidnapping. Brett gave me a big hug after dinner and told me he hoped that Ben and Cassie would come home soon.

"Ben's really strong. He'll beat up those kidnappers, and he'll be home soon; you just wait and see," he told me.

I smiled indulgently. "Yes, he will," I answered. I wished things really did work that way and that my kids did have superpowers to overcome their captors. I sighed wistfully and fought back more than a few tears.

I wish I had played closer attention to my gut when I thought about getting out of Philadelphia and moving someplace far away. I just had to stay in this city, where my kids were easy targets for those thugs. Jack has to be lying about being involved. In fact, my panic would be far greater if I believed any differently. What is all of this supposed to mean? Are they scaring me, or is Jack planning to take his millions and hide somewhere with the children? With his money and connections, he could take them to some foreign country where I'd never see them again. I'm pushing to the back of my mind the thought of never hearing their sweet voices again or feeling them once more in my arms. The police have to come through for me this time. They need to get my children back. I'll do anything after that to keep them safe. I'm seeing an EFT practitioner tomorrow; I have no idea what to expect. Perhaps I should have picked up some literature on it before I actually did it, but what choice do I have? Nothing else is working—I might as well try it.

Chapter 6

I slept better at Connie's house than I had at my apartment with Officer Dave looking over me, and I got up as the sun rose. It was just past 7:00, and I was disheartened that no one had called yet except Kyle, who phoned me at 9:00 the night before to find out if Ben had been found yet. Apparently, their disappearance was already the talk of the school.

I took a long shower, letting the water cascade over me. The hot water was giving me a sense of renewal: I felt I was washing away the memory of all the bad things that had been going on around me. I dressed comfortably, not knowing what to expect with EFT. I could hear movement on the second floor, and I knew the family was up. I made coffee and drank a cup before Connie and Brett came downstairs for the day. Gavin was already on the move; I saw his car pulling out of the driveway as I came out of the guest room. I sat at the kitchen island sipping my coffee and getting some solace from the early morning quiet. Birdsong filtered in from the yard. Suddenly the house livened up as Connie and then Brett made their way into the kitchen.

"Ooh, coffee." Connie's eyes lit up. "I don't often get this luxury in the morning."

Connie gulped down a cup while Brett ate his cereal. Once breakfast was over, we left the house together. As I would be leaving the clinic after my treatment, I took my own car and followed Connie, first to the school as she dropped off Brett, and then to the clinic—a small, single-story white building tucked behind a strip mall. Not very glamorous, I thought, but who was I to say?

I parked next to Connie and we walked in together. The waiting room was neat and pleasantly decorated, with soft blue chairs and several pieces of modern art that made the place look extremely fashionable. I commented on the art to Connie. She told me that if I looked carefully, I'd see that each piece included the seven colors of the rainbow. Their effect was to reach out to each client on the vibrational level that he or she was at when they entered the clinic. That had me scratching my head; I didn't have a clue what she was talking about. I decided just to nod and stay quiet.

A lithe, twentysomething woman with a long brown ponytail and lovely brown eyes sat behind the counter. "Hey, Connie! How are you this morning?"

"Hi, Amy," said Connie, taking her jacket off. "I have an emergency client for Ken to see today. Does he have any room this morning? Any time to squeeze in my friend here?"

Amy didn't miss a beat. "Well, he just had a cancellation at 9:00, and his 8:00 client is Mrs. Abrams. She never usually takes the whole time, so he should be free fairly soon." She turned to me. "Are you the emergency client?"

I nodded, wondering what I should do next. I didn't know if this was like a regular clinic or if I had to do something special besides registering.

"I've got some paperwork for you. The practitioner you'll be seeing—his name is Ken March—likes to have his new clients fill out a few papers before seeing him." She handed me a clipboard with several sheets of paper attached. One of the papers was a one-page hand out entitled "What is EFT?" Given my novice status with this stuff, that caught my eye.

"Here," Connie said, opening the door that led behind the counter and into the back portion of the office. "Amy, Sondra is going to fill out those forms in my office while I get started."

"No problem; just give them back to me when you're done," Amy said.

Connie led me to her office at the end of a short hallway. Client rooms lined the hallway on the way to her office. I noticed a records room and a couple of cubicles in the room across from her hallway. We turned left and entered Connie's office. She had a large desk with a nice chair and a couple of guest chairs that matched the ones in the waiting room on the other side of the desk. The room was a bit cluttered, and Connie explained that her office also doubled as the library. "We're running out of space. The room that had been our library was taken over when our most recent acupuncturist joined us a month ago, and I haven't had these books organized yet."

I had a seat on one of the blue chairs and started to fill out the forms. The first form asked for my name, age and all my personal information. As I signed at the bottom, I wondered how much all of this was going to cost me. I was sure it wasn't covered under my insurance, but then, I was so miserable, I realized I didn't care what it was going to cost. It went through my mind that I was a millionaire on paper. I had yet to spend a single dime of my fortune; in fact, I had barely thought about the money until this moment. Maybe I was frightened by the consequences of having this wealth. Given what had happened to Dr. Richardson, I decided not to tell this Ken March person about that part of my life—it would be safer for all concerned.

The next several sheets of paper amazed me. Ken March wanted to know a great deal about me, including details about my sleeping and eating habits, if I took herbs or vitamins and exactly which symptoms I had. Even my GP, Dr. Wiley, didn't know—or want to know—that much about me. It was a good start, I thought, and I felt my tight muscles begin to relax a bit. Why had I been so tense about coming to an alternative health care clinic? I guessed it must have been the fear of the unknown. I had been raised to respect and indeed revere the medical profession. When I was a child, whatever our doctor said my parents took to be an absolute truth. Any medicine we were given had to be taken with no questions asked. So I think my parents had influenced my belief system by teaching reverence toward medical doctors and also, as I began to reflect, inadvertently to the pharmaceutical industry that supplied and sponsored the traditional forms of the medical profession, to the detriment of any alternative. Thought of rationally, what harm can a practitioner who does not offer you drugs do? Suddenly, on a rational and emotional level, I felt pleased to be here. The fear was diminishing. It wasn't totally gone, but it was definitely lessening.

It took me so long to fill out the forms that it was past 8:30 when I handed the information to Amy and went back to Connie's office to wait for my appointment. The clinic was buzzing with clients by that time, and I wanted so badly to check out what was happening. I knew they had a couple of acupuncturists, and I had never seen that technique before, not even on TV. I sat down in front of Connie and decided to read the handout, which turned out to be a reproduction of an article from the *Philly Times,* which I guess was a good endorsement.

EFT – What Is It?

You may well have heard of EFT—the Emotional Freedom Technique—but you perhaps don't know what it really is. If you knew what it was and how it could help you in all aspects of your life, you would try it. It's simple to learn, even simpler to do—and the potential benefits of EFT are enormous.

EFT evolved from Thought Field Therapy during the 1990s, through the work of Gary Craig and his colleague Adrienne Fowlie. Just like Thought Field Therapy EFT works on a system of "meridians"

What are meridians?

These were discovered over five thousand years ago by the ancient Chinese have been used in Acupuncture ever since. They found an energy—invisible to our senses—which flows through everyone's body. This energy flows along the meridians; these are a bit like the copper wires on an electrical circuit board, carrying this energy to all parts of the body.

Disturbances in this energy flow are likely to cause physical and mental problems and so it is on freeing up these energy flows that EFT works. There are 14 such meridians in the body, which the Emotional Freedom Technique works upon. By really focusing your mind and tapping on these specific meridian points—points on which acupuncture and acupressure therapies also work—you can rid yourself of many physical, emotional and mental issues which may be holding you back and causing you distress.

How does EFT work?

This tapping rebalances the energy flow that has been disrupted, causing the unpleasant symptoms you are feeling. Focusing on the problem you want to tackle allows you to tune into the frequency of the disturbance in the way that tuning into a radio does.

Then you tap—or have your EFT therapist tap—on specific points near the end of each meridian associated with the particular problem you are facing. This acts to unblock that particular channel and allows the energy to travel effectively again, thus correcting the problem.

How is EFT so effective?
EFT has undoubted success, perhaps largely due to the fact that it treats the subconscious mind as well as the conscious mind and the body. Your subconscious mind can so often hang on to old beliefs, which hinder and block your healing process.

What is EFT useful for?
EFT works also upon the subconscious mind and breaks down these beliefs so that you are no longer unwittingly sabotaging your attempts to heal and to change. Emotions and subconscious thoughts play a huge role within people feeling pain, too—something that therapies other than EFT often fail to appreciate.

As well as psychological trauma, fears and phobias, physical pain can be healed through EFT in this way. Sometimes one session is enough, sometimes it takes several, but long-term, EFT has a great success rate. It is a gentle technique during which you should feel calm and in control, and afterwards, you should emerge feeling refreshed and relaxed.

EFT is also something that you can learn to do for yourself, so a lifelong healing technique is quite literally in your hands through EFT. It is definitely something which you should consider learning more about.

The article included a photo of the discoverers of the therapy, Gary Craig and Adrienne Fowlie. They looked like a nice, all-American couple.

So I'd now seen it in black and white. It really was true—EFT was a real live therapy and made a difference in people's lives.

I asked Connie if she wanted me to help her organize the books that were mostly sitting in boxes around her desk. I thought I might come across a useful title along the way. And although I was excited to be starting EFT, I had never sought the services of an alternative therapist before, and I truly felt nervous at the expectation of what was to come. I thought that doing something constructive would help calm me down.

Connie looked up. "Yeah, if you want; see where we have the topics labeled on these shelves? You just need to put the book where the matching topic is listed. Sondra, stop worrying—you'll be on the mend very shortly."

"God, does it show that much?" Connie's intuition was pretty sharp.

Even assuming Mrs. Abrams didn't take up all her time, I had a few minutes, so I grabbed some books and started trying to match them with where they went on the shelves. I had finished emptying two boxes when Amy came back and said that Ken March was ready to see me. I looked at the clock; it wasn't quite 9:00, so Mrs. Abrams had been true to form, and I was going to get a few extra minutes in my session.

My heart did a flip-flop as I followed Amy down the hallway and into a client room. I was surprised to notice that, rather than the harsh, fluorescent lighting of a doctor's office, this light was more like Dr. Richardson's office. There were several lamps casting a soft and soothing glow. Some new age, peaceful music was playing in the background. A trim, graying man with a nice smile and rosy cheeks was sitting in a comfortable chair, reading the papers I had filled out.

He stood, shook my hand and introduced himself. I sat down on the only other available chair except for the lounge-like chair in the center of the room.

"It looks like you've been under a great deal of stress lately," he said, "and that's an understatement."

I laughed. "I was just going to say that." I was glad he had a nice sense of humor.

He read a bit more and then turned to me.

"So, Sondra . . . before we start, I like to give my new clients a very brief history of the therapy we are going to use. I am an energy psychologist, and I practice several of the many energy psychology models that are out there. However, I prefer to use EFT most of the time, because it's easy to use here and at home. Are you okay with hearing the background?"

"Yes, sure. As Connie may have told you, I'm a newcomer to your world—and a skeptic."

"Well, I'll do my best to change that view. Feel free to ask questions whenever you want. This session and those that follow are all about you, Sondra. The term energy psychology refers to energy therapies that are based fundamentally on the Chinese Meridian Energy System of medicine, including acupuncture—something that's been in use for more than 5,000 years. From my experience, energy psychology effectively and easily releases emotional stress by massaging, touching or tapping known points on the body while holding or verbalizing the toxic thoughts that bother you. We are all more than what bothers us; I hope you can see this simple truth.

"I won't go into too much of the science of it, as that part could be confusing. Briefly, this process reduces the neural connections in the amygdala, which is a tiny part of the temporal lobe that plays an important role in your emotional self. The amygdala is located deep within the medial temporal lobes of the brain. Research has shown it performs a primary role in the processing and memory of emotional reactions, so it's a vital part of you."

The gentle tones of Ken's voice were lulling me into a trance-like state. I felt so relaxed just hearing his soft-spoken voice filling my mind, taking over my senses.

"So, put another way, EFT is a psychotherapy tool based on the premise that negative emotions are caused by disturbances in the body's field of energy. Physical intervention on the meridians while thinking of a negative emotion or event returns the body's energy field to a positive state. It often works when other processes have failed. Most times it is rapid and long lasting, and it is always gentle, though sometimes you need to associate quite closely to the problem, but not always. The big benefit is there are no drugs or equipment involved. You'll find that EFT is easy to learn, and you can use it by yourself quite easily as well. Years ago, when these discoveries were made, the original pioneers faced a lot of hostility to get their work recognized. However, the efficacy of energy psychology has long been recognized, even though it remains an alternative therapy. Are you okay with that brief explanation, Sondra?"

"Yes, thank you," I said, but in truth the whole explanation had flown right over me and I didn't care. I was just so relaxed after the talk.

"First of all, I want you to recognize that you are responsible for your own healthcare and well-being, both on an emotional and physical level. I want you to go into only as much detail as you feel comfortable with, and if something is difficult, you can speak in metaphor if you don't want all of your secrets out here on the table. For example, let's say you want to clear the effects of sexual abuse; you may prefer to use a metaphor rather than tell me all the private details. So you only need to say 'that darkest moment,' and you and your emotional self will know exactly which event in your life you are referring to. Is that okay?"

I smiled benignly in approval.

"You don't need to believe in this technique for it to work, and sometimes we have to tap and say to ourselves, 'Even though I do not believe in EFT, I am still okay with myself.' Does this make sense?"

I nodded, not really knowing what to say.

"Actually, Connie told me you might be coming with some reservations about EFT, just as you said." He pointed to an easel next to his chair that had a picture of the human body on it. "That's why I brought my informational material into the room. I want to answer all your questions before we begin."

I gulped. Sure I had questions, but I wasn't sure he was ready to answer them. I gathered my strength and decided to go for it. "Pardon my ignorance, but what exactly is EFT?" I asked sheepishly, hoping that his answer would clarify the words on the handout I had just read. "I know what the letters stand for, but beyond that, I'm a novice."

"Okay, Sondra, let's put the larger energy psychology intro to one side and just consider EFT. You've heard of acupuncture, right?" he began in a soft and gentle way.

I nodded. I'd never had it before, but I knew a number of people who swore by it.

"EFT is based on the same principles as acupuncture. Remember what I said about meridians?" I nodded, although I was still unclear. "Both acupuncture and EFT are based on the principle that the body has lines of energy—those are the 'meridians'—located throughout the body." Ken leaned over and used his pen to touch the chart he had on the easel. He pointed to a number of lines drawn on the human body that extended up and down the whole person, including the arms and legs. Around the head and upper torso there were specific tapping points shown; there also was an inset of a hand showing additional tapping spots. "See here there are 14 specific points that I may tap on—are you okay for me to do this tapping for you?"

I nodded, and he turned to the next page on his easel. "On a very basic level, EFT is intended to calm and relax you; it will enable you to see your problems in a calmer and more relaxed way. It sounds like things are very difficult for you right now, and that you really need your wits about you. Am I right?"

He didn't know the half of it, I thought, but I just nodded. I still hoped to protect him from some of the really dangerous, sordid details of my life.

"Now," he said, pointing his pen in the general direction of the page. I could tell he'd had a few clients like me before. "At its more advanced levels, EFT can help you dissolve negative emotions and bring about a positive state of well-being for you." He went on, "I should mention that EFT also works on physical pains as well as emotional ones, in the belief that the cause of all negative emotion is a disruption of the body's energy system. In fact, often we find that physical pain is underpinned by an emotional problem."

"You mean like my headaches?" I asked. I thought of how my headaches had started when I made the painful decision to leave my marriage.

He smiled. "Exactly like your headaches. Do you recall, by any chance, when the headaches began?"

I looked at the floor, somewhat embarrassed. "My husband had been involved in certain activities that he kept secret from me. As soon as I decided to leave him, the headaches started, and they haven't gotten any better, even with medication."

"I'm not surprised," he said. "The actual event that brought about the headache is what we call the 'aspect.' To cure your headaches, we will deal with the underlying cause.

"So before we begin, I need to tell you how we are going to know if you're making progress. We do this using 'SUDs,' which stands for 'subject units of disturbance.' We have a scale of zero to

10, where 10 is the worst you could feel and zero means you aren't upset about the problem at all. Now tell me, on a scale of zero to 10, how intense would you rate your experience of leaving your husband?"

Memories flooded back of having to basically sneak out on him and all the guilty feelings I had about disrupting my children's lives and bringing to an end what turned out to be a horrible relationship for me, because of his huge deception. What made me feel even worse was that he had a good relationship with the kids, and by taking them away, I felt as though I were ruining that good relationship. "I'd call that one a '30,'" I told him.

"Great. I'll remember that when the time comes," he said soothingly. "We'll see if we can get it back to a more respectable level." This was like meeting with Dr. Richardson, except I knew it was a different approach altogether. Even so, my comfort level was improving by the minute.

He continued, "EFT practitioners cannot change the event that happened to you. They can, however, change your emotional and physical *response* to the event. EFT has a very high success rate, and in my own practice, the success rate is more than 80 percent, and that usually occurs in just a few sessions. You stand a good chance of making progress with EFT treatment."

"What is EFT treatment like?" I had seen Connie, her son and other people use a sort of tapping technique, but I couldn't figure out exactly how such a thing would help me.

"EFT is sort of a combination of activating the meridians of the body, through tapping on specific areas we've come to know are helpful, and using affirmative statements while holding a thought that will help you heal from whatever is concerning you. As I said, the science of it is very ancient, but in today's pharmaceutical climate, doctors turn more often to pills to treat conditions that may not actually need medication, and these medications can have unwanted side effects," he explained.

I thought about all the pills I had been taking and how terrible most of them made me feel. If there was a way I could feel better without having to "white-knuckle it" or take pills, I was willing to give it a try.

I thought of another question. "What really allows this to work?"

Ken sat back in his chair. "It's tuning in to a bothersome thought while, at the same time, tapping into the meridian energy system inside your body. The more specific the thought, the more likely it is that the tapping will help achieve a positive outcome. Thinking of global thoughts can take the edge off of the anxiety you're having, but specific thoughts are the 'zinger thoughts' that give you the best results."

I had come to the conclusion that I finally understood how this form of therapy worked and was ready to begin. "I have a few more questions, but I think they can wait until later. I feel comfortable enough to get started," I said, although I didn't know how much time we had left.

As if in response to my unspoken concern, he said, "We have an entire hour this time, Sondra, and you can decide whether or not you need to come back."

He had me sign a consent form stating that I would allow him to tap on me, and he told me that, before long, I'd be doing the tapping myself.

"Can we start with the issue we talked about earlier with your husband?" he asked, leading me to the comfortable recliner-type chair. I was anxious just thinking about when I left Jack, even though it had been a couple of months by now.

"Tell me what else has been going on in your life around that," he said in a soft and soothing tone.

That opened the floodgates for me; even though I had planned not to, I ended up telling him everything—about the murders, the break-ins and the kidnapping of my children. I felt like I was going to scare him away with all of this chaos in my life.

"Let's start with a global thing, such as when you left your husband. That seemed to start all of the rest of the issues."

He seemed to be getting what I was saying and wasn't scared off by it.

"Now, as I start tapping the various areas, I want you to say this sentence out loud: 'Even though leaving my husband was traumatic, I now completely love and accept myself.' Okay, Sondra, let's say the words together."

So I repeated what he said and then allowed myself to relax as he began to tap on various spots on my body. It didn't hurt at all, and I actually thought it very calming. I repeated the sentence, concentrating on the words and feeling less and less anxiety about being there. I just let go and hoped everything would work the way it was supposed to. He checked my SUDs level regularly; bit by bit I started to calm down and the SUDs number diminished as well.

He asked me to do more: "Even though I am sad at having to part from my children's father . . . Even though I am unwillingly leaving my home of 13 years . . . Even though I am being set up against drug dealers, including my husband, Jack . . . "

We did about a half dozen statements, all designed to tackle the issue, the overall problem and its multiplicity of aspects.

Before I knew it, we were done, and he asked me if there was another issue or "aspect" we could discuss. I thought immediately of Jim Pruitt and told him what had happened, including how angry and guilty I felt. I rated the aspect of Jim's murder as a "10" also.

He repeated the same maneuvers while I said, "Even though I feel guilty about Jim Pruitt's death, I completely love and accept myself." At first, it was hard for me to say that, but it definitely got easier over time.

Where to go next? My life was filled with "10s," as far as I was concerned.

We went on with my guilt over children's recent kidnapping, Dr. Richardson's death and my anxious feelings I had about work ever since vandals broke in and trashed the place. I had been feeling so guilty about dragging others into the situation that I had become almost nonfunctional.

Finally, Ken sat down and asked me how I thought things went. I couldn't believe the time was nearly up. I got up and sat on the regular chair next to his. I did an "anxiety check" and found I felt much better. I wondered if any of this would last; I prayed it would.

He asked me to rate how I would feel now, after the EFT session, about seeing Jack in person. I gave it a five—a definite improvement, but I could see I still had work to do.

"I'd like to see you again, if that's okay with you."

"I'd like that," I said, genuinely feeling good about the experience.

"I have some homework for you," he said. He handed me a few sheets of paper, some of which just had lines on them. "Your homework is called doing a 'personal peace procedure.' I'd like you to think through your life as it is now; including issues from the present or the past, and I'd like you to think of any people, places, things or events that still hurt you as you give thought to them today in your life. If you wish, you can use metaphors to describe something so that I, as the practitioner, don't have to know. Believe it or not, it only matters that you know what it means. Write down all of the things that have hurt you. Most people come up with about 80 to 90 aspects. Number their intensity from zero to 10. We'll be able to deal with approximately five or so of the 10s in a double session and get you on your way to personal emotional freedom. Would that be okay?"

Tears welled in my eyes and I dabbed them with a Kleenex, yet at the same time I felt happier than when I arrived.

He pointed to an instruction sheet. "That sheet teaches you the various areas on your body that you'll tap, similar to what I have done for you today, except that this information is the self-help modality, which uses setups and rounds of tapping. Practice it and see if you can try some of the same verbal techniques we used today. I hope I'll see you next week."

I looked at the instruction sheet. It looked fairly straightforward, the difference being that Ken had tapped while we verbalized the problem, but at home I would tap on the side of my hand saying and thinking the complete setup sentence, then use a shortened reminder phrase around the other points. I could see that each round of tapping barely represented a minute of time, so it didn't seem arduous in the least.

"Oh, and before I forget," he said, "here is a sheet on the best diet for those with anxiety. You should be drinking several quarts of water per day, especially on days we see each other."

I looked at the diet sheet. It said to avoid tobacco, social drugs, caffeine, alcohol, white sugar, white flour and highly refined foods, among other things. Boy, had I failed in that department, I thought. I noted the part where it said to drink lots of water, especially on the day of a session, and to avoid strong fragrances.

"Do you feel okay to drive?" he asked me suddenly. I had shed a few more tears, but I didn't feel particularly dizzy or confused, and I told him I was fine.

I shook Ken's hand and immediately went over to Amy. "Can I make another appointment for next week?" I asked her.

"Sure," she said. She scheduled an appointment for exactly a week from that date, at 11:00 a.m., and handed me an appointment reminder card.

I had left my coat in Connie's office, so I walked down the hallway, hoping she would still be there. I found her sitting at her desk, looking over a stack of papers. She stood up when she saw me in the doorway.

"Come on in," she said, waving me inward. "How did it go?"

It was then that I realized I didn't have a raging headache for the first time in a very long time. "Well, I'm headache free. I feel better, and I'm coming back next week," I smiled as I spoke.

"Excellent," she said, rounding her desk to give me a big hug. "I'm so glad you gave it a shot."

"I think it might work for me," I told her honestly. "I've got some homework to do, and I have to practice this tapping technique, but I think I can handle it."

"I'll help you. Are you spending the night again?" she asked me, the tone of her voice suddenly changing. I was suddenly thrust back into the reality of my life and the terror of losing my kids forever rose up inside me.

"Yes, I think I will," I told her. "I'm going to stop by the apartment and see what's going on first. I forgot a few things when I left yesterday, so I'll get those as well." I wondered who was on duty in my home, and I thought I'd call Detectives Murphy and Littleton to see what was going on.

I said goodbye to Connie, threw on my coat and headed out to my car. On the way home, I flipped open my overused cell phone and called Detective Murphy.

"This is Sondra Ackerman. I just wanted an update on everything."

"Good timing," he said. "I was going to call you today. We're working the case on multiple levels. We've got a GPS tracker on Jack's car, and we have a tail on him, just in case he takes a taxi anywhere or uses a different car. We're using a newer program that triangulates the location of his two cell phones so it's not possible to lose him. We still firmly believe he knows exactly where those children are, and when he visits them, we'll have him nailed. I don't think it's going to take long." . . .

. . . Frank phoned my cell. "Hiya, Jack. I cleared out of the apartment, so your old lady is going to be in for one hell of a surprise when she gets home." Frank spoke with his typical nonchalance, even though he had just finished stripping everything from 214 in record time.

"Sure as hell," I replied and said threateningly, "Whatever you do, Frank, you treat my kids with absolute respect. Don't go trying to use that guinea charm of yours on my Cassie when my back is turned. Is that understood?"

"Of course, Jack. She's just a kid! The thought never entered my mind."

I snapped the phone shut. . . .

. . . "What about the narcotics ring?" I asked Detective Murphy.

"Of course our work with that is completely secondary to finding your kids, but we did hear back from one of our undercover officers. He said it's going to take a little longer to completely document the extent of the business but, fortunately, none of our guys have been pegged as narcs by the organization. Everything is going as planned."

I felt like I'd heard all of that before. "So how long do you think it will take?"

"I think it will be just a couple of weeks," he answered. "And, Mrs. Ackerman, I think that when your children come back to you, until the case is settled, you and your family belong in the witness protection program. We can't afford to lose your testimony, even though we have Jack basically giving up the organization on tape, thanks to you."

I sighed. Why couldn't things be easier for a change? "Yeah, when my kids return, I'll be happy to go into the program." I liked that we were talking "when" while we were referring to my children's return. It gave me hope.

"We'll talk about that later," he said before we said goodbye and I hung up. I decided that I'd wait to talk to Detective Littleton. I wasn't sure he had much more to offer. I turned in to the parking lot of my apartment complex. . . .

. . . If Sondra escaped into the witness protection program, I would need to go underground. If I didn't disappear, I could end up in jail or being wasted by the Brothers. I knew the smartest thing I could do in this situation was to own up to the whole thing and throw myself on the mercy of the Brothers—and see if they could think of some way out of this that I hadn't. Should I call or visit Los Archos? If I called, at least I would be on home

129

turf, at a safe distance from them. If I went to see them and they turned on me, coming home to Philly might not be an option. Calling sounded like the better idea. I had to get it right or I could lose everything; Carmen and Canada could all go up in smoke before my eyes. Maybe I should ask Carmen to marry me and explain to the Brothers that Sondra was a problem that needed to be taken care of. That way I wouldn't come across as having screwed up the situation. They said they knew everything, sometimes even before it happened. I didn't doubt it. These guys were clever, always have been. How else could two guys, both under 40 years old, from some poor backwater Mexican village, build up a 30 billion dollar a year enterprise, no stock or shareholders? All they did was supply buyers with what they wanted and keep all the profit. . . .

. . . It was snowing lightly when I got out of the car and headed for my building. It was early for snow, I thought; maybe we were in for a hard winter. Halfway up the stairs, I was blocked by a man carrying a ladder. He was wearing white pants and a white t-shirt flecked with different colors of paint.

"Hi," I said, in a much better mood now that I wasn't riddled with headaches and had heard some good news from Detective Murphy. "Which apartment are you painting?"

"We're painting 214 this morning," he answered.

Dwight's place? He hadn't told me he was having his apartment repainted. "Oh, I know the person who lives there. I didn't know you guys would paint an apartment that was still occupied."

"It's not occupied, ma'am," the painter said. "The tenant moved out late yesterday and the management wants us to get the place ready for showing as quickly as possible."

What? Surely he had gotten the apartment number wrong. But as we approached the second floor landing, I could see that Dwight's door was wide open, and the entire place appeared to be empty. "Can I take a look?" I asked, confused.

"Go ahead. We haven't started yet," the painter told me, maneuvering the ladder through the door.

I followed him inside and was stunned to find that the apartment was indeed completely empty. The only things left were the indentations in the carpet from the entertainment center and the feet of the couch where Dwight and I had sat only two days earlier.

I walked into the kitchen, which was also completely cleaned out. The bedroom and the bathroom were bare, too. Something was really wrong, I thought. Bemused, I walked through the rooms again as if I needed to make sure that they were really empty.

"Could you hold off for a second?" I asked the painter, who was setting up his ladder. "I need to make a quick call to the police."

The painter looked at me strangely as I dug out Detective Littleton's card and my cell phone. "Detective Littleton, this is Sondra Ackerman. I'm not certain, but I think I have some information related to my children's kidnapping," I told him, wondering if he would believe me. I explained that I had developed a close friendship with a man by the name of Dwight Osborne and that he had suddenly moved out of the apartment next to mine the night after my children were taken. Something told me that Dwight Osborne wasn't his real name but, for the moment, I didn't really want to think about that.

"Tell the painters to get out of there. I'm sending a forensics team to see if we can figure out who this guy was," he instructed me. "And, while you're waiting, go down to the manager's office and see what you can find out about this neighbor of yours."

I told him I'd do my best. "I hate to break it to you," I told the flustered painter, "but I'm passing on a police order for you to get out of here. The guy who lived here was probably involved in a double kidnapping, and the police are sending a forensics unit to this apartment to collect evidence." Even as I told the painter this, I realized I was tapping my gamut spot on my left hand, the emergency tapping point Ken March had given me to do if I felt anxiety approaching. Right now I was definitely anxious.

The painter shrugged, and I could tell he didn't really know what to think. "Well, it's no skin off my nose. Do you think they'll mind if I keep the ladder up here? I'd hate to drag it downstairs and then back up again later."

I told him it would probably be okay. We left the door to the apartment open, and I followed the painter down the stairs. We both headed to the manager's office in building A. It was a tidy, comfortable space, a converted studio apartment. A clean-cut dark-haired young man sat behind the desk. He stood and shook my hand. He had a firm grip.

131

The painter just stood there and glanced over at me, looking like he was hoping I'd speak first.

"Hi, I remember you," the fresh-faced young man said. "You live in 215 in building C, right?" He had a good memory for faces, and I hoped he could help me out when it came to finding out something about Dwight.

I caught a glimpse of the flashing lights of a squad car outside. "Yes, that's me," I told him. The police car pulled up close to the building. "I'm Sondra Ackerman. What I'm about to say is really complicated, but it's important, too. I'm the lady whose kids have been kidnapped from my apartment. I'm here—as are the police officers, who are on their way in right now—to ask you about the tenant in apartment 214. We believe he's involved in the kidnapping. The police have told the painter here to stop what he's doing so they can collect some forensic evidence from that apartment."

The smile left the young man's face, and he looked positively ill when two uniformed police officers stepped into the office. He told the painter to find something else to do and dismissed him.

I introduced myself to the officers and updated them on what I knew. I also told them about meeting Dwight Osborne. I told them that he had been a new—but close—friend of mine and that he and I were watching movies in his apartment when the kids were kidnapped. I explained that he had intentionally invited us over for dinner and that I had made sure the kids were locked in the apartment the evening they disappeared. The guilt of my actions flooded through every cell of my being as I told the story; I was tapping my gamut spot unobtrusively, as my own support mechanism, I guess.

Now it was time to find out what we could about "Dwight Osborne." The manager had already pulled Dwight's file and told us that Dwight had moved in on October 1, about a week or so after I had moved in. I thought it was strange that I hadn't noticed him moving in, but I realized he had probably done so while I was at work. I also noticed it was a far cry from the year he said he'd lived there.

The manager said that Dwight had given them proper identification but had paid his rent in cash. He was on a month-to-month lease but hadn't given his notice or even mentioned planning to move out. Damn, I thought. He knew he'd be able to get to my kids, and he knew exactly how and when he was going to do it. He must have called his accomplice when he was out of my sight that night—in the kitchen, in the bathroom . . . I could barely recall the events of that evening, my head was swimming with all this new information.

It turned out that the references he had given the management were bogus, as was the work number he gave them. It seems that Dwight had been deposited into my life by the organization to keep tabs on me and help someone kidnap my children, after which he would simply disappear into the huge population of Philadelphia—or wherever he came from.

I felt so cheated and so dirty. I hated that I had let him kiss me and that I had trusted him. On the other hand, I never told him much, so the organization still hadn't been able to find out how much I knew about them. I wondered if he was responsible for the bugs in my apartment and for trashing the place. One thing I did know for sure was that if I ever met that sleazebag again, I'd want to give him a dammed good beating.

The forensics team was already in Dwight's old apartment when I got back to the building. The door was open, so I walked into the apartment and introduced myself to a small, wiry, older man who was using some kind of chemical on the living room windowsill. I sincerely hoped Dwight hadn't wiped the apartment clean before he left.

"Oh, hi," he said, not stopping what he was doing. "You spent some time in this apartment, then?"

"Well, I wasn't here as much as he was, but I'm sure I touched a few things. If it helps, I have already been printed," I told him.

"That's good to know," he said. "Thanks for the information."

Still seething about the situation with Dwight, I left his old apartment and entered my own home. Officer Martin was sitting at the dining room table with headphones on, enjoying his coffee and a large jelly donut while he worked. He set down the donut and removed the headphones before standing up and shaking my hand.

"Good morning," he said, still chewing. "How's it going?"

I sighed. "As good as can be expected," I said, taking my coat off. "How about you?" . . .

. . . Once I had Ben and Cassie, I suddenly realized I didn't want them to see the swanky home that Carmen and

I had in Lancaster. Taking them there would have been admitting that I lived a double life, and that my other life was far better than I had ever allowed them to have with their mom. So I decided to send them to the hub—our distribution point for most of the east coast—in New Jersey. We had a few rooms there that we used for sleepovers for some of the couriers. I could use those rooms and the basement to stash the kids until I was ready to move them farther away. If I was going to get them to Trinidad in less than a week, I needed to get on the stick and get them some fake passports. I'd maybe hire a Lear jet, make it special for the kids. I sure couldn't use a regular airline, that was for sure. Once we got to Trinidad, we could hang out there for a month or so while I got their schools arranged. . . .

. . . Officer Martin sat back down. "Well, the good news is that your phone isn't ringing off the hook. The bad news is that we haven't heard anything."

"Well, most people have my cell phone," I explained.

"I noticed," he said, absently moving his finger around the rim of his coffee cup. "Remember? I listen in on all your cell phone calls, too."

I was suddenly embarrassed, wondering if I'd said anything stupid. "Oh, I forgot. I guess I lead a boring life," I told him.

"Ma'am," he said looking up at me, "considering all that's happened to you, I wouldn't call it boring by any stretch of the imagination."

"I guess you're right," I said. I suddenly remembered I had an important question for him. "You were on until 7:00 last night?"

"Uh-huh," he said, going back to his jelly donut. "You want one of these?" He pointed to a box donuts. I was hungry by this time, so I helped myself to a chocolate glazed.

"Thanks," I said, taking a big bite. I asked him, "Did you see the guy next door moving out last night?"

"Yeah, I think so. There was this big moving van outside when I went to leave, and I saw about four burly guys hauling a couch down the stairs. I had to wait until they got the couch out before I could get down the stairs myself."

I described what Dwight looked like. "Did you see anyone who looked like that?"

Officer Martin shook his head. "No, I didn't see anyone like that. In fact, two of the guys were black, and I think the other two were Latino," he said. "They looked like regular moving guys with a regular moving van."

Maybe they were regular moving guys, but that was the only regular thing about it, I thought. I was dumbstruck that a police officer watched an occupant moving out the day after a double child kidnapping. Was the man stupid? I asked him if he remembered anything identifiable about the truck. There had to have been scorn in my voice.

"Yeah, it was a Mayflower van—a pretty big one," he said.

I reached for my cell phone and made a call to Detective Murphy. I told him about the situation with Dwight Osborne and the fact that the forensics team was looking for prints and hair samples. I also told him about the Mayflower van and asked him if he could look into it.

"No problem," he answered. "I'll have one of my guys check it out."

I explained that, while I was technically with Dwight when the kids were taken, I was sure now he had lured me into his apartment in order to make it easier for someone else he knew to take the kids.

"Well, I hope they get some prints on the guy or that we can get some hair samples for a DNA analysis. In the meantime, we'll check out the moving company," he assured me. He paused for a moment before adding, "I'll put a new request in for an update on the case; this is a very important development. Thanks for calling me so promptly."

"So you mean this Dwight guy was moving out, right under the noses of the police?" Officer Martin asked me incredulously after I had ended my call. "If I had I known there was a problem, I'd have put a tail on the truck or at least checked around a little bit. But how was I to know?"

"The scary thing is that Dwight set me up. He played me like a fool, and I fell for it. The entire time, all he wanted was to get me away from the kids. And I thought he was a decent guy who really cared about me." It was a hard thing to admit. I remembered Dwight's look the night the kids were taken, and I felt so stupid for believing him.

"At least we have a few leads on him," he said. "Want another donut?"

I remembered what Ken had said about processed foods and anxiety, and politely declined. "No thanks," I said. "I'm going to work for a couple of hours. I'll see you later."

I needed to go to work. Taking solace in a job I loved was better than sitting at home waiting for the phone to ring. Spending some time at the office, then staying at Connie's house for another night, would help me keep my imagination from running wild with thoughts of where my kids were and what might be happening to them as I sat, helpless.

My coworkers were so sympathetic and kind to me when I arrived that I almost started crying again. Shelly's eyes were already red. It was close to lunch, but the donut had taken the edge off my appetite. I just asked Shelly for a cup of coffee and told her I'd work through the lunch hour.

"Okay, then," she said, "I'll grab a sandwich and work alongside you."

I didn't tell her I wanted to be alone; she was so sweet that I hated to hurt her feelings. "That'll be great," I answered.

Shelly and I ended up working for three hours straight, getting as much work done as possible before I got tired and decided to head for Connie's house. She had given me a key, and I wanted to look at my homework in private before she got home. I thanked Shelly for all her hard work and, leaving her to get on with the filing, left my workplace.

The lack of activity on my cell phone was starting to bother me, and the only thing I felt good about was that the police were carefully tracking Jack all this time. There was nothing more I could do. My car was parked just as I had left it. The tires were intact. That, at least, was good news. I drove out of the parking garage with a heavy heart, knowing I was not going to my own home to be with my children. I quickly brought my attention back to the road ahead of me.

Detective Murphy called me on my cell phone as I was driving to Connie's house. He told me the moving van must have been bogus, because the real Mayflower company had no record of a move at my apartment building yesterday. I was disheartened at the news but not very surprised. Jack's organization had a great number of resources; it would be easy to do up a van to look like a legitimate moving company and get some men to move Dwight's stuff out of his apartment. I hoped the forensics team had better luck.

Fortunately, no one was at home at Connie's house, so I grabbed my EFT homework, sat down in the living room, and started writing down some "aspects." At first, it was easy.

1. My guilt over trusting Dwight who subsequently abused that trust: 10.
2. My terror over my children being kidnapped: 10. (That was like a 30; I decided to ask Connie about that.)
3. My embarrassment over my work being ransacked: 10.
4. Jack's physical abuse of me: 9.
5. Jack being in organized crime: Definitely 10.
6. Jack's emotional abuse of me and the kids: 9.

I kept going with the current issues in my life, but then I started thinking about parts of my life that I thought were long past. I remembered my father being emotionally abusive to me and telling me I was only good for housework. I felt like that still affected me, even though I was a manager at a major company. I thought about feeling guilty that I didn't take the time to visit my mother in Cincinnati very often and how she used to be so strict with me, telling me I was a lazy slob and would amount to nothing. I wrote those things down, too. It could be that it was these toxic memories that prevented me from being closer with her now. I slowed my thoughts down to enable myself to examine this new problem and its various aspects. The list seemed endless.

I pulled a well-thumbed textbook, *Emotional Freedom Technique Unraveled*, out of my bag. Connie had recommended I borrow it from the clinic's collection to help me understand EFT better. I had noticed a section about the "generalization effect" as I flipped through it in her office and now found that part and skimmed it quickly. This was EFT speak for the collapsing of the lesser distressing memories as the larger aspects are dealt with. So as the big numbers—all those nines and 10s that had caused me the most distress—collapse, the smaller numbers collapse beneath them. Looking at my ever-growing list, I was truly hopeful that this was about to happen for me too.

I continued to list aspects for about an hour, and I surprised myself at the sheer number of them: more than 90, many to do with my relationship with my mother. And I knew that, with a little more time and thought, several more issues would come to mind.

I put those sheets away and turned to the instruction sheet on tapping. I was glad no one was expected home for a while yet. I wanted to get used to doing the tapping on my own first, because even though I was sure Connie's family had seen her tapping, I knew I would feel self-conscious practicing in front of other people.

I looked carefully at the sheet and read it through once before starting at the beginning again. It talked about tuning in to a specific issue, physical feeling, emotion or problem. If I had trouble, I was to picture the problem in my mind as a short one-minute movie and to pay attention to what comes up when I "watch" the movie. Images of Dwight's false sadness when he heard about the children being gone came to mind, and rage filled me when I did that. I could even smell the lingering scent of the apple pie he had made.

There was a sheet that talked about what I should do when I'm doing EFT by myself. I took a look at it:

> STEP 1. Sit in a chair or lie back upon a couch—relax and undo/loosen any tight or restricted clothing. Choose the SPECIFIC incident or issue for treatment or if ultra distressed go global and close in gradually to a specific aspect.
>
> STEP 2. Determine the intensity of the distress on a scale from zero to 10 where 10 is the greatest amount of distress and zero nothing at all.
>
> STEP 3. While tapping the outside edge of one hand with the fingertips of your other hand, repeat the following statement: "EVEN THOUGH (ET) I HAVE THIS (xxxxx problem), I DEEPLY AND COMPLETELY LOVE MYSELF AND ACCEPT MYSELF." Do this three times.
>
> Examples of presenting issues might be:
> ET I have this headache . . . or searing head pain . . . etc. (reminder phrase "this pain")

ET I am extremely angry with XXX . . .
(reminder phrase "this anger")
ET I am profoundly sad about losing my XXX .
. . (reminder phrase "my loss")
ET I am terrified of being without a life partner .
. . (reminder phrase "this loneliness")
ET I am upset that my family may never be
together again . . . (your reminder phrase)
ET I am STILL smoking/drinking/taking meds .
. . (your reminder phrase)
ET I am overweight/underweight/stressed
beyond compare . . . (your reminder phrase)
Now go around the individual points on the
head/torso or the head/torso and hand using a
shortened reminder phrase while tapping the point
such as "this anger . . . "
After each round sit back, close your eyes and
inhale a deep breath and then rate your SUDs level.
Keep tapping until you reach a zero or a number
that suits you; 2 or below is ideal.

Then there were the tapping spots. I first tapped the fleshy side
of my hand with the fingers of my other hand. Just to make it
realistic, I said, "Even though Dwight betrayed me that night, I
deeply and completely accept myself." I then said the same thing
while tapping between my eyebrows with three fingers on my right
hand.

So far so good, I thought. Then, with two fingers, I tapped the
spot at the inner end of my eyebrow, the bony area on the side of
my eye, and said the same statement over again as calmly as I
could. I tapped with two fingers of both hands under both eyes,
saying my statement out loud. Then I tapped with two fingers under
my nose, followed by two fingers under my lower lip. I looked at
the paper, and this time I said, "I am releasing all of my guilt and
shame related to Dwight's betrayal of me."

I moved on to my chest and tapped with all the fingers of my
hand just off the upper middle chest. I said, "I am releasing all of
the sadness related to Dwight's betrayal of me." After that, I had to
read carefully. I found a spot about four inches under my armpit
and tapped with all my fingers, saying, "I'm releasing all of my

resistance and blocks related to Dwight's betrayal of me." Finally, I tapped on the crown of my head with all of my fingers and said, "I release all of my grief related to Dwight's betrayal of me."

I set the paper down and leaned back. I *did* feel better about the issue. I also felt happy that I was really doing something myself to help me feel better. I thought I could learn these tapping points by heart after a few practice runs. I realized I needed to trim my nails, though, as they were a bit too long for this work.

I ran through the tapping points one more time before putting the papers safely in my room next to my journal. I felt like it had been a very long day but one in which I learned a lot and, in particular, I had learned that this EFT process had its merits. I didn't have a single headache all day long. And even though my kids were still missing, I felt I was better equipped to handle it. I reminded myself to thank Connie that evening and to apologize for being so bull-headed about trying EFT in the first place.

I took a leap of faith today, and I think it really paid off for me this time. I took a medical technique that I hadn't even heard of several weeks ago, and I allowed myself to trust in the process. My reward in the end, I think, will be much greater than what I initially put into it. I learned that people, including me, harbor a great many issues that cause physical symptoms and emotional pain that EFT can help manage. How lucky I am to have Connie as a friend—she led me to this technique that I think will help me greatly. I know without a doubt that I still have much to go through until my issues are resolved, but tonight I have the faith that I have the ability to handle them. I think I'll buy a book on EFT while I'm not working full time, and I'll take the time to understand this unique technique to its fullest. My only regret is that Dr. Richardson isn't around for me to share with him how much I've been helped in just one day by Ken March and EFT. I think Dr. Richardson would have been pleased.

Chapter 7

I woke early the next morning; I was the first one up. I was finding it increasingly difficult to be away from Ben and Cassie, and my heart ached with longing for my two lovely children. I wondered where they were at that hour. Were they safe? Were they being treated well? Pain started to well up in me, and I decided I had to do something to lift my spirits.

After making a pot of coffee, I grabbed the worksheets Ken had given me and put down a few more aspects I had thought of the night before. It was interesting how so many things in my past had interwoven to make my life the way it was now. Even issues from my childhood were coming up—things I hadn't remembered for decades.

Once Connie and her family came downstairs, I gave serious thought as to what I needed and wanted to do for the day. I didn't want to go to the office right away; the stares of my coworkers had been unnerving the day before. No, I decided, I'd let Shelly hold down the fort while I found something else to do that morning.

In the end, I thought I'd stop by my favorite bookstore downtown to see if they had any books on EFT. I couldn't help being such an analytical person; I didn't want to simply take this type of therapy for granted without really understanding what the experts had to say. I waited until everyone else in the house left before gathering my things and going out to my car.

It had snowed about half an inch the night before, and I shivered in the frigid weather. It didn't take very long to dust my car off and, with the heater blasting, I worked my way downtown.

The saleswoman knew right away what I was looking for. "I've used EFT for many years," she offered. "In fact, my husband does, too. We swear by it."

The EFT books were on the lowest shelf of a section on alternative health, so I sat cross-legged on the floor in front of the bookcase and allowed myself the luxury of browsing through each one. In the end, I found one entitled *Emotional Freedom*

Technique: Healing Negative Emotions. It seemed like the perfect book for me.

I walked down the street to a coffee shop, chose a scone to go with my coffee, and settled in the back of the shop, ready to begin reading my book.

I found myself intrigued about "aspects." The book said that an aspect could be something with a single part or that it could consist of many interweaving parts. I think that explained why I had some aspects that I rated as a 30, when I knew I was supposed to rank them from one to 10.

I started looking at the kidnapping of my children differently; now I could see the different parts I could list as different aspects. I learned, too, that an aspect could be a feeling, a thought or belief, a bodily sensation, an event or a combination of these. That explained why I had seen some people use EFT for physical pain, while I was using it for events and my emotional reaction to them. I sipped my coffee as I studied again the various tapping points and how to do them.

I was almost to the second chapter when the jangling sound of my cell phone disturbed my relative peace. I could see from the caller ID that it was Detective Murphy calling, and my heart started to pound.

"Hello?" I said nervously, nearly dropping the slender phone.

"I have good news," Detective Murphy said. "We've got the kids and they're fine." My heart nearly jumped out of my chest. "We triangulated Jack's cell phone to an old house in Jersey. Our officers grabbed him as he was coming out the door and they stormed the house. We found the kids with a man I think you might be able to identify. The kids said you know him."

I think I stopped listening after he said the kids were unharmed. I had this sudden feeling that I couldn't get to see them fast enough. "Where are they?"

The kids had been taken first to the hospital, as was standard procedure after rescuing children from a kidnapping, he said, but neither of them had been harmed physically. Now they were at the Fifth Precinct, where Jack and the other guy I was supposed to know were being held. "I need you to go down to the precinct as soon as you can," Murphy told me. I grabbed my purse and my book and raced out to the street.

The kids were fine, he had said. Thank God! I couldn't believe I was going to see them in a few short minutes. I jumped in my car and wound my way through the streets until I pulled up to the familiar two-story brick building with the words "City of Philadelphia" and "Fifth Precinct" above the front door; it was the same precinct where I had given my statement several nights before. I parked next to a squad car and ran into the building.

Ben and Cassie were drinking colas and eating donuts in a conference room. Above their heads, the Seal of The State of Pennsylvania adorned the wall. I burst in before the officer who showed me the way could even let go of the door handle. Both kids were still dressed in the same clothing they were wearing when they were kidnapped. They both burst into tears and rushed over to me as soon as they saw me. Ben flew across the room so fast he sent Cassie's cola spinning across the elegant conference table.

"Mom!" Ben gave me his biggest bear hug—something he had recently been too "grown up" for. "We were so worried about you!" he exclaimed. Cassie was crying a little, and I put my arm around her and squeezed her tightly. I never wanted to let either of them go at that moment.

"Worried about me?" I said, holding Ben even tighter. "I was terrified about you two. What happened to you both?"

"Ma'am," the officer behind me said. "I need to get a statement from them. Perhaps we should talk about what happened together."

I allowed myself to relax a moment and asked the officer, "Could I have a diet soda?" He nodded, disappeared for half a minute and came back with a soda for me as well as a replacement for the one Ben spilled in his rush to get to me. I ushered the children back to their seats and sat between them, stroking their hair the whole time. Cassie was shivering, so I took off my jacket and slipped it over her shoulders.

The officer, whose last name was Blake, had several sheets of paper. He sat down and I could see he had already started by writing their names, birthdates and addresses. "Let me start with Cassie. I realize you both have basically the same story but I need to hear it from both of you."

Cassie was calm by this time and had even resumed eating her donut. "Okay, go ahead."

"On the night of the 16th, three nights ago, where were you and your brother right before this incident happened?" The officer was being really calm and respectful of my children, and I appreciated that.

Cassie cleared her throat. "Well, Mom was over at Dwight's apartment, and my brother and I were locked in our apartment for our safety. We were messing around and doing some homework, and I heard a noise like Mom was coming back. I said, 'Hey, Mom—why are you back so soon?' and then I turned around and it was Dad instead. There was this big, nasty-looking guy with him and Dad told us we had to walk down the stairs really quietly or he'd slap us." Cassie's voice broke as she said this. I could see she was upset at her own Dad talking to them like that. "It was like it wasn't my Dad. And he wasn't upset at all when he told us Mom was in the hospital."

"I was what?" I couldn't help interrupting.

Cassie looked up at me sadly. "Dad said you had had an aneurysm at Dwight's and were in the hospital. He said we were going to stay with him in the meantime. We were really upset and wanted to ask if we could go to the hospital to be with you, but he just kind of . . . gave us that dirty look again and told us to shut up and get in the car."

Cassie's voice dropped to a whisper as she picked at her donut. "I'm sorry, Mom."

"What? Why?"

"Because I feel so stupid for believing him. If you had really had an aneurysm, Dwight would have knocked on the door to tell us. We would have heard the ambulance siren, and the EMTs come into the building. But we never thought of that till later."

My heart went out to them; they must have been so frightened. I hugged her again. How could Jack have terrorized his own kids like that? I was furious. I made a mental note that this was another aspect to write down on my EFT sheet.

"Then what happened?" the officer prompted Cassie.

"They put us in the back seat of a car; I couldn't tell what kind of car it was, but it wasn't Dad's car. The mean guy drove and kept telling Ben to shut up because he was crying a little bit."

I saw Ben give Cassie the meanest look. I knew he was trying to be brave, but he was only 11—of course he'd be upset. I pretended not to notice what Cassie said, for Ben's sake.

"Then what? It was dark by then, right?" Officer Blake was writing furiously.

"Yes. I couldn't tell where we were going, but we drove for about half an hour, it seemed, before the mean guy got out and told us to get out of the car. He almost pushed me down on the sidewalk in front of this big, dark house. Dad was behind us saying that everything was going to be okay," Cassie explained.

"They took us into the house and pushed me and Ben up the stairs. Dad said we had to stay there for a few days and that he was taking us to a really cool place—like on a vacation—after that," she said.

"Did they ever hurt you or forget to feed you?" the officer asked.

"Well, they put us both in the same room. It was like a bedroom, with a bathroom next to it. There were some snacks and sodas on a dresser, and the mean guy told us the food had to last us for three days. Nobody really hurt us, but they locked us in there and me and Ben had to sleep in the same bed." Cassie made a face at the idea of sleeping with her little brother. "We were really scared."

"You forgot to tell him about the pictures," Ben cut in.

"Oh yeah," Cassie said, suddenly remembering. "The first night, Dad came in with this camera and made us stand against a wall, and he took a bunch of pictures of us one at a time."

Officer Blake finished what he was writing before turning to me. "We found falsified birth records, fake passports for the kids and several tickets to Trinidad in the house where the children were found. The photos likely were for the passports."

My heart sank as I realized I had come perilously close to having my children disappear out from under me—to another country, no less. I decided that this fact was an aspect all its own.

As Cassie spoke, Jack's plan became clear: The children were locked in that same room with a minimal amount of food for their entire stay as he arranged to take them out of the country. Ben and Cassie didn't see their Dad after the first night, until he showed up this morning with the airline tickets and the false papers.

Cassie explained that she and Ben were never left alone, however. She told the officer that the "mean guy" never came back, but he was replaced by another man who watched them the rest of the time.

"Mom," Cassie said excitedly, "you'll never guess who took care of us in that horrible, old, stinky, rotten house."

According to Cassie, it was Dwight himself who showed up the next day and who was their "prison guard" during much of their time at the house in New Jersey.

"He was so different, Mom," Cassie explained. "He was mean to Ben, and he kept calling us brats. It was like he had turned into a different person."

For some reason, nothing could shock me by this time. I knew for certain that Dwight was somehow involved in the kids' abduction when the painter showed up, and it just didn't surprise me that he was intimately connected to the crime. Another aspect, I decided, as I thought about what I really wanted to do to that jerk now.

"Ma'am," Officer Blake interjected, "after this interview and before you take the children home, we need you to verify that the man we have in custody is the same man who lived in the apartment next to you."

Only if I can kick him in the nuts afterward, I thought to myself. I could feel the slightest hint of a headache coming on, and I reminded myself to practice my EFT techniques later, if I got the chance. It seemed like such a reasonable option when compared to popping painkillers.

Cassie finished her interview by explaining that, when the officers stormed the house, Dwight tried to hide them in the basement, but that he was caught and arrested. "I skinned my knee, Mom, when Dwight tried to push me down the basement steps," she told me, rubbing her right knee. I didn't see any bleeding through her jeans, so I told her I'd take a look at it when we got home.

"They looked at it at the hospital, and the cops already took a picture of it," Cassie explained.

Then it was Ben's turn. His statement corroborated much of Cassie's story but, as he's such an observant child, he offered a great deal more detail. Officer Blake continued writing it all down.

". . . And I heard Dad calling Dwight 'Frank' this morning," he told the officer. "I don't think his real name is Dwight."

"Thanks, kids," Officer Blake said kindly. "I need to check on something and I'll be right back."

Officer Blake left for a couple of minutes; in the meantime, the kids chattered about how good it would be to get home. Even though they both looked tired, the excitement of being in a downtown police interview room had them hyped up. They seemed to be easily getting over the trauma of the past few days. I realized, however, that this would only be on the surface, and I worried about their near future—when their deeper emotions would surface and when they'd start thinking about the fact that their father had kidnapped them and given them a rough manhandling. I couldn't tell if they were completely aware of the fact that he was intending to take them out of the country. That was another issue we would need to talk about. In the meantime, they both needed showers, a change of clothing, a nice meal and their own beds.

When Officer Blake came back into the room, he had another officer with him. He asked me to go with the other officer while he kept an eye on the kids; I was needed in another room for a few minutes.

I followed the officer who had the name "Archer" on his nametag, and we headed into an elevator and up to the second floor. "What are we doing?" I asked him.

"I have the other guy they arrested at the house in a viewing room. You'll need to tell me if he's the guy who lived next door to you," Archer said blandly. "It won't take long. It's all set up."

He took me to a darkened room with a one-way viewing window. On the other side, dressed in gray sweats and a black sweatshirt, was Dwight, sitting at a table talking with another officer. I had no doubt that it was Dwight, of course, and I wished I could confront him to tell him what I thought of him instead of being silenced behind this window. I wanted him to look me in the eye; I wanted the scumbag to apologize.

"Yeah, that's Dwight," I said, sighing and allowing myself to slip into one of the plastic chairs in the room.

"He had ID on him that said his name was 'Charles Martinez,' but we think it's a fake," Archer explained.

"Yeah, and the kids said my husband had called him 'Frank,'" I told him as I got to my feet again. I wanted to get out of there; I didn't want to waste any more time on that jerk.

I called Detective Murphy before I went back into the conference room to collect my kids. I wanted to thank him and all the police officers for everything.

Detective Murphy humbly accepted my thanks. "You realize, though, that we need to have a serious talk within the next couple of days. The kids can't go back to school until I can arrange for someone to guard them, and I think you need a bodyguard, too."

I was confused; I asked him what he was concerned about now that Jack and "Dwight"—or whatever his real name was—were in custody.

147

"Listen, Sondra," he said, "with your husband behind bars, Los Archos doesn't have him telling them to keep you and the kids alive. All three of you are in more danger now than ever before. They'll just kill you to shut you up. That's why we need to discuss what we're going to do to keep you safe until we wrap this case up. Can you come by first thing tomorrow, around 9:00?"

I was stunned. In my mind, I kept thinking of Jack as the enemy. It never occurred to me that he was the one who was keeping the kids and me alive. Detective Murphy waited a moment for my response, but my mind was miles away. When he prompted me with, ". . . Mrs. Ackerman?" I jumped.

I collected myself enough to say I thought that I could meet with him tomorrow, and he continued, "Okay. We've also got some good news in the case: The prints we lifted from your place turned out to be Jack's, which matched some unidentified prints we had on file. One was from a package of coke we seized, and another was a partial that we lifted during a raid on a building that was being used by drug traffickers. So these two records clearly place your husband at the site of three crimes: the kidnapping and two drug-related crimes.

"The house he was holding the kids in belongs to him. He and his 'company' use it to ship drugs out. Also—and I am sorry to have to tell you this, but it's better you find out from me now instead of from the media in the near future—we found out that Jack was two-timing you. He was cohabiting with a Latina woman by the name of Carmen. They share a swanky house in Lancaster. She's the sister of the big boss of the Tijuana connection, Los Archos Hermanos cartel. So the two houses we know of, along with your old home, will have to be seized by the court."

Jack with another woman? I was past caring, but I felt stupid that I didn't pick up on it myself.

The kids had finished their donuts and soda, and were patiently waiting for me when I got back to the conference room. "Can I take them home now?" I asked Officer Blake.

"Yes, ma'am; we'll call you if we have any questions," he answered.

I stopped for a second, realizing I had an important question of my own. "What's going to happen to my husband and the other guy?" I couldn't call him Dwight anymore.

"Well, ma'am," he began, "after they've been interrogated, they'll go down to central lockup, and tomorrow they'll see the judge."

"What if they get out on bail?" My heart did flip-flops in my chest at the thought.

"Well, I can't say for sure what the judge will do, but given the circumstances, they'll either get a really high bail or they won't be allowed out on bail at all if they're considered flight risks."

That made me feel better, and I thanked him. "Let's go home, kids." It was so good to be able to say that. . . .

. . . I had been arrested. For kidnapping, of all things. My attorney was going to have to make that judge understand I had rights as their father. How could I be arrested for getting my kids back? Sondra did the wrong thing, here. She took them away from me first. And we sure didn't sit around a table discussing parental rights before she did it. She left me, and she stole the kids, not the other way around. I'm just a father who took back what was stolen from him. How could anybody call it kidnapping?

The downside now for me is RICO. I don't think my lawyer can stop the prosecutors from bringing up my business in the case with my kids. But if I can get the kidnapping charges dropped before the drug investigation starts, I'll get out on bail and just disappear, get over the border with a new identity in just a few hours, no questions asked. I just got to get out of this place.

I still don't get what happened in the bust. I hear nine of us got nailed. Somehow our security got breached; how sloppy was that? Maybe the Feds had an insider working alongside us . . . but that's next to impossible. Everyone in the organization works their way up the ladder bit by bit, earning the Brothers' trust. An undercover agent would have been involved for years. Would have had to have killed people, sold drugs or stolen girls off the streets. How could a government agent get in good with the company without doing stuff like that? They couldn't have. But somehow, we got infiltrated.

This whole bust is just lousy timing. Me and Carmen were going to get married once Sondra was out of the way, and the Brothers had promised me a huge promotion, too. After all, I'd be their brother-in-law. And now this. I've got to be able to buy my way out of this. Everybody has a price.

One thing I have to make sure the Brothers know, and that's that I'll never turn states evidence on them, mainly because they could get to me even if I was in jail. I'm not going to risk that.

I need somebody to get a cell phone to me. It won't be easy, but I'm sure I can bribe a guard or maybe an inmate with connections. The most important thing is that I call the Brothers as soon as I can and let them know I'm cool—that I won't start talking.

I also need to ask the Brothers to help me out from the outside, so I can get off. I need both the kidnapping and the drug charges against me dropped. I know they can do some serious witness intimidation, or even worse. I know they'll help me out; we have all the power. . . .

. . . On the way home, I called the office and told them my kids had been found and I wouldn't be in today. I talked to Shelly about what I wanted her to do today but she wouldn't stop crying; she was so happy for me. I gave up trying to talk to her and just hung up.

Next I called Connie, who was thrilled and relieved that the kids were home. I told her I needed to pick up my things at her house in a few minutes, but that I'd leave the key on the kitchen counter and lock the door on my way out.

"Do you need anything, honey?" she asked.

"Yes, Connie, I need to see Ken as soon as possible," I said. She sounded really happy to hear me say that and said she'd talk to Ken about bumping up my appointment.

I realized it was Thursday already. This time next week would be Thanksgiving. What a week this had been. I left the kids in the car while I raced into Connie's house, grabbed my belongings, including my EFT homework, and left.

"So that was really Dwight, wasn't it?" I was trying to get the kids to talk more about what had happened. They were both so quiet in the back seat of the car.

It was Ben who finally spoke up. "Yeah, he sure fooled us. I just about died when he showed up at the old house. I thought he had done something bad to you."

Poor kids. They must have been terrified. "No, he never hurt me one bit. I didn't even know he was involved until he moved out all of a sudden. The apartment is empty now."

"Whew," he said. "I was pretty worried about that."

"Me, too," Cassie said quietly. "I thought Dad might have hurt you, too."

"You know," I told them, "Dad hasn't really been all that good a dad lately. He's been really selfish, and I know he hurt your feelings a lot."

I could see Cassie nodding in the rearview mirror. "Mom? Was he really going to take us to another country?"

I sighed. They were smart kids; they knew what was going on the whole time. "I'm afraid so. He wanted you all for himself, and he had figured out a way to do that, by taking you far away from here."

"We would never have seen you again, huh, Mom?" Ben speculated.

"I would have looked for you forever if that had happened. But now you're back where you belong, and your father is probably going to prison for a very long time."

We finally arrived home. The kids helped me carry my things up the stairs, and I opened the apartment door. To my surprise, the dining room table was empty. The police officers and their monitoring equipment were gone, and we finally had our apartment to ourselves again.

"Who wants to take a shower first?" I teased them.

Cassie begged Ben to let her go first. Soon she was brushing her clean, wet hair, sitting on the couch and watching a soap opera in a clean pair of sweats and a t-shirt.

While Ben was getting cleaned up, I sat next to Cassie on the couch and put my arm around her. "You know, Cassie, I feel terrible that I left you guys alone and let those guys steal you. I've been worried sick about you."

Cassie stopped brushing her hair and gazed down at the brush, fiddling with the bristles. "I feel bad, too. I feel like I should've gotten away somehow, but I didn't, because I was scared and because . . ." She hesitated, and I could tell she had something important to tell me. Finally, she buried her head in my chest and started to cry. "That guy we thought was Dwight and even Dad told us you died in the hospital. Dad said we just needed to go live with him now and that our new mom was named Carmen. I was so scared."

I just squeezed her tight and murmured, "It's okay. I'm fine, and everything is going to be all right."

I later had a similar conversation with Ben, who also had failed to disclose this vital fact to the police. I was so angry at Jack by that time, I could have strangled him.

I let the kids watch whatever they wanted on TV and called the school. I told the secretary that they wouldn't be going to school for another few days, but they were fine. She said that she might be able to get some makeup work from their teachers, and I told her to call me if she was able to do that. Our lives, in the meantime, were on hold.

I spent part of the afternoon adding aspects to my list. The events of the day had really helped me fill out the form. Connie called late in the afternoon and told me she'd made an appointment for me with Ken the next day at 4:00. I told her I'd take it.

When I realized my Friday was going to be so busy, I called Marge and gave her the good news before asking her if she'd take the kids all day tomorrow. She often did that on days when school was out, but this was a bit short notice for her. I didn't need to worry, though—Marge agreed without hesitation.

"They'll probably be a bit quieter than usual, Marge," I told her. "They've had a bad experience, but I know they will feel safe with you. I've already explained to them that they need to spend some time at your place, and they're fine with it."

"It's no problem, Sondra," said dear, sweet Marge. Nothing seemed to ruffle her. "I'll be delighted to take them for the day. I'm just so relieved they were found so quickly."

We said our goodbyes, and I went back to hugging my kids. We had all sat very close together for what seemed hours. We all needed each other so much at that moment. It was good to be home and complete.

Later, I ordered some Chinese takeout from a place on North 10th Street, and we watched a movie on cable. The kids were so exhausted after their ordeal that they were perfectly happy to go to bed by 8:00.

After they had gone to bed and the apartment was quiet, I stretched out on the couch and reflected on all the events of the day. I was so tired from all the emotional highs and lows of the past several days, but I couldn't go to bed just yet. I just let my mind drift for a while, relaxing, and thinking about what I had to do the next day. At 9:00, I needed to meet with Detective Murphy. After that, I needed to run down to the courthouse; I was told that the mysterious "Dwight" and Jack would be arraigned on kidnapping charges at 1:00. Dwight was supposed to be charged with third-degree assault as well, for pushing Cassie down the stairs. At 4:00 I had my EFT session with Ken. I didn't know how he'd react to my coming back to see him so soon after my first appointment, but a lot was going on, and I was developing a moderate headache again. My homework was done, and I realized I still had time to read more about the technique in my new book before going for my next session.

I sat up and dug around for the book in my bag. I started on chapter 2, which talked about the meridians in detail. I began to understand why the tapping points were located where they were. I learned about the "floor-to-ceiling eye roll" technique, which is used to get a stress level all the way down to zero, and practiced it a few times. I reminded myself to ask Ken more about that technique when I saw him tomorrow.

I ended up falling asleep on the couch with the book on my chest, and woke up at 7:00. I realized as I lay there, with the sleep still in my eyes, how fortunate I had been and that I needed to show my gratitude for getting my kids back so quickly. It had been many years since I had prayed. In truth, I didn't really know who to pray to, so I just started to whisper how grateful I was. In those moments, praying for the first time in what must have been about 12 or 13 years, I realized it felt good to be making contact with a higher someone or something. I decided there must be something bigger out there. I didn't know a name for it, but I felt "God" was as good as it could get. So I thanked God, not as a Jew, but as a grateful mother.

I took the first shower and let the kids sleep a while longer. I stayed under the fast-flowing water for 20 minutes, maybe longer. It seemed the most wholesome way of just letting go of all the bad things that had been in my life recently. As the water flowed over me, all those bad things just went down the drain. I thought of how I picked this up from the EFT books I was reading, and how the therapy was doing more than helping me get rid of headaches.

I actually enjoyed getting the kids out of bed that morning. It's funny how the little things become so important after you realize you came close to losing them. Both Cassie and Ben gave me big hugs when they got out of bed, and I was pleased to see their old personalities coming out again. I reminded them they needed to stay with Marge today, and for once I got no argument about them being too big for a babysitter.

I made it to Detective Murphy's office just before 9:00. Finding a place to leave the car was a challenge as his precinct was downtown and the parking garages were all full by the time I got there. I finally found an empty meter close to both the precinct and the courthouse, so I knew I would make it to court on time as well.

Detective Murphy greeted me warmly and took me to a small conference room next to his office, apologetically saying his office looked like a tornado had gone through it. He offered me a cup of coffee and brought his own cup as well. He sat across from me at the conference table.

"So, the kids are doing okay?" he asked.

I nodded. "They're doing better. They were terrified during much of the ordeal, even though neither was really injured. I found out after we got home that Jack and Dwight told them that I had died from an aneurysm and that Carmen was going to be their mother."

"That's awful. No kid should have to go through that," he said. "And by the way, based on the forensic prints we got from the apartment that we matched with your friend Dwight, we found out his real name is Frank Albert Traynor. He has a long rap sheet, and he's done time for drug dealing. He's probably in the same trafficking ring that Jack is in, and most likely they'll both be going away for a long time—and that doesn't count the drug charges pending against them and the previously unsolved crimes we have them on now. Traynor is already in violation of his parole in New York."

I told him I was going to their felony arraignments to see what would happen; I was worried they'd get out on bail.

"I highly doubt it. I know the judge scheduled for the arraignment. She's tough—and she's very well versed in the charges being brought against the two of them. She won't let them go," he reassured me.

"I hope not," I said, feeling better about the situation.

"So," he said firmly, "let's talk about how we're going to keep you safe until we put the rest of the gang behind bars."

I cringed; I already knew what he was going to say.

"I want you to—for a short period of time, mind you—to enter the federal government's witness protection program." He saw me wince, and he leaned a bit closer, folding his hands on the table. "You have to realize, Sondra, that the witness protection program takes care of many witnesses and their families whose lives are in danger because they will or have testified against the likes of drug traffickers, organized crime members and other types of criminals. Your testimony is vital to our being able to put these people away, and we don't want anything like the kidnapping of your children, or worse, to happen.

"I think you should bear in mind that no one who has gone into the witness protection program and who followed all the security guidelines has ever been harmed. Please, Sondra, for your own peace of mind, and before anything else happens to you or the kids, please consider it."

I was stunned by how somber and how concerned he was. "How long do you think we'd have to be in hiding?" I asked him, imagining spending months and months with different names, in a different state where we knew no one.

"I don't know," he said honestly. "Ideally, we'd keep you under wraps until the trial, which could be pushed up to about three months after we make the arrests. We're expecting to make the bulk of the arrests within a couple of weeks. It's possible you could come back then, but I wouldn't recommend it."

I'd heard all sorts of horror stories of people living isolated, lonely lives in the witness protection program. How would my children deal with a new place, under different identities? They'd been through so much already.

"What about bodyguards—wouldn't assigning us bodyguards accomplish the same thing?" I asked hopefully.

He shook his head. "I'm afraid that would be a poor substitute."

I sat back and took a sip of coffee. This was so overwhelming; I was having a hard time wrapping my mind around it. "And what would happen to all of our stuff—things in our apartment?"

"We'd keep the rent paid up. You can take some clothes and a few personal belongings, but you'd leave behind your vehicle, any photos or anything else that could identify you. And, of course, you wouldn't be able to contact your friends or family members while you're in protective custody."

"I understand," I told him. "I'll tell you what—can I let you know my decision on Monday? I really need to think this through."

He frowned and after a second or two said, "Monday would be the absolute latest. We can't protect you here—you understand that, right?"

I was immobile, paralyzed with fear as I once again realized the magnitude of danger we were in. He knew I understood. I didn't need to say anything; my body language spoke volumes. Even so, I still thought I needed several days to think about it before making a decision.

We parted ways shortly thereafter, and I wondered if I'd see him at the felony arraignments. I had a couple of hours before I needed to be at the courthouse, and I really wanted to talk to someone about all this. I found myself heading for Connie's office.

"You're early," Amy said brightly as I entered the clinic. I explained to her that I was just here to see Connie, and she sent me down the hallway to her office. Connie's door was open.

"Sondra!" she exclaimed as she jumped up from her desk. "Come here, let me give you a big hug." As she embraced me warmly, she asked, "How are the kids?"

I closed the office door behind me and took off my jacket. "Do you have a minute?" I asked, starting to feel desperate.

She looked alarmed and led me to a chair. "What's up?" She sat down in the chair next to mine and leaned on the armrest.

I began to tearfully explain in detail what Detective Murphy wanted me to do. "It just seems like so much to go through," I told her.

She reached over and took my hand. "Honey, look—this might sound harsh, but none of what you, Ben and Cassie have gone through will be worth it if you're dead. Those guys need to be put behind bars for everything they've done, and you play a key role in that."

I started to cry harder. "I just don't know if I can do it."

"You've been through so much, but you're strong—otherwise you wouldn't have been able to deal with everything so far. I know you'll get through this next phase just fine. I'd miss you, but at least you'd be safe. That's all that matters."

"What about the kids?"

"You could treat it like an adventure," she smiled.

I knew she was trying to help me feel better, and I knew that I really didn't have much choice in the end. I was just being stubborn, trying to hold out until some other option presented itself. And I was getting frustrated at the negative feelings that were mushrooming inside me.

Connie got me a bottle of water from the break room and sat down again. "So, when is this going to happen?"

I took a sip. "I'm giving him my decision on Monday."

"Well, now you know my opinion. And I think Gavin would agree with me," she said.

I thought about my job, but for some reason it didn't seem all that important to me anymore. I could get another job when I returned, or I could start my own business with the two million dollars no one but Connie knew I had yet. That was one thing I was going to keep secret, I promised myself. I had already decided I deserved to keep that money—especially after what Jack had done to my kids. No one else besides Jack would have any idea I had taken it, and he might not even know himself. And he'd never find out if he went to prison, I reasoned.

I had another hour before I had to leave for court, so I asked Connie if I could sort some more books for her, just to keep me occupied. She laughed and then heartily agreed. "Sondra, you can sort my pencils if you want to," she teased me.

I found several good EFT books while I emptied more boxes, and I started to ask her if I could borrow them before realizing I might not be around to return them. Monday was only three days away. After an hour of shelving dusty books, I thanked Connie and told her I'd see her later that afternoon.

I didn't see Detective Murphy at the arraignment; in fact, I didn't see anyone I recognized. The courtroom contained a couple of reporters—identifiable by their voice recorders, notebooks and poised pens. The rest, I guessed, were family members or other visitors, but none of Jack's family was there.

He didn't have many family members left; his parents were both dead. He had a brother living in Florida, but they never spoke to one another. Milton was much younger than Jack and Sol. Their mother's favorite, Milton was a doctor and played the violin, which set him apart from his street brawling brothers. Where Sol had got to, I had no idea, and didn't care as long as he stayed out of my way. I never did tell Jack that his gay brother hit on me more than once some years ago; apparently he played for both sides. He always was greedy like that—never wanted anything to pass him by. I might let that pearl slip if and when the time was right.

A little after 1:00, several prisoners in orange jumpsuits were led into the courtroom. I saw Jack and Dwight—Frank, I corrected myself—in the lineup. I was glad I had chosen a seat in the back corner of the courtroom. A few moments later, we were instructed to rise as the judge entered the courtroom. Judge Cortez was an older, gray-haired Latina woman who I hoped was as tough as Murphy had claimed.

Jack's case didn't come up for nearly an hour. I was surprised to find myself daydreaming of how Jack had been grabbed and cuffed, how he probably reacted to being read his Miranda rights and being thrown in jail. He always hated being denied his freedom for long periods—something I hoped he was going to have to get used to. I also hoped that during his short, overnight stay in jail he had started regretting his decision to become a drug baron.

The court clerk called Jack's case, and he stood up and gazed at the judge. Although he had looked around the courtroom a few times as he waited for his case to come up, he hadn't seen me. I prayed that he never did, and made sure I was hidden behind the person in front of me. His attorney was named Clyde Parker. Parker was a tall, broad-set African American wearing a dark blue suit; the quality of the cut showed he was not from a pro bono practice. He exuded expensive taste.

It was no surprise that Jack cockily answered "not guilty" to all the charges against him. I wouldn't have expected him to respond any other way.

When it came time for bail to be set, the prosecutor, a petite blonde woman with a short haircut, sporting a gray wool skirt and suit jacket, said, "Your Honor, this is an unusual case involving both Mr. Ackerman and a second defendant here today. Mr. Ackerman is accused of kidnapping his two children from their home and taking them across state lines to New Jersey, where evidence suggests he was planning to take them out of the country. He's charged with two counts of aggravated kidnapping and two counts of neglecting a child. He's an extremely high flight risk. We ask that he be denied bail."

I could see the reporters scribbling furiously as the prosecutor spoke. Parker then leaned toward the microphone on his table. "Your Honor, it has yet to be established that the taking of this gentleman's own children was in fact a crime. This man has a clean felony record and has been employed with a shipping firm for over five years. I do not believe he's a flight risk at all."

The judge sifted through a couple of pieces of paper, scanning them quickly. "Thank you both," she said. "I'm ordering that Mr. Ackerman be held without bail."

Parker leaned forward into the microphone again. "In that case, ma'am, I'd like to ask for a speedy trial on the defendant's behalf."

"So noted, counsel," the judge said. . . .

. . . What an insult! I'm used to getting more respect from dealers and drug runners than I got from our so-called legal system. That bitch of a prosecutor saying I needed to be kept locked up because I was such a bad boy. . . . That ugly old Spic of a woman judge denying me bail. . . . What'd I do? I got my kids back, because they were taken from me while my back was turned. Sondra should be on trial, not me. She didn't have my permission, not the court's permission or I bet even my kids' permission either to drag them off to that apartment she was holed up in. So if no one with authority over the jurisdiction of my children gave her the okay, why wasn't she standing up there today? Why didn't they get it—she stole my kids and was walking away scot-free. Where's the justice in that?

Still, we're not done. I've got people on the outside who can do what I need to be done. My brother Sol will steal my kids back for me. He won't screw it up. Sondra's life was hanging by a thread before, but now she's done. I ordered for her to be hit as soon as I got back here. With her gone, the kids will get picked up and driven to Mexico. They'll grow up in Mexico, and arrangements have already been made for them to visit me regular—at least once a month. I know Carmen won't wait 30 years for me, but the bosses can arrange for someone else to bring them to see me. Goddammit, I'm so pissed off. Just yesterday the world was my oyster—Canada as good as mine, becoming a billionaire just around the corner . . . well at least well on the way, 10 or 12 years at the most . . . a billionaire at 46, now that would have been something. . . .

. . . With Jack remanded to prison without bail, I felt immensely relieved. Next up was "Dwight"/Frank. It was a bigger slam dunk than Jack's case. He was already in violation of parole in New York. He pleaded not guilty, and he, too, was denied bail.

Just before Frank sat down, he looked in my direction. He smirked at me before turning around. I immediately turned my head away as soon as I realized I had been seen and, before the next case was called, I grabbed my purse and slipped out the door.

As I walked away I started to think that it was just about over between Jack and me. Just the divorce to go and the split would be complete. . . .

. . . Once back in the lockup, an inmate smuggled me a cell phone, and I called my Tijuana bosses. "It's Jack. I want you to set up some stuff for me. Get the contract on Sondra Ackerman going, no delays—just go right ahead and fix her, then get my brother Sol to get hold of my kids and get them to Carmen, you got that? Good. Don't let me down. Adios, amigo." . . .

. . . As it turned out, I had plenty of time to get to the clinic to see Ken. I was so lost in thought over Jack's and Frank's arraignments that I almost forgot to bring in my new book and my homework papers. Inside the office, I asked Amy if I had time to say a quick word to Connie before I had my appointment.

"No problem," she said. "You go on back and I'll call you when he's ready."

"Thanks." Comfortable now with the clinic, I headed back to where Connie was enjoying her afternoon cup of coffee and thumbing through trade journals stacked on her desk. "Hi," I said, breaking her peaceful silence.

"Oh, hi, Sondra! How'd it go this afternoon?"

I sat down and relayed the entire afternoon's events, including how pitiful Jack and his cohort looked in orange jumpsuits. "It doesn't look like they're getting out any time soon."

"What about Murphy?" Connie asked. "Did he have anything more to say?"

This, for me, was a sore spot; I didn't want to have to talk further about Detective Murphy's recommendations. Even so, I went over every detail again and reminded her I didn't think I was going anywhere soon, even though I technically needed to tell him my answer by Monday.

"Oh, Sondra," she said, with a quizzical look on her face. "Just go! What's wrong with you? You have to go! What if those other guys working with Jack get it in their heads that you aren't worth keeping around—that you're too much of a liability?"

"I know, I know," I conceded. "I just think there are ways to get around actually going into hiding. Between the police and the FBI, they have to have the resources to protect all three of us, and it wouldn't uproot the kids."

"Sondra, they're not the Secret Service!" she protested. "I just don't want anything to happen to you before your testimony—or ever, for that matter!"

"I said I'd think about it."

At that point, Amy showed up with my chart in her hand. "Ken will see you now," she said.

As soon as I stepped into the hallway, I could see Ken's familiar figure at the other end of the hall. Amy approached him first and handed him my chart.

"Come on in, Sondra," he told me, ushering me into the same office as last time. He had soft Asian music playing in the background, and the lighting in his treatment room was again soft and pleasant. "It's nice to see you again so soon," he said, sitting in his padded chair and gesturing for me to sit down. "I heard things have been hard for you lately."

I told him I had redeveloped a slight headache that had gotten worse when I learned that my husband and the man I knew as Dwight had been intimately involved in the kidnapping of my children. "Even though I've got the kids back, I feel like all of the issues around the kidnapping are still so huge. I don't feel like the stress has left me."

"It seems like the entire kidnapping issue is one of those giant problems that you need to break down into its component parts— what we call aspects, remember? When we deal with each part, the whole thing will seem much easier to handle," he calmly explained. "Can I see your homework?"

161

I handed him the pages and he looked over them very carefully. "I see you've done some of the work in breaking down the kidnapping issue into smaller pieces."

I told him about the book I had purchased, and how much it had helped me with some of my homework; he congratulated me on getting interested enough in EFT to buy a book on the subject.

"Why don't we take some of these EFT aspects and work on them, okay?" He stood up and helped me get into the comfortable reclining chair. I immediately felt more relaxed and confident that he would be able to help me.

"On this first one," he said pointing to one of the 10s on my peace plan. "I want you to just go for it—let me be an observer so I can see how your tapping technique is coming along. So if it's okay with you, I'll have you do the tapping. How does that sound?" he asked.

My setup phrase was "Even though I almost allowed my children's kidnapper to make love to me and I now feel such pain at being deceived this way, I deeply and completely love and accept myself." Round and round I went, using the now-familiar tapping technique. I continued with this aspect until gradually the intensity I felt neared zero. When I felt I was finished, I nodded and waited for him to speak next.

"How about this: 'Even though I'm angry that my husband Jack was responsible for taking my children, I love myself and I fully accept myself," he suggested.

We went through that one, and he gave me some pointers on how to make the tapping of the meridians more effective. Then we addressed several more aspects. I could feel my anxiety and low-grade headache start to release from my body as I relaxed into the chair and felt my EFT tapping technique become more and more automatic. I was no longer self-conscious about saying the affirmations, and I felt comfortable that I was tapping correctly.

"I think there may be one here that you missed," he said, out of the blue. I looked at him. "Try this," he suggested. "Even though I feel guilty about my children being kidnapped, I love and fully accept myself."

I smiled. He was right; it was a big issue—one I truly felt bad about. I had been feeling foolish and guilty about the fact that I had allowed myself to trust Dwight when I shouldn't have. "Let's do that one," I said, my cheeks reddening.

Ken didn't seem to notice that I was embarrassed about the topic, so we went through his suggested affirmation. As soon as we finished and I was relaxed, however, he suggested we do an affirmation having to do with my embarrassment over trusting Dwight. I smiled to myself; he didn't miss a thing.

The hour went by quickly, and I felt considerably better as I got up and sat in one of the smaller chairs. I didn't have a headache anymore, and I was impressed by how much work we had done.

"Will you be back next week?" he asked me, gathering the loose papers, including my homework, and placing them neatly in my chart.

"I already have an appointment on Tuesday. Is that too early?" I grabbed my coat and slipped it on.

"No, I don't think so. Do you still have some blank sheets left over so you can write down any more aspects you come up with?" he asked.

I told him I did and let him open the door for me. I could see that it was getting dark; I was running late. I thanked Ken and quickly paid Amy before running out to the parking lot to my car. After another 20 minutes of Philadelphia rush hour traffic, I finally pulled up in front of Marge's small brick house. Children's toys littered the driveway; Marge babysat for younger children, too.

Ben and Cassie were happy to see me. I paid Marge for the day plus the money she would have gotten if the kids hadn't been kidnapped. She tried to refuse, but I insisted. Before long, we were headed back to the comfort of our apartment.

I still hadn't gotten a chance to buy any groceries since the kids came home, so we stopped at a popular fried chicken place and took home a bucket of chicken and a number of sides. We didn't even bother getting out the real plates; instead, we loaded up paper plates with the chicken, mashed potatoes, biscuits and corn on the cob before heading to the living room to find something fun to watch on the television. Somehow I hadn't been able to sit at the table and eat since the police had commandeered that space for all of their telephone equipment.

After dinner, I called Ben's friend Kyle's mother and asked if she would please watch the kids the next morning while I made a much-needed trip to the supermarket. She had heard the kids had been found and said she would be happy to watch them. "Bring them over anytime; I'll be home," she told me.

I spent the rest of the night reading, while the kids watched television. I finished my book on EFT and went back to reread several passages that interested me. I wondered if I'd have time to swing by a bookstore tomorrow morning to look for another book on EFT before getting the groceries. This subject was so fascinating to me that I just had to learn more. I had always been like that: whenever a topic interested me, I would read everything I could find out about it. EFT was clearly working for me and, after going to two sessions and reading up the subject, I could tell I was becoming a loyal convert to this type of therapy. I couldn't wait until my next session, and I was eager to learn everything there was to learn.

By 9:30 I was tired, and I could see that Ben had fallen asleep on the floor in front of the television. I sent Cassie to bed, covered Ben with his favorite blanket and fell into bed.

Tonight, I feel hope. My children are back in my arms, and I've found a therapy that is actually helping me feel better. I can't believe I have been such a skeptic all this time. Ken March and EFT are two of the best things that have happened to me lately. I feel lighter than I've ever felt before, in spite of the enormous stressors that are still facing me. When all of this is over, I hope I won't forget what the gift of EFT has brought me and how much it has done to improve the quality of my upside down life.

164

Chapter 8

The kids woke me up early the next morning, complaining that the milk had gone bad. I rolled over and groaned at them to eat one of the oranges or apples in the refrigerator. I was pretty sure they were still fresh. I later found them devouring the remnants of some old pizza that they'd microwaved. I felt too guilty about having so little food in the house to even complain. I also was feeling bad now about my recent reliance on takeouts. Was I no longer capable of cooking fresh, wholesome food for my family? I would have to tap for this very negative feeling I was holding about working in the apartment's kitchen. For some reason it just seemed to represent the seat of all my bad feelings. Definitely a tappable issue. I needed to get over it.

At 10:00, I asked Ben to call his friend Kyle just to make sure they were home. His mother said they could come right over, so I gathered my things and walked them over to their building in the apartment complex.

I greeted Kathy, whom I'd met a couple of times, and she invited me into their apartment. I'd heard that she was a single parent, too, and I made a mental note to get to know her better when things settled down. She offered me a cup of coffee, which I eagerly accepted. The children had retreated to Kyle's bedroom, and Kathy and I sat at her dining room table. I looked around. Her apartment was laid out exactly as ours was. A lonely television set sat in the corner of the sparsely furnished living room. What she had was sorely mismatched; it looked like she shopped at a lot of yard sales. . . .

. . . Without any warning, I got transferred from the central lockup to Graterford State Prison. It was an imposing old place, but the security seemed up to date. They put me in solitary, and not even the guards spoke to me—they just growled once in a while. I was expecting a welcome meeting with the governor or at least the warden, but it hasn't happened yet. Doesn't matter, I figured. Those guys aren't really in charge of the prison. It's the inmates who run the place, and the best thing to do to protect yourself is find out who the gang leaders are and show them respect, then stay out of their way.

I didn't know what kind of influence I was going to have in here, but I figured that as a major East Coast drug trafficker, I'd be able to get some respect of my own. Prison is all about cash or drugs, after all, and the more you have of either one, the more favors you can get. What I needed to happen was to have my bosses or my brother Sol arrange for someone to visit me and get me some stuff so I could distribute it in here to make my rep. That would mean buying a guard or two, but that shouldn't be a problem.

In the meantime, I managed to hold onto about a hundred bucks. How far that would get me in here remained to be seen. I was figuring this place could be my home for the rest of my life. That thought was pretty depressing, but I didn't want to get down about it. I've heard that what you think, you get in your life, so I've got to stop thinking stuff like that—but how? Maybe I could ask for books. I've never been much of a reader, but it was boring in here—got too much time on my hands—and it would be a good way to keep me from thinking too much. When I get my meeting with the warden or whoever's supposed to welcome me here, I'll ask him for books. I know a good joke—maybe I should ask for books called *How to Dig a Tunnel* or even the original book from that old *Prison Break* series. Still, I need to be careful; maybe they wouldn't appreciate my sense of humor in this dump. You never know how these dumbasses are going to react. I remember seeing a movie where a guy was kept in a cold cell and the guards would hose him down with cold water. I didn't need crap like that.

I didn't think I was going to be treated that way, but with drugs on your rap sheet, you never know. If one of the guards had a kid who was a junkie or something, he'd get his revenge on the nearest dealer, and that could be me. So

I figured I'd better be smart and polite—don't be a wise guy. I had to play this right. . . .

. . . "You must be so relieved to have your kids back," Kathy murmured, fingering the rim of her coffee cup and looking somewhat past me as she talked. I wondered what her life was like—what she did for a living, or if she was a stay-at-home mom. She seemed really shy and a little nervous.

I smiled warmly, hoping she'd open up a little more. "I'm so thrilled, Kathy. You have no idea how terrifying it is to have your children stolen right out from under you."

Kathy cleared her throat and stared into the cup. "I . . . uh . . . I wanted to talk to you after it happened, but I figured you'd be busy with the police and everything. I wanted to tell you that I actually really do know what you've gone through."

I was shocked and curious as to what had happened to her. I decided to be as straightforward about it as possible. "You do? You mean something happened to Kyle . . . ?" I was at a loss for words.

She nodded. "My boyfriend—Kyle's father—took him for the day when he was only 5 years old. He was supposed to bring him back that night around 7:00, but . . . he just never showed up." Her voice started to shake as she recounted what happened. "The worst of it is, you sit there and wait for them to come back, and as every minute goes by, you think up different excuses as to why they're not back yet. Maybe traffic is bad. Maybe they lost track of time because they were having fun. You know? But at the same time, you've got this little voice inside you saying it's all going wrong. We just don't listen to our instincts, do we? So I waited for hours before I called the police." Kathy paused, fighting back tears.

"Oh my God," I exclaimed. "How did you get him back?"

Kathy was shifting uncomfortably in her seat, but at least she was starting to look directly at me. "I called the cops that night around 10:00, and at first they said they couldn't do anything until Kyle was missing for 24 hours. But when I told them my boyfriend had violent tendencies and could be a danger to Kyle, to himself, or even both of them, they said they'd start looking for them."

"That sounds unbearable," I told her, my own ordeal still fresh in my mind.

167

"It was," she agreed. "We were living in Seattle at the time, and they finally found them at a motel in Nevada almost a week later. Kyle was all right, but he's had trouble sleeping ever since."

"What happened to the boyfriend?" I asked, curious as to how my own situation would turn out and what kind of prison time Jack might face.

"He got 20 years. He probably won't get out until Kyle is an adult, but I didn't want to take any chances. We changed our last name and moved out here. I never even let my family know where we went." She looked at me as if to see if I believed her or if I was shocked.

I touched her arm. "Kathy . . . thank you for telling me this. And for what it's worth, I think you did just the right thing for your son." Even as I spoke, I felt a pang of guilt, wondering what was keeping me from making the right decision for my own children.

"Well, anyway . . . I just wanted you to know. . . ." Her voice trailed off.

Kathy stood up, and the intimate moment we had just shared, two mothers protecting their children, was broken.

I stood up as well, and grabbed my purse. "Thanks for watching the kids for me. I think I'll only be gone an hour. I haven't gone grocery shopping for more than a week."

She walked me to the door. I thought about saying goodbye to the kids, but I could hear them laughing and talking in Kyle's bedroom, so I just said goodbye to Kathy and slipped out the door.

I actually had fun shopping that morning. The supermarket was busy, but I was feeling great, and I wanted to spoil the kids as much as possible. I planned to make peace with the apartment kitchen and start cooking healthy meals for them, so I bought all of the staples I used to keep in our old house, plus some treats. I knew they'd love the gallon of chocolate ice cream and the bag of their favorite cookies.

I ended up hauling out six bags loaded with groceries. It was a lot, but I could enlist the kids to help carry them once we got back to our own apartment building. I knew Cassie and Ben would help; they were such good kids when it came to things like that.

I thought about stopping at the local bookstore to pick up another book about EFT, but I had taken so much time at the supermarket that I felt I needed to head for home instead. Plus, I had forgotten my cooler, although I thought the ice cream would make it as long as I didn't get stuck in traffic. It was still early, so the streets weren't busy with the usual Saturday traffic yet, but I made sure I didn't speed. It wasn't worth a ticket.

I turned on the car radio and found myself humming to the music as I took the now familiar route to our new home. At the last stoplight before the entrance to the apartment complex, I heard a loud noise, like another car on the road had backfired. It sounded like it came from my left. But as I looked in that direction, all I could see were the broken windows of a rundown brick building that must have been a factory at one time. The only car I saw was the one in my rearview mirror. . . .

. . . I was told that Sondra would be wiped out Saturday morning. The two hit men had a plan, and I was told it couldn't fail. They knew their business, I was sure, plus they guaranteed their results, so I expected to be a widower sometime soon. Maybe I'd be allowed to go to the funeral, and I could use it as my chance to break out.

What about Cassie and Ben, though? In some ways I wished I could call the cousins off; in other ways, I just wanted it over with. Being in this shithole changes a man's perspectives. When I put out the contract on Sondra, I was pissed at her, because it was her stupid high morals that got me in trouble. But if I was put away for a long stretch, which could happen, I had to make arrangements for Ben and Cassie that might be less than perfect. Sure, I want them with Carmen, but she's not exactly model mother material. What if she ditches them because taking care of them would keep her from having a good time? What if the Brothers adopt them? Even if I did decide to turn states evidence, I wouldn't be able to; they could use the kids as a bargaining chip. . . .

Sol. Sol was the key. I needed him to take over with the kids. Would he accept that? It was tricky, what with his lifestyle and all. He'd be just like Carmen—not wanting to give up his love of partying. It was all falling in on me. . . . I didn't know the answers. . . . I knew I should just go with the flow, wait for news and then react, but it was so hard to sit tight and wait. What a mess. . . .

. . . I didn't really feel pain, exactly. The small welling up of blood on my coat sleeve caught my attention. And then I saw the tiniest of holes in the driver's-side window and the glass beginning to star outward in several directions. It didn't really register that I'd been shot until the car behind me honked to tell me the light had turned green.

Just then I looked up to see a Hispanic guy standing in front of my car and slowly, as if in slow motion, he was raising his hand. He had a gun. Without even thinking, I hit the gas as hard as I could. I clipped the guy at around the same time a slug tore through the upholstery right beside me.

I thought I heard another shot go off just after my car lurched forward into the intersection. Forcing myself to take my eyes off the wound on my forearm, and trying to see what was ahead of me through the shattered glass of the windshield, I gunned the engine and tore down the street, past the apartment complex. I couldn't let the kids see me like this. . . .

. . . I had been pacing up and down in my cell, waiting for the call. My phone vibrated in the pocket of my jeans.

"Jack?" It was Nesto.

"Yeah. Give me good news."

"Jack, it didn't go well."

I demanded all the details.

He said, "I took a shot from the side; I thought it hit, but if it did, it didn't take her out. Pablo stepped up. He had the Ruger Rimfire; it's his favorite piece. He never misses with it. He fired directly at her, but the shot went wide because she hit the gas. Clipped Pablo on the hip even though he jumped out of the way. He was really pissed at the miss. He was sure he had a hit, but she got away. We both got off another round, but. . . . Jack, this is not our way. She had luck with her. We got away; nobody saw us. We'll try again—don't worry." . . .

. . . I drove like a madwoman in spite of the fact that, by now, I realized the bullet had only skimmed my arm. Even so, I wanted to get as far away from that intersection as possible. Plus I couldn't shake the fear that whoever did this was following me. Actually, my head cleared enough that I knew exactly who "whoever" was.

I drove up to Graduate Hospital and resisted the temptation to pull right up to the emergency door. Calming my mind and wishing I could drive and do EFT at the same time, I found a nearby parking spot and started walking toward the entrance. I was still so flustered that I almost left my keys in the car. I took a deep breath and called Kathy to tell her I was going to be late. I didn't tell her why. The kids would find out soon enough.

The doctors and nurses in the emergency room acted swiftly when I told them the story. Not long after I arrived, I found myself in a patient gown and an intern was cleaning my wound. I heard a nurse tell the doctor that the police would be arriving any minute.

The bullet tore through my jacket and grazed a neat linear gouge through the flesh of my forearm. One doctor said my forearm had kept the bullet from hitting me in the chest. I was grateful that I wasn't seriously hurt, because I needed to get moving—to get us into witness protection. I had made my decision.

As the intern was flushing the wound with sterile solution and an attendant was asking me for my insurance information, Officer Dave walked in with his partner. Officer Dave recognized me right away.

"So what happened?" he asked, peering at the wound. "It doesn't look too bad; you were lucky."

I told both officers the same story I had told the emergency room staff—about going grocery shopping and how I was stopped at the intersection of Waverly and 16th when I heard a loud popping sound and saw that I'd been shot. I told them about seeing the man with the gun in front of my car and how I had hit him as I sped away from the scene. "I think I know where the first shot came from, but I can't be certain," I told them. "All I could think of was driving off as fast as I could and getting here to the hospital. I didn't know what else to do."

This whole incident had knocked me off balance. I could barely remember what it felt like, only an hour or so before, to be cheerful and content, buying groceries for my family. Now I had to face the thought that my children had nearly lost their mother.

I wanted to get back to my kids more than anything. I was sure that the medical personnel around me were working as fast as they could, but it wasn't fast enough. I just wanted my wound cleaned up so I could be home with Ben and Cassie. I wanted to feel their arms around me—then I would know I was still alive.

"We need to take some photos and examine your car for bullets," Officer Dave told me. "And there could be some DNA or fibers on the car where you bumped the guy. Where are you parked? I'll send Officer Avery here out to do the dirty work while we talk for a minute longer," Officer Dave winked. He turned to his partner and said, "Have Mrs. Ackerman's car taken to the impound lot and do a full forensic sweep. Keep me posted on the results."

I handed over my keys and told Officer Avery where my car was parked and what make and model it was.

"Can you get my groceries out of the trunk?" I asked. Strangely, my thoughts were on the ice cream and how it probably didn't make it.

The intern covered the wound, saying she'd be back to put a dressing on it. Officer Dave now moved in close to me and spoke candidly. "Mrs. Ackerman, this is the last time I want to have to respond to a call that you're in the hospital—or worse. Do you understand?" Before I could answer he went on, "You need to get the hell out of here until this case is settled. I don't want to see you or your children in the morgue one of these days." His look was serious, and I knew he really was thinking of my and my children's welfare.

"You need to act now—not tomorrow or any other day," he said. "Let me call Detective Murphy and get you set up to enter the program."

I sighed. Somehow I knew it would all come down to making an on-the-spot decision, that I wouldn't really have time to sit down and weigh the pros and cons. And here it was—the moment of truth. I was scared beyond belief this time, and I wasn't afraid to admit it. What choice, really, did I have?

"Call Murphy," I said quietly.

The intern dressed and wrapped my wound and told me how to take care of it. "Change the dressing every day, and come back or see your own doctor if you see any signs of infection. It will leave a nasty mark to start with but it should turn out okay," she reassured me.

Officer Dave had gone out into the hallway to make the call to Murphy, and when he returned he handed me a piece of paper with a telephone number on it. "Normally you would be met by a U.S. Marshal at this point, but given the circumstances and the fact I am here now and you know me, I have been asked to give you the information. Go home and pack your things—you're allowed one suitcase per person. Then call this number as soon as you're ready. A van will pick you up and take you to a safe house, where you'll start the process of entering the program."

I took the piece of paper gently, as though it would bite me if I held onto it tightly. I tucked it in my wallet and asked Officer Dave if it was okay for me to go home now.

"Yes. Avery found bullet fragments in your car and took some photos, but your car is going to be at the impound lot for a while they run the tests. You're going to be long gone before it's ready to be released; I think we can get clearance from the department for you to leave it there while you're out of town. We'll run you back to your place now. They're expecting to hear from you within a few hours. So consider yourself and your children as being in protective custody starting now."

After signing the papers handed to me on a clipboard by the emergency department attendant, I collected my blood-soaked coat and followed officers Dave and Avery to their cruiser. My six bags of shopping were in the trunk, but I couldn't see us using them now. Once back at the apartment, I had to get my kids and take them to who knew where. I didn't know what I was going to say to Ben and Cassie, but once I saw them and hugged them, I was sure the right words would come.

Kathy was the beneficiary of my six bags of groceries that the officers helped me carry to her apartment. As soon as I saw Cassie and Ben, I held them as tightly as I could and told them what happened. They both burst into tears. They knew that their dad was involved in the shooting.

I told Kathy very little, but I knew she understood. She never asked me a single question and just thanked me profusely for the groceries.

"I don't know when we'll be back," I told her. "But I'll give you a call when we are."

Kathy gave me a huge hug without saying a word. I walked away with my kids.

Still crying, Cassie walked next to me on the sidewalk that led to our building, while Ben trailed behind. After his initial burst of emotion, he stayed silent. Once we were inside the apartment, I calmly told them everything that had happened and explained why we needed to go into hiding. I told them how serious the situation was, and I could see they were truly frightened. They kept stealing glances at my bandaged arm, and I knew it was real for them.

"Now, just remember, we have each other, and that's the most important thing," I said firmly. "We are going to be just fine. We're going to turn this into an adventure." I was trying to reassure them with more confidence than I felt at that moment. "Now, let's pack so we can get going as fast as possible."

"But will we ever be able to come back home?" Ben asked, tears springing to his eyes.

I hugged him again. "Of course we will. We just can't be around here for a while, because Dad's been keeping company with people who don't like us very much."

"But Mom, they tried to shoot you!" Cassie burst out, coming out of her tearful trance. "How do we know they won't just keep coming after you?"

I explained that that was the very reason we needed to enter the witness protection program. I told them how the system worked and that, once the federal officers busted the entire organization and put them in jail, we would be safe again. I hoped they didn't ask me how long that was going to take, because I truly didn't have an answer.

"We need to pack a suitcase—one for each of us. I'll dig them out of the hall closet while you guys grab some clothes. Remember—only pack the stuff you absolutely need. And pack a few summer clothes as well," I told them.

"Summer clothes? Where are we going, anyway?" asked Cassie. Ben's surprised look showed he was as bewildered as his sister.

"For once, will you do as I ask without questioning everything!" I retorted with unusual ferocity. In my urgency, I could feel myself becoming impatient with the two of them. "We don't have much time. Just pack a few summer clothes and a few winter clothes." I thought they understood we were probably traveling far away from here, but maybe I wasn't clear on that part. "I don't know where we're going, okay?" I answered sharply, my voice rising even more.

Ben started to open his mouth, but before he could ask any more questions, I prodded him along to his room. I dug out the suitcases, which were packed tightly in the back of the hall closet. I threw one into Ben's room and took the other two into the room I shared with Cassie.

Cassie was gathering her things, and I started to collect what I thought we'd need, ripping items off hangers in the closet and pulling others out of dresser drawers, and stuffing everything into the suitcases without worrying about how well they were folded.

"Mom, I'm scared," Cassie said quietly as she placed her favorite teddy bear into the half-empty suitcase.

I didn't stop what I was doing and simply answered, "Me too, honey."

She turned and grabbed me around the waist, giving me the biggest hug she had given me since she was rescued after the kidnapping. "Why can't our lives be normal?" she sobbed.

I started to feel bad about being so short with the kids. "I'm so sorry, Cassie," I told her. "When this is all over, I promise you we'll have the greatest life ever." I was still thinking of the two million dollars I had. I planned to take them on as many vacations as they could handle . . . as long as we didn't get ourselves killed first. "Now go finish up."

In half an hour, all three suitcases were sitting by our apartment door, and I used my cell phone to call the number Officer Dave had given me. A very kind-sounding woman answered and told me the van would be at our apartment in 15 minutes.

I went around unplugging electrical devices and tidying up the apartment, mostly because I didn't want to just sit there on the couch with my kids. I thought about calling Connie or even Shelly, but I didn't think our "keepers" would want me to do that. In fact, because I didn't know what power Jack's organization had, I shut my cell phone off for the first time in a long time and put it in my purse.

Within a few minutes, our doorbell rang. I hit the access buzzer and two men were at our apartment door only seconds later. The flashed their federal IDs and told us it was time to go. The men, who never introduced themselves or made small talk, carried out the suitcases for us and let me lock the apartment door before marching down the stairs behind me. A few steps ahead of me, Cassie and Ben held each other's hands. . . .

. . . My cell phone vibrated in my pocket. It was Nesto. He and Pablo had put their backup plan into action.

"Just to be sure Jack, it is apartment 215? What do you want us to do when we get there—waste all three of them if they're all in there, or just kill the woman and grab the kids?"

I drew in a deep breath. I didn't want my kids harmed physically or mentally, so this was a really tough call. After a minute I said, "If all three of them are together, split them up. One of you keep the kids in 215, then whoever is going to waste her, drag her into 214, do it there, and close the door behind you. Make sure that snot-nosed kid of a manager doesn't see you leave. Take the kids to one of the safe houses, then call me."

I pocketed my cell phone and sat and thought about Pablo and Nesto. I'd met them last year, at a Los Archos management meeting. Hard, physical Latinos, they were the type who parted crowds on the sidewalk. They always wore Ray Ban sunglasses that formed a seamless band of black across their eyes into their long, slicked black hair.

Not much later, my cell phone vibrated again. It was Nesto again. "Jack, nobody was in 215. We wasted the manager, but before we did, we got him to tell us that the three of them and what sounds like some federal agents all left here in a van just a little while ago. They were carrying suitcases. Looks like we missed 'em." . . .

. . . The black van, nondescript except for the tinted windows, was crowded with the three of us in the back seat and the luggage stowed behind us. As the van took a circuitous route through the downtown streets on that cloudy late November day, I wondered where we'd be spending Thanksgiving—and probably Christmas—this year.

The van pulled into an underground parking garage near Detective Murphy's precinct where I had met with him the other day. I watched as the driver, who hadn't spoken a word since we left our apartment, punched some numbers into a keypad. The gate went up, and the van entered the parking garage.

Once the van pulled into a parking spot, the driver told us we could leave our suitcases in the van and the other Fed helped us get out and instructed us to follow him. The Fed we were following, whom I'd mentally named "Curly" because of his sandy-colored wavy hair, led us into what looked like an ordinary office complex. We took the elevator up a few floors, and then he led us into a conference room. A woman in her late 20s, with auburn hair and glasses, was studying some paperwork.

She looked up as we came in. "Hi," she said, standing up to shake each of our hands. "I'm Aubrey; I'm one of the coordinators of this program. I'd heard you might be joining, but I hadn't anticipated it would be this soon," she said, glancing at the bulky dressing on my arm, which was revealed as I removed my coat. "Please, sit down."

"Curly" closed the door and disappeared down the hall, leaving us with Aubrey and the mound of paperwork on the table. There was a large padded manila envelope next to the pile of papers.

Aubrey addressed us, "Now . . . you all realize that you're voluntarily entering the U.S. federal Witness Protection Program?" Without waiting for an answer, she proceeded. "Detective Murphy told me that you might remain in the program until your testimony is required in court and, at this point, we don't know exactly when that will be. You'll have the option to return home, unless you feel staying away is best for you and your family. We'll be advising you the entire time, of course."

I nodded and hoped the kids weren't understanding a word of what she was saying. I glanced over and saw that they both looked dazed—like deer in headlights—and I decided I'd explain only as much as they needed to know later on.

"I have filled out most of your current biographical information, but I'd like you to look it over in a minute to make sure everything is correct," she went on. "I have your new identities, birth certificates, some money and your airline tickets here. We have you on a flight out of Philadelphia tonight, bound for Phoenix. You'll then be taken to Tucson."

Ben, who didn't dare say anything during the meeting, looked up at me and grinned. I could tell he knew where Tucson was and was now finding this whole "hiding" thing to be more interesting. Cassie still looked dazed.

"Now," Aubrey said, with an air of anticipation, "here are your new identities." She pulled out three social security cards, three birth certificates and three note cards from the manila envelope.

"Sondra, you'll now be Sondra Collins. Here's an Arizona driver's license in that name, with your new address. This is your bio, on this card, and here are your other credentials. You'll need to open a bank account so we know where to send your stipend."

I took these foreign objects that would soon need to become part of who I was. I was impressed at the speed these IDs had been put together. I picked up my new license, and we all looked at my picture. Then the kids looked up at me. Then we looked down at my picture again. It was hardly a match for how I looked right now; I looked years older than the photo. The children's good manners kept them from making more of the obvious difference between the two looks. All in all, it felt strange holding these items. I glanced at the biography I apparently was supposed to memorize.

"That reminds me, Sondra," Aubrey said. She reached over and took my purse. "I need to go through this entire purse and keep anything connecting you to your life or identity here in Philadelphia. Don't worry; you'll get that stuff back when you return."

I was shocked when she just helped herself to my purse, but as all of this was clearly under her jurisdiction, I knew I didn't have any right to protest. I wondered how often she did this—ripped people out of their lives and put them somewhere else. It was a brand new thing for me, but obviously she was used to the process.

She went on to tell Ben that his new name was Benjamin Collins and told Cassie that she was now Cassie Collins. They both took their bios, but neither did more than glance at them.

"Cassie, Ben, you'll want to memorize everything on those cards in case people ask you about your life," she explained.

Aubrey hesitated, probably because of our stunned expressions. "Maybe I should explain our process better," she said. "As witnesses entering the program, you get new names and new places to live, provided by the government. We usually encourage witnesses to keep their first names, but sometimes they opt to change them. I'm sorry we didn't have time to check with you to see if you wanted different first names. Are you okay the way things stand?" We all nodded dumbly. "Okay," she went on. "As part of the program, we provide new documentation like your driver's license, Sondra, and help you with a place to live and a stipend. The stipend helps, but it's not much, and probably won't pay all your bills. We encourage everyone in the program to get a job, and in fact, there's the possibility that we would cancel the stipend if it turns out someone in the program is not trying to get a job. Sondra, are you okay with supporting your family this way?"

"Yes, that's fine, Aubrey."

Aubrey went on to explain that under no circumstances were we to contact any family or friends from our old life until we were told that it was safe. "That means no contact with your relatives over the holidays, okay?"

She told us where we would be living and said we'd find a car there as well; the keys would be hanging on a hook in the kitchen. "Here are the house keys. It's a lovely Spanish style home in a modern housing development. It has three bedrooms, two baths and a community swimming pool."

I saw Ben's eyes light up and knew he was envisioning endless sunny days in a warm pool. Maybe this wouldn't be so bad after all, I thought. I dreaded, however, telling them that they had to go to school while we were living there.

Aubrey then pulled out a cell phone. "This phone is registered to Sondra Collins in Tucson, and you can use it to contact me at the number I'll give you. I'll also be contacting you on this phone. You can't use it, however, to call anyone from your old life."

After another hour's worth of paperwork and instruction, "Curly" returned and said that our suitcases checked out—that nothing we had packed would give away our true identities. I didn't realize they'd be going through our luggage, but again, I was in no position to argue.

Aubrey gave me $1,500 to start and said we'd have a stipend of $1,800 per month deposited directly into the bank account I was to open. Although we were going to be living in the house rent free, I could see where getting a job would be in our best interest.

Through the window next to the conference room door, we saw the dark-haired driver of our van appear in the hallway. He looked in and pointed to his watch.

"It looks like it's time to head to the airport," Aubrey said. "Let me put the things from your purse into this envelope. We'll keep them safe until you return."

There was a great deal of swapping old items for new and double checking them as they were slipped into the large envelope, which Aubrey folded over and sealed. When my purse officially belonged to Sondra Collins, we were ready to go. I tucked the kids' bios in my purse as well and told them we'd study their new identities on the plane.

We were ushered down the hall, into the elevator and back into the van, and soon we were on our way to the airport to catch an evening flight to Phoenix. The three of us settled into the back seat again. Our two guards removed their outer jackets before climbing into the front seat, and Ben's eyes widened to the size of saucers at the sight of the guns tucked neatly into their shoulder holsters. The kids, I think, were still stunned by the whole thing, and the sight of real weapons took them one step further into the land of adventure I had proposed. I wasn't so sure I was completely together at the time either. I glanced out the windows at the passing scenery, dulled to a monochrome by the window tinting, and wondered when I'd ever see Philadelphia again. I had so wanted to call Connie to tell her we'd be okay, but it was too dangerous. I knew she'd understand. . . .

. . . Sondra and the kids had disappeared off the face of the earth. My best guess was that they had gone underground, into the witness protection program. The two hit men the bosses sent down missed them by a whisker— twice, if the news I was getting was accurate. I'd had to pay the one million dollar fee for Sondra's hit up front. For that money, the hit was supposed to be guaranteed. That was the rule. But I was stuck in here, and I couldn't get the answers I wanted—or get the money back.

If she was under government protection, it might be a long time before we had another chance at her. Those marshals who run this thing are no schmoes. They've got a pretty good track record of keeping witnesses alive to testify at trials, so we had our work cut out for us.

As for my situation, my lawyer told me that the drug charges alone could get me 20 plus years. If they got any hint of how many people I've offed, I could be sitting in here till the day I died. I was thinking more and more about turning states evidence. I definitely had a lot of stuff on the Brothers, and I could do some serious damage if I spilled it all.

Still, I wasn't sure what I should do. I sure couldn't ask my lawyer—he was paid directly by Los Archos and worked exclusively for them. He wasn't looking out for my best interest, that was for sure. He was a company man through and through. He was owned. Maybe I should talk to the Feds directly, in private. The only problem was that every time they wanted to interview me, they called the lawyer first. It was the rule. I had to figure out a way to let them know I wanted a private meeting, no lawyer. But how? The guards couldn't be trusted. If I tried to tell a guard I wanted to see the Feds on my own, I'd have had no guarantee where that information would end up. It would for sure be worth a grand or two to a guard to finger me to my bosses. Then you could bet my cell door would just be left open one night. A shiv can be as simple as a sharpened toothbrush—that's all it takes to end a man's life in a place like this. I needed to keep my wits about me and my mouth shut, tell no one what I'm thinking. . . .

. . . Our flight to Phoenix was uneventful. The kids and I studied our biographies, and both Ben and Cassie peppered me with questions as to why we had to do this, when they could talk to their friends and whether they really had to be the "Collins kids" the whole time they were in Tucson. I got so impatient that I pointed to my injured arm as a reminder and told them it could have been worse.

"Unless we do this for now, none of us will be safe until the criminals are sent to prison," I explained. Once again, neither of them asked how long that would be, and I was glad, because I didn't have an answer; I wished I knew, myself.

We were met at the gate by more federal agents and were escorted to yet another van. Our guards, for that is what they were, looked after our every need. We made one restroom trip between cities. At the service station where we stopped, they watched us closely in case we were tempted to call someone back home.

Our first two weeks in Tucson were a whirlwind of stress, interesting surprises and careful planning. Our home turned out to be a lovely, newly built, moderately sized Spanish hacienda-style house close to the Tucson Country Club. There was more than enough room for everyone, and I was grateful for the space. As decent as our Philadelphia apartment was, it was cramped compared to this home. When we first got there, we dashed through the house, excited to find all the amenities we had lived without for so long: new kitchen appliances including a dishwasher, a central vacuum, and a garage with a late-model Toyota parked inside.

My favorite spot was the screened-in porch. It was the perfect spot for me to do my EFT work. On our first full day in Tucson, we drove around to familiarize ourselves with the neighborhood, and we visited a small bookstore in a nearby plaza. I purchased several books on EFT and spent my evenings on the porch, reading, tapping and meditating. I also had picked up a book on meditation. The promise of being able to find the real me was too good to ignore.

Thanksgiving rolled around quickly, but we decided not to have a traditional turkey dinner. Instead, we had a picnic out near the pool, just a block from our new home. I realized it was the first time in my life that I had not had a full Thanksgiving dinner on the holiday, but I didn't really care. It's strange how a date on the calendar can be so meaningful in some circumstances but in others mean nothing at all. Where was home now? Where was the rest of my family? It was the three of us now, and I was going to be there for my kids so maybe, just maybe, Thanksgiving would be back on our calendar next year.

I made sure "Ben Collins" and "Cassie Collins" were signed up for school before it closed for the holiday, but I didn't see the need to have them start until the following Monday, and the district agreed. So in the meantime, we enjoyed the warm weather, visiting parks and going to the pool quite a bit. It was just so good to be able to be in the great outdoors and out of danger.

The most fascinating landmark in the area was the "A" Mountain. Its true name was Sentinel Peak, and every year this massive "A" on the side of the mountain, which stood for the University of Arizona, was painted by the students. I enjoyed the drive to the top and the fabulous view from there. It also was fun to experience nature out west, seeing the famous saguaro cacti and the sun baking the orange rock formations. It may as well have been a million miles from Philadelphia.

I also noticed that I found myself feeling more at peace the more time we spent in nature. I decided to keep myself grounded that way in the future—making time for nature, which meant making time for me.

Tucson was a nice city, very multicultural, which I liked. Despite Aubrey's warning about being careful with our stipend and encouraging me to supplement it by getting a job, I wasn't about to pinch pennies—we needed to enjoy ourselves for a little while, so we ate at restaurants and saw a lot of movies—and besides, I thought, Aubrey didn't know about my little nest egg.

I decided that there was no possible way anyone could trace the money from the Cayman Islands. I also figured what I spent couldn't be gotten back by anyone—authorities, mob bosses or, for that matter, Jack—so there was no reason not to use it to get everything we needed for our stay in Tucson. I opened a bank account near our home. (This was the first time I had to produce identification as Mrs. Collins, and it was both strange and exciting at the same time to pretend be a different person.) I transferred $2,000 of the money to Sondra Collins's new account. I had tucked the account number and password into a small rip in my wallet and, fortunately, Aubrey hadn't discovered it. I realized later that I should have memorized the most important 16-digit number in my life instead of taking the chance that a government agent would discover it, but it had all worked out anyway. I got the feeling that the universe just wanted me to have the money.

I took us all on a shopping spree. The kids got plenty of clothes appropriate for winter in Arizona, and I got a few things for myself as well. We each bought a swimsuit so we could actually go in the pool instead of lounging beside it, as we had been doing. Ben insisted on having swim goggles. It was a typical thing for an 11-year-old to do, and I loved him for it.

Ben and Cassie were really good sports. They started calling each other by their assumed names at home so they wouldn't slip up in public. It became a game between them: "Mr. Collins?" "Yes, Miss Collins?" Kids can be really smart, and they had figured out a fun way to familiarize themselves with their new family name. The Collinses had arrived in Arizona.

I sent them to school with brand new school supplies on the Monday after Thanksgiving. I wasn't worried about them keeping busy and making new friends, because they were the type who managed that easily. That wasn't true for me. I found myself bored with being at home all day. I had been used to a busy life. I needed something to do. I decided to tap on all the mental blocks that seemed to be haunting me. I made my list; "scared to face the world" was at the top—a 10 if ever there was one—followed by a few lesser aspects.

I settled in and started the now familiar EFT procedure. It was just so amazing how this thought field therapy, along with energy tapping, released pent up and unresolved feelings. My tapping lasted most of the day. I broke up the tapping with a 20-minute meditation. I felt wonderfully rejuvenated and didn't even feel guilty that I decided to take the kids out to eat instead of stopping what I was doing in order to cook dinner. Was my newfound good mood due to the tapping or the food here? I had read that chili peppers can make you feel good, so maybe the tapping and the meditation combined with the chilies was a new super cure. It felt so good to think ridiculous things and laugh without worrying that somebody was about to shoot me.

A couple of days later, I got the employment section of the newspaper and started hunting for jobs. I could have asked for assistance from our "handlers," but I decided to do my own thing. I wished we had a computer, but that was the one thing denied us— just in case any of us were tempted to send a friend or family member an email. Still, there were some job opportunities in the paper that caught my eye, including one for a receptionist at a local wellness clinic.

I called the clinic and got an interview for that Friday. I typed up a quick resume for Sondra Collins at the local library and thought up some answers to standard interview questions. On Friday, after seeing the kids off on the bus, I dressed in my nicest conservative outfit and got into the white Toyota the government had given us. It was much nicer than my car back home, which still sat in the police impound lot, I presumed, still untouched, with bullet holes in the windows and my blood splattered on the front seat.

The clinic, called Mind Body Therapies, was just outside Tucson proper. I loved the name and, when I got there, I was delighted to see that the sign in the front window said that it offered energy psychology, which I knew embraced EFT. I had been studying at home, but I was hoping to find a clinic nearby in case I had trouble doing it on my own. Although I did my best, I could see the possibility that I might get in my own way, so to speak.

I met with Stephanie James, the clinic manager. She was tan, had a warm smile and the brightest platinum-blonde hair I had ever seen. Stephanie took me to her office and looked over my resume.

"So, have you ever heard of any of the alternative therapies we offer clients?" she asked me as she was going over my resume.

I explained that I'd recently discovered EFT and that I had not only been to a practitioner, but I'd also been studying it at home.

She seemed to like that answer a lot; the interview went very successfully after that. Stephanie was so easy to talk to and was very enthusiastic. It seemed we talked more about the study and practice of EFT than the duties of the job; all my efforts to come up with a background for Sondra Collins were practically wasted, as she barely asked me about my job skills at all.

"If you're really interested in learning more about EFT, you may want to look at some of our master's courses," she said. "You see, we not only offer EFT as a therapy at this facility, but we also train people to become qualified EFT therapists."

"Stephanie," I said. "You may be onto something. EFT has helped me out so much that I think I want to learn how to do it with others. What can you tell me about the training?"

"You could take courses to become a master EFT practitioner while working as our receptionist; all the extra training that our staff takes on is arranged around their jobs. And we offer the courses at a special reduced rate for all our employees. As the receptionist job is part time, you'd have plenty of time to study. So you'd come out of this with a qualification that will enable you to work here at the clinic or independently."

She explained that there were several training sessions and workshops. The introductory session was starting in a week and there were still spaces available. I was thrilled. The receptionist job would satisfy the conditions of my stipend, and to pay for the course I could just take out some more money from my foreign bank account and become a student again. The thought of learning these skills professionally really excited me. I thought back to my vision of opening my own shop in Philadelphia. Maybe in time, when I had completed my training, I could open my own healing facility instead. No doubt about it—as soon as Stephanie mentioned the idea of being a practitioner, I was hooked.

Plus, it looked like I had the job.

As it was, I left the center not only with a job but also with an appointment for an EFT session, as well as some reading materials for my EFT training, which started a week from Monday. I found myself dancing on the inside the whole way home. I was happier than I had been for a long time. I felt I had a purpose now.

The kids were pleased to hear my good news when they got home from school. To celebrate, we decided to go for a swim. As the kids swam, I studied my reading materials.

I found myself riveted by a passage on the subject of something called "tail enders"—the things we say when we feel we should have done something, a viewpoint that often was derived from our upbringing. I had tons of issues about that. I looked down at my healing arm as an example. "I should have stayed with Jack and been a loyal wife" was the thing that had gone through my head so many times since the incident. I could almost hear my mom saying this to me. Added to that, as I thought about it, were "I should have gone into the witness protection program before the kids were kidnapped," "I shouldn't have trusted Dwight," . . . the list went on. I made a mental note to ask about "tail enders" at my EFT appointment.

My cell phone jangled deep in my purse, and my heart leapt in my chest. As I struggled to find it, I realized I couldn't ever remember it going off before. It had to be from the FBI in Philadelphia; nobody else had that number.

"Sondra? This is Aubrey. I have some news for you."

"Hi Aubrey. Good news I hope?"

"Sure is. The FBI raided a meeting of the drug trafficking ring, and most of the members were there. Several others were rounded up soon afterward. Detective Murphy spoke with our undercover officers, and it sounds like they've managed to get everyone we know of behind bars except Sol Ackerman. I just thought you should know."

"So, am I needed back? Can we come home?" I asked her. I realized I had mixed feelings about the idea. "That Sol was always a slippery guy," I threw in, almost without realizing I was looking for an excuse not to return.

"You can always come home, but we'd prefer it if you stayed where you are until the trial. It could be as long as three or four months," she said.

I thought about the life we had just started in Tucson and the fact that I had a golden opportunity here, at least for the present. "I'll call you if we really want to go home, but we're doing fine here, so I think we'll hold out a little longer."

"That's the spirit. Good work, Sondra," she said, before saying goodbye. I still was very unused to the witness protection process; it felt unreal talking to Aubrey, like another world that I had found myself involved in and which I couldn't escape from. But, in some ways, it was a small price to pay.

The kids asked me what the phone call was all about, and I explained that we'd probably have to stay in Tucson for another few months. Ben shrugged and went back to swimming, while Cassie asked me if we'd really be able to go back to our old lives again.

"Yes, honey," I said. "I know this is tough, but I promise it will be over before too long."

Satisfied, Cassie went back to playing water polo of sorts with her brother.

Chapter 9

I started seeing my EFT practitioner, Judith Schmidt, the following week and, after I told her I was attending some training sessions, she even offered to mentor me and have me follow her around for a couple of days a week. I gladly accepted and waited in happy anticipation for the first course to begin. . . .

. . . Where the hell were Sondra and the kids? I'd been stuck in the slammer for months wondering what the hell was going on. Still, my life in prison wasn't bad. I had a good cell. I had a "job" as a medical assistant in the infirmary, but it's not like I'd actually been on a work detail yet. I mean, come on—I had a reputation to build, and it didn't have anything to do with working where they told me to.

I had been able to put together a gang to rival the blacks, the Hispanics, and the Italians. A little bit at a time, we took over the drug trade in here. My line of supply was just as good on the inside as it had ever been on the outside. I found a guard who had had been passed over for promotion twice and so figured it was only fair he got a little extra cash out of me—he thought he deserved it, and who was I to tell him no? Given Los Archos controlled the very fields that our Acapulco Gold was grown in; we could deal with the inmates at bargain basement prices. The other teams couldn't keep up. One of the leading blacks was already six feet under, and the message was loud and clear: Get out of my way or join your buddy as worm food. Needless to say, the others fell in line. The more business me and my team took, the more their contractors left and joined me. Now I had plenty of money, and it was only a matter of time before the rest of my opposition gave up and the joint would be mine. . . .

. . . The following Monday, I met my classmates: a dozen fascinating people who would become good friends of mine—or, rather, good friends of "Sondra Collins"—while we learned from Judith the intricate details of how Emotional Freedom Technique worked and how best to handle certain situations.

One of the first issues she covered was why we should be therapists for a healing modality that is freely given away and so easy to use as a self-help tool. Judith explained that nobody was wasting their time learning how to be EFT therapists.

"Imagine you are the client," she said. "You have a problem that you want to solve with EFT. You have read that EFT is a really effective tool for self-help on all sorts of physical and emotional health issues. It is easy to learn using EFT downloads, CDs and DVDs. However, there really is a case for it being better to get your EFT therapy from a trained professional.

"First, and most fundamentally, EFT always works. If a person using EFT is not getting results, it's often due to inexperience and the inability people have to get over their own emotional energy blocks. Even trained EFT professionals can get stuck when they try to perform EFT tapping techniques on themselves. There is a good chance that an EFT professional would be able to help with that kind of a problem.

"Next, an individual can learn the EFT tapping technique— watch a video, study a chart, take a course to see the techniques in person—but EFT is so much more than tapping points. The core of EFT therapy success lies in being able to get to the real root of a problem. Often this is a subconscious issue, which makes it very difficult for a person to find on his or her own. By its very nature, the subconscious is hiding the problem. An EFT practitioner is trained to ask the right questions to uncover the fundamental emotional issues, which have led to that problem and its many aspects.

"Another reason to use an EFT therapist is that EFT therapists are fully qualified as practitioners, which means they have been trained in all the tapping points. Now, all of these points can in fact be easily accessible to EFT newcomers. However, as you will discover and as I have already mentioned, people get in their own way, which in turn can slow down the self-healing process. So an EFT therapist's help can always be used to work on stubborn problems.

"And speaking of stubborn problems, an EFT therapist will be able to ask questions that uncover all sorts of emotional aspects of a presenting problem, which a person may not think of. A good EFT practitioner is a good detective."

Judith took a sip of water before she continued. She glanced at her notes and continued, "If a person is using EFT therapy for deep-seated trauma and abuse, although EFT does not make it necessary to revisit these past painful situations, an EFT session may unleash a lot of emotions and thoughts which are very difficult to clear alone. An EFT therapist can be a really big help with these issues. A practitioner can also be very gentle in approaching sensitive emotional areas, which may be handled less effectively by someone without EFT practitioner training.

"Just as 'two heads are better than one' in most situations, so it is with dealing with the emotions that block our energies and cause us so many problems. An EFT professional is another head, another pair of eyes and another perspective on the presenting problems of the client. That's why trained EFT professionals sometimes even work together. In other words, sometimes it just helps to be able to talk about issues to begin to see things differently.

"Last, EFT is an energy therapy. Just imagine the power that two people—the client and the practitioner—have when they combine their energies with the intent to heal. That's what really happens when you visit an EFT professional. Two people have one purpose: to heal the client's particular emotional issue that is manifesting itself physically as well as mentally. Together, you are so much stronger, and you really do have the power to change a person's life," Judith concluded.

Our courses consisted of instruction from Judith, as well as sessions where we practiced on one another and group meditations to relax after several hours of study. My own experiences of meditation were enhanced in this group of a dozen like-minded students.

The introductory course lasted a week, and the following week, I shadowed Judith as she worked with her own clients on Tuesday and Thursday.

On a personal level, my own problems, including my "shoulds and oughts," along with the very toxic thoughts that had been troubling me, were all fast hitting zero. I am sure that this was my first life experience of group consciousness. I had read about the power of the group, and I was sure I was now the beneficiary of the group working together.

The kids and I welcomed the holiday break and enjoyed our small celebrations in our government-funded hacienda. We were never much for Hanukkah, but we got back to lighting the menorah, which brought us closer together as a family. As we had always embraced Christmas and all its trappings, this year I took enough money out of the offshore account to provide the kids with brand-new Nintendo games and other goodies, as well as a tree we decorated Arizona-style with Southwestern decorations, including a Santa Claus dressed in tropical clothing on the top.

Relaxing with the kids on a warm Christmas Day, comfortable in our new house and with plenty of money in the bank, not to mention all the wonderful things I had going on in my professional and spiritual life, I started to think how easy it would be to learn to like it here permanently.

Once the kids were back in school in January, I signed up for another EFT course to study the therapy in depth. Judith continued to mentor me and, at one point, she offered me the chance to take on my own clients one day a week. I was nervous about that, but I realized I needed to start somewhere.

By mid-February, I had several clients of my own. My first was a woman who struggled with food addiction and who wanted help controlling her weight and her behaviors. I had seen Judith work with someone with a similar problem, so I felt I knew where to begin, but I needed to tap for myself and my confidence before seeing her.

As Lisa apprehensively sat down next to me in Judith's office, which she let me borrow for my own clients, I saw myself sitting with Ken March all those months ago. Because I could empathize with Lisa, I knew what I had to do in the session, and I found myself relaxing. I started with a reassuring smile. This lady desperately needed that reassurance. She was so nervous she could barely speak. I could see she was already struggling to control her emotions.

"Now that you have taken this step to control your problem, Lisa," I began, "let's talk about just what could have caused your weight to become a problem to you."

I quietly explained that weight gain usually happens because we have developed bad eating habits, often underpinned by emotional problems—we eat for comfort or to relieve boredom. Lisa, still silent, nodded quickly and seemed to visibly relax at these words, but tears, I noticed, were not far away. I could see she was starting to face her problem.

"The therapy I use, Emotional Freedom Technique, raises awareness of your feelings and emotions. So this technique can help you learn what triggers your poor eating habits," I said.

"I can't help reaching for the cookie jar when I get upset," Lisa burst out. "It can be the simplest of things, like when my husband criticizes my cooking, or worse, when the kids come home and say the other kids in their school were making fun of my size. I just can't cope. . . ." Lisa started to cry.

"Okay, Lisa," I said gently. "So that's when you feel a snack attack coming on, right?" She nodded through her tears. "Now, just listen to me for a while, and let me explain this incredible therapy. If you know how to use the Emotional Freedom Technique, you are then better prepared to decide whether you are really hungry and therefore need to eat, or whether you're eating purely to mask some other emotion. If the latter is the case, you definitely haven't got emotional freedom, have you? Instead, you're a slave to your emotions, which dictate your eating desires and so your weight."

By this time, Lisa was crying openly, but nodding at the same time.

"Listen, Lisa," I said, leaning forward to hand her a Kleenex, "EFT is so easy to learn and to use. You can do this yourself. You can carry it with you wherever you go. It's simple, and it will work for you." Lisa stopped crying and was starting to listen attentively. "You can use it as part of a daily affirmation, which I'll talk more about when I give you some homework. With EFT, you affirm your desire and ability to lose weight, as well as when you feel your willpower wavering, and you think you may eat in a way you no longer wish to.

"A huge part of why people overeat is emotional. All of these emotional concerns can be addressed by EFT, which is why it can rightly be called a holistic approach to healing. Whenever you feel yourself about to slip back into an old, undesirable habit, like overeating, you do a quick round of EFT. You'll start with a few deep breaths and an affirming message about what you want to happen, such as, 'I do not really need that cookie.' The round of EFT can take less than 30 seconds, but it can easily be enough to break your thoughts away from that unhealthy snack you wanted, and put you back on the right track toward healthy weight loss.

"We use something called setup phrases. Your setup phrase at the beginning of an EFT session can be something like, 'Even though I am overweight, I completely love and accept myself.' This is essential, because maintaining a positive attitude about yourself is important, for two reasons. First, negative emotions block the energy flow, and second, having a positive attitude increases your motivation. Once you accept yourself in this way, you feel you are worthy and capable of gaining control of your emotions, and so your weight. Does that make sense, Lisa?"

Lisa nodded, now clearly focused on what I was saying.

"What do you think stops you from losing the weight that you want to lose? Think of that, then think of a positive statement that asserts that you can get over this problem, like 'I am worthy of self-love, and I don't need to eat to comfort myself.' Repeat this affirmation to yourself throughout your EFT tapping routine. The tapping will disrupt your habitual neural pathway, and you'll find that the next time you're about to fall prey to this negative thinking or behavior, your thoughts will be disrupted, and it will be easier to resist temptation or to fall prey to the negativity that makes you eat.

"I'm going to show you the tapping routine you should follow for any EFT healing. You should tap each of these points on the meridians seven times, then complete the whole tapping routine again, all the while repeating your affirmation statement that you can overcome whatever it is that you want to address. Try it with me now."

Lisa, self-consciously at first, followed my lead in both tapping and saying her setup statement and reminder phrases.

"Begin on the inside corner of your eye, near your nose. Tap seven times. Move on to the outside corner of your eye and again tap seven times." I watched her do it, then I said, "Okay, now tap seven times on each of the following points: under your eyes . . . under your nose . . . your chin . . . just below your collarbone . . . and finally under your arm. Find the spot that's about a hand-width down from your armpit, right about where your bra hits. The tapping should be gentle, but hard enough to notice. Remember to repeat your affirmation sentence to yourself, saying what you will change, as you tap in each place. Pretty soon, you should have your eating and weight under control."

Lisa responded with a smile that I recognized as a release from her emotional state.

"So, Lisa, that is a round of EFT; as you can see, it took no time at all. Now what we have to do is rate your emotional intensity, give each a number value. We'll be checking these numbers, note how they change over time, to measure our progress." I explained the SUDs scale in just the same way Ken March had explained it to me all those months ago. Lisa was now ready to begin her treatment.

And so the session went on. I was a little worried I had bombarded my client with too much technical jargon, but I was reassured when I saw a very different Lisa leave my therapy room that day. The session had gone well, and she said she'd see me in a week. She was smiling. I had given her hope and the chance to regain a hold on her emotions. Suddenly I was no longer a manager of an insurance company; that was a past life. I was a working EFT therapist, and it felt great.

I saw several other clients that day. I tapped myself before meeting each one, to allow myself to be confident and intuitive so I could assist them correctly. Judith had also taught us to have the firm intention to heal our clients to the best of our ability, which I strove to do. And as I helped my clients, I felt uplifted myself. For the first time in a long time, I truly felt I had contributed something to my community, which is what I now considered Tucson.

Cassie and Ben did well in school, and they quickly made new friends who often visited our house and sometimes came over for sleepovers. We even had a barbecue and pool party of sorts one Saturday afternoon, with several of the kids' newfound friends. The kids had fun, and I met some of their parents. Little by little, we were developing a nice life in Tucson, however temporary it would be.

Fitting my training in with my job worked better than I had hoped, and I was able to take all of the master's training programs available. By spring, I felt ready to take on the challenges of a full-time practice in EFT. As it wasn't going to be in Tucson, however, I maintained my mentoring with Judith and continued to see clients once a week.

It wasn't until early April that I got the call from Aubrey that they needed me to give my testimony at the grand jury hearings. It was time to go home. Frankly, I was anxious to get on with my life and was more than happy to find out that our stay in Tucson was over, however pleasant and rewarding it had been.

I went to the EFT clinic and met with both Stephanie and Judith. I explained our situation and told them that we were leaving. I felt relieved somehow to share my story; I felt almost as though we were nearing the end of the nightmare. They were both very shocked when I told them, but they were understanding.

"My God!" gasped Stephanie. "To think you and your kids have been keeping this to yourselves!"

Stephanie offered to have my EFT certificates put in my real name, which I readily agreed to. She then suggested that the three of us join together and use our EFT to give me courage and strength to speak the truth in the face of adversity. That my teachers would do this for me and with me was so humbling that I burst out crying. We sat together for quite some time, doing rounds of tapping. In those moments we created a unique spiritual bond that was uplifting in a way I had never experienced before.

As we finished, Judith gave me a hug and told me I was as ready as I ever would be for what lay before me. She said, "I know you can handle testifying in court, Sondra, but I'm concerned about the kids having to testify too—how it will affect them. Look, let's just step into my therapy room for a moment. I want to give you an insight into EFT and children. It's outside of the training you've had so far, but this is a situation we shouldn't ignore. We have to make sure they receive as much help as possible."

Judith got us both cups of coffee and we sat down in some comfortable chairs. I could tell that she was very concerned about Ben and Cassie, and I was touched that she was taking the time to advise me. It made me feel less alone in a trying time. We were going to have to step back into that nightmare shortly, so I welcomed any guidance she could give me about the kids.

"Let's examine how you can help Ben and Cassie get through this," she said. "Because they're young, they're going to need a lot of support. It's great you're there for them, but they have to be feeling totally betrayed by their father—someone they should have been able to trust. They've had to move twice, and now they have to move again. After all your study, Sondra, I don't need to tell you that we all carry with us frustrations and negative energies that have all sorts of negative effects on our health and our feeling of well-being. Children are no different; in fact, often it can be worse for them, as they often have less freedom in their lives than adults do. When you couple that with the knowledge that children often have not yet developed the communications skills to express themselves well, it's no wonder they have their positive energies blocked and they end up having a meltdown." Judith spoke gently and smiled at me, and I smiled back, but I could feel the tears welling up. Her soft, kind words had struck a chord. I sat silently as she continued.

"I'm sure you know by now what I'm going to say, but I'll say it anyway. EFT can help with this in all sorts of ways—both physically and mentally. Your kids can benefit from the same emotional freedom that you've gained, either by using the EFT tapping routine themselves or by having you help them with the healing. It will help whether they are angry, upset or just plain ill. The great thing is that as their Mom and as an EFT practitioner, you can teach them how to tap, and you can help them when they get stuck. It won't be easy, Sondra. You might uncover emotions in your kids that could be too much for you to handle. If that's the case, maybe another practitioner, someone not involved in your situation, would better able to deal with any of the emotions that may pour out. That will be your call, once you get started with your kids."

"This won't apply to your kids, as they're older," Judith continued, "but it's worth keeping in mind if you see other kids as part of your own practice: When youngsters find something difficult to talk about, they'll often talk through a toy. If you're asked to help a troubled child, using a toy can really help with the EFT tapping routine. You can use your inner energy and intent to help them, and the tapping routine will help to free up the child's routine."

Judith pulled some papers from her side table drawer and thumbed the pages.

"I want to bring your attention to some really interesting work done on EFT for children, which involved the use of tapping on toys. Ah, here it is," she said as she reached the section she wanted. "It's fantastic. You can get a special stuffed animal, called 'TappyBear.' It was invented by EFT practitioner Till Schilling and his daughters, and has all the meridians of the EFT tapping routines marked on it."

Judith read aloud from the page, "This bear has all sorts of uses. As well as the obvious use as an educational toy to show children the EFT tapping routine, it can actually be used as a healing technique with the bear being tapped instead of the child. If as a healer your intentions are good and you are tuned into the illness and distress of the child, you can focus on that and tap the bear or another toy on the meridian points, if it is not appropriate or possible to perform the EFT tapping routine on the child. You'll be amazed to find out that the EFT therapy will be just as healing as when carried out on the child."

"Simply be close with the child, looking at them and focusing on their pain and distress, stating setup phrases appropriate to the problem they are facing, and tap the toy you are using as a surrogate for the EFT tapping routine."

"To effectively help a child in this way, you have to distance yourself to some extent, but still feel their distress. You must control your feelings while you are healing, so that you do not also become angry and upset, which will focus your energies destructively back inside you again, instead of projecting them out positively to heal the child. But you can do this for a child you love. Show them the Emotional Freedom Technique and you have given them a great gift for life."

Judith closed the article she was reading from and placed it on the table by her chair.

"Sondra, don't forget your kids and their emotions in this traumatic situation. Take good care of them and yourself. You've learned enough now to get through all this. Teach them what you can, and if you can't handle it, get some help from another practitioner. There are plenty of us around!" Judith said with a broad smile.

All this time I had sat in complete silence. I realized that now that I had started the healing process myself, I was able to be strong for my kids. Now what I had to do was pass my knowledge on to them to help them recover from what had gone on in their young lives. I thought back to seeing Ben following the tapping routine his soccer coach had led; how long ago it seemed, and how foreign the tapping was to me at the time. But now I knew I could build on what Ben learned simply for sports, and have him and Cassie apply it to their personal lives to help them in the future.

Judith and I stood up and hugged again. "I've learned so much. I can't tell you what a different woman I am now," I said.

"You don't have to. I can guess!" she smiled warmly. "Good luck, Sondra. You will come through this. You've come a long way, I can see that now. Call me sometime, and feel free to visit. We'd love to see you again. It's been a pleasure."

I left the clinic feeling exhilarated. Yes, I had come a long way. It wasn't over yet, but I would handle it with a lot more wisdom and skill than I had had months earlier. . . .

. . . My trial was coming up soon. It was about time. I thought they had forgotten me in here. So now that the date was set, that meant Sondra would be coming home to squeal like a piggy against the big bad wolf who just wanted his kids back.

The Feds had a habit of bringing folks back close to the date they were needed to testify. So we had to get started, get some of my crew on the outside to watch the airports, bus stations, train stations. This was a job for Sol. He knew them for real, not just from a photo, and could pick them out of a crowd better. I should call him, tell him to get some feet on the streets. I'll call him tonight, make it happen. Find her before she can testify against me. Maybe we could take a hostage. Maybe snatch her sister Laura. Or her friend Connie—or, even better, that brat of a kid of hers. I always hated that kid. Whoever can give me the most leverage. Sond was always so noble, there was no way she was going to let somebody else suffer for something she did. And that's my way—always find the weakness and work it. This was not over. . . .

. . . The kids had mixed feelings about leaving Tucson. They had made new friends and were reluctant to leave them, not to mention the nice house and pool. Even so, they'd always known that all of this was just temporary, and that we all had an important job to do in court. Aubrey had some good advice about how the kids should deal with the move back; she said that it would be okay for them to be honest with the people they had met—tell them the truth about why they had been in Tucson and why they were leaving. It sort of renewed the sense of adventure. And it wouldn't do any harm, because if for any reason we had to go back into the witness protection program, we'd end up being sent somewhere else anyway. So Cassie and Ben had fun telling their new friends in Tucson a little of our story and that they would be moving away and not returning. . . .

. . . I was put in Graterford early on for a reason. The DA said I had to be in a secure lockdown because I was a flight risk and a risk to my family. She was right, of course. Plus the Feds were hoping I would turn states evidence, which I never did, but if I had, I would've been targeted by my former bosses.

My big hope was that at my trial, witnesses would disappear or change their stories. But I knew Sondra would never do either one. In all honestly, I was afraid of what she was going to say, how she would implicate me. "A woman scorned" and all that—she was just waiting for the trial so she could nail me, get back at me big time for everything I had done to her. I totally understood why she would hate me, but something else was going on. Something happened to her after she left me—she was different, stronger.

If the Brothers couldn't find her and shut her up permanently, she would nail me with her testimony, and she'd make sure the kids did, too, because of the whole thing with the kidnapping. And once the three of them put the final nails in my coffin, I'd never see the kids again, for the rest of my life. Even if I got out, there was no guarantee I could track them down; they might even change their names and move away so I couldn't find them. That was something I was afraid of, I had to admit.

Hopes and fears . . . being stuck in prison gives you plenty of time to think about those things.

I know it's too late now, but in a stupid way I wish the whole thing had never happened.

I blame my father. He made me and Sol what we are today. We were made in his image, and for all I know, Pop was made in his father's image. Who knows? For my part, I became what my father wanted me to be—tough, hard, dishonest and yet, in his mindset, a provider for the family.

You think about it for a while, you realize that our yesterdays created our todays.

199

Carmen used to visit me a lot, but it's been a while since I've seen her—nearly four months. If we had been able to get married before this whole thing happened, I would have had a claim on her. But now I didn't know what she was doing or who she was doing it with. All I know is, she's sure doing it with someone. The way she was when I got thrown in the slammer . . . at the peak of her sexuality, and all that Latin fire to boot, I knew she wouldn't wait for me. She needed some every day, like food on the table. She was crazy, and I had loved her for it.

Now all I had were these four walls and an exercise yard for company. Hardly compares. It's tough to think about doing 30 years in here—I'm already going stir crazy. Maybe I need another lawyer—not Parker, not a lawyer sent to me by the organization.

Thirty years . . . makes turning states look pretty good. I should think about it for a while. Might really be more of an option than I thought.

In the meantime, I had a new shipment to distribute, get my cash. Sol was doing better than all right as my supplier. I just wish he could visit . . . but that would be impossible. . . .

. . . The trip from Tucson to Philadelphia was all set up for us, just as our trip to Arizona had been. I went to the school to get the kids' records and hoped the school back home would understand that these were their real records, in spite of the name change. I reminded myself to ask Aubrey about this during one of our frequent phone conversations before we left Arizona for good. We ended up bringing back a whole lot more than we had taken out to Arizona—more clothes, the kids' Christmas presents—but that was all we had to worry about. Aubrey arranged our trip back, which was the same as when we came out, only in reverse. Two Feds picked us up in Tucson and drove us to Phoenix, and once again, we flew commercial out of Phoenix. All we had to do was walk away—leave the house, leave the car. The Feds took care of all of it.

The flight was uneventful, and I spent the time trying shake my feeling of sadness about leaving my "new" life behind by meditating on what Judith had said about helping the kids with EFT. Although I knew I wanted to work with them using EFT, I let it be for the moment. Despite what Ben knew about it, I wasn't sure they would understand about using it for emotional issues. Or maybe I had just come up with a tail ender of my own, something I needed to work on for the future. What I could do, as an experienced therapist, was to give my intention to their cause and tap in my mind for and on behalf of them both.

I was surprised to see "Curly" at the airport in Philadelphia when we returned. He took us back to the federal offices and put us in the same conference room where we had given up our lives so many months before. Aubrey gave me all of my things back, took back the phone and retrieved the Arizona IDs. We were debriefed for some time, and she surprised me by saying I was needed for testimony in just two hours.

"What do I do with the kids?" I protested.

Aubrey looked over at "Curly." "Do you want to watch the kids during the testimony?"

"Ma'am, I don't think you're asking me for my permission," said "Curly" with a kindly look on his face.

Aubrey pretended she hadn't understood what he said and turned to Ben and Cassie. "Guys, this is Ed. Ed's going to take you to an arcade around the corner for a while—on the government. How does that sound?"

Both kids just smiled and Cassie looked over to me to see if it was okay. I nodded and then asked Aubrey if I could make a couple of phone calls.

While the kids headed off to play video games with Ed, I called Connie at her office. She was almost speechless when she heard my voice.

"I figured you'd be able to call me now that the arrests have been made. It's been all over the news," she told me. "I have loads of stories I cut out of the papers."

I told her that the kids were fine and that I couldn't wait to see her. I also told her a bit about our life in Arizona and that I completed my master's training in EFT.

"I'm not surprised you found a way to keep up your interest in EFT. Let's get together this weekend, okay?" she suggested. "We can take the kids out for a nice meal, my treat, and you can tell me all about it."

I didn't tell her that I thought that my interest in EFT was just beginning. There was plenty of time for that. What I did say was, "Know what I would love?"

"What's that?"

"A good ol' cheesesteak from Pat's! Are you okay with that?"

Connie laughed. "You have been away a while! No problem, if you don't mind standing in line—it's busier than ever there nowadays. How about if we do Pat's for lunch and then a good restaurant in the evening, okay? I'll call your cell Saturday morning, not too early."

Next, I called the president of my insurance company to fill her in.

She said, "Don't worry, Sondra. We all know what's been going on. It's been all over the news. Will you be coming back to us?" Before I could answer her, she continued, "I should tell you that we had to fill your job, but you know you're welcome back as soon as you feel strong enough. We can always find an opening for someone like you."

She was being so kind, but I knew I couldn't string her along. I told her right then that I would not be coming back. She sounded disappointed but said she understood, and the door was always open for me, and she said I had a standing offer for a glowing reference whenever I needed one. We chatted for a few minutes more and agreed we should meet for coffee sometime soon. Although it sounded like one of those empty promises that no one ever makes good on, I knew I really did want to meet with my old boss in the near future. With more than a thousand employees in the company, I knew it was a great opportunity to help any of them who were under a lot of stress or had any emotional problems in that building. I was ready to introduce EFT to my former coworkers.

My final call was to Marge, as I was certain she had worried about the children every day we were gone. She sounded so relieved to hear we were okay, she almost shouted with happiness. "Sondra, did you know you have been headline news everywhere? I just can't imagine what this has been like for you and the kids."

I told her, "Yes, I know we've been in the news, but I just can't face watching any of it or reading about it in the papers. Cassie and Ben have been so brave. But now I just want them to be settled. I just want us to get on with our lives."

"Of course. Give them both a big hug for me. You know they can come here anytime."

"Of course I will, Marge. And I'll give you a call when I need you next, which probably will be soon. The kids will be so glad to see you again. Thanks so much for all you've done for us."

I could tell that spring was finally coming to Philadelphia as the sight of dogwood blossom and marigolds gave a wonderful sense of renewal to the city. I wished that I could roll the car window down and breathe in the scents of spring as Aubrey and I rode to the federal courthouse on Market Street. At Aubrey's insistence, I was wearing an auburn wig, a wide-brimmed hat and some seriously large sunglasses. Aubrey assured me that it was usual for witnesses to wear a disguise. . . .

. . . I had heard that the Feds had the whole routine of keeping witnesses safe while getting them in and out of court down to a science. My people hadn't been able to get so much as a hint of when Sondra would be testifying—the kids either. With an absolute fortune stashed away in banks all over the world, I still couldn't buy what I wanted; I would have given every cent of it to be able to walk away right there and then—have the slate wiped clean. I've never really had much to say to God or whatever's out there. My family wasn't exactly religious. My bar mitzvah was just about showing the family and friends we had money. Not that Pop ever put it that way directly. There were just those small remarks that stayed with you, like "Nothing too good for my boy," and all that, instead of more spiritual lessons for me. It was the same for Sol.

I hadn't seen my brother for a while now—he's been hiding real good. He should've been busted with the rest of us, but he didn't make the meeting where we got raided because he was in bed with his latest pubescent conquest and overslept. I talk with him pretty regular on the phone— he's been taking control of everything I built up, stepping out from the number two spot and grabbing the limelight. He's just the type to enjoy being numero uno—he's always wanted to have lots of respect.

It was Sol who got me into the business in the first place. I've got to admit he made a good move around the time Pop's firm went down. We were just vegetating when the drug thing came our way, but Sol saw the opportunity and grabbed it.

And once you got your hands on as much money as I had, what did you do? Me, I kept it secret and used it to have a good time; when you had drugs to sell and money to squander, girls were just available—really beautiful ones, too. Sure, it was exciting, but did any of it really make me happy? Considering where I am today, I would say probably not. I wonder if Sol would call me a baby for how I feel now: I wish it had never happened. I wish I could just start over, me and Sond and the kids, and just live a simple life.

Now I had plenty of time to really think about what's important in life. Being in prison really makes you think about who you are as a person. . . .

. . . I sat quietly with Aubrey in a private room until it was time for me to testify. She talked a bit about how I should make sure I told the complete truth at all times. She needn't have worried on that score. As we waited, I tapped ever so unobtrusively, firm in the knowledge that EFT helps maintain calm—and if ever I needed to remain calm it, was now.

Soon enough a guard came to escort me to the courtroom. I swore to tell the truth and sat on the witness stand; I was nervous, yet completely in control. I answered questions from the prosecution and the defense regarding the activities of my husband, the information I had gotten from Jim Pruitt and the validity of the recording I'd made with Jack in the park the previous autumn. It all seemed so foreign to me after spending more than five months in Arizona. It was like I turned into someone else, up there on the stand, testifying against a load of drug traffickers. I can remember feeling totally detached from any feelings that it was my own husband who was one of them, but then it wasn't every day you found out the man you married had crossed the line from loving husband and father to a ruthless, heartless criminal.

I barely looked at Jack the entire time, although I got the sense that he was glaring at me from his seat at the table with his defense attorneys. But as I stepped down to leave the courtroom, I couldn't help but sneak a glance his way. He was practically a stranger to me now. More important, he didn't frighten me. I had no regrets about leaving Jack, and I had no regrets about putting him in jail for a long time.

I felt almost as though all the experiences I had gone through in the past several months had made me grow up. They had shaken me out of a safe world and dumped me and my kids into a life of fear and uncertainty. Not the best way to find where your strengths lie, I had to admit, but that's just what had happened to me. I had found strength I never knew I had, and I had learned to live without the man that I had never thought I would want to be away from.

I later learned that nine people, including the two Latino cousins who had tried to shoot me, had a combined total of 36 charges against them as a result of their drug trafficking business, attempted murder and related activities. Along with my testimony, there was the testimony of plenty of others—more than enough, in fact—to confirm their guilt. The large number of witnesses gave me peace of mind for my personal safety; it wasn't just me who was revealing what this "organization" had been doing.

I also had to testify at Dwight/Frank's trial. Ben and Cassie testified as well, and I was so proud of both of them.

For the kidnapping charges alone, Jack received 20 years in prison, and Frank received 25 years. Once they had their trial for the drug trafficking charges, Jack and Frank got another 20 years on top of that. . . .

. . . I got the news that Los Archos Hermanos cartel was dead. A lifer in my cell block, one of my most trusted runners, gave me the news. He only knew me as his boss and may have never heard of the Brothers, so his details were a bit sketchy, but as I understood it this is what happened: Apparently, after the Philly franchise was exposed, other franchises across the country fell like a house of cards. It sounded like the Feds had had undercover agents in all our cells for many years—that was the only way the cartel could have been destroyed so completely.

At the same time, it turned out, the Feds got in league with the Mexican government to storm the Tijuana ranch, They rounded up everybody, including Carmen and her brothers.

I was concerned that this was going to cause a major disruption in my supply line, but Sol told me not to worry about it; he had taken care of it. Turns out Sol had taken off to Canada. He had a new identity and lived and worked out of Montreal, and he was still able to get me stuff. He called me the other day and told me to start charging more. With a thirty billion-dollar hole in the supply market, prices on the street had shot up, which meant the same in here.

So what would happen to my million-dollar contract on Sondra now? Everybody involved was in the slammer. I'd never get the money back, but what the hell. Honestly, I wanted to cancel it, in case another firm had picked it up. With my whole circle locked up, my children were best off with their Mom. I wouldn't want them to be orphans and get dumped into the foster care system. It didn't have a great reputation and was no place for my kids. I had to get word to Sol to have the contract cancelled. He could manage to get a message to the Brothers and the two cousins even though they were in the slammer; Sol was very resourceful.

Besides, Sondra's evidence was against me, not the Brothers, so I bet they wouldn't even bother with her now. I had been very loyal to them, never turned states evidence, so they owed me. If they still wanted to go after Sondra, I could let slip that I still could squawk about what I knew, which would make sure they stayed in the slammer for the rest of their lives. I hadn't thought about it for a while, but maybe, just maybe I could use that to get out of here. . . .

. . . It was all over. It had all seemed so unreal for so long, but the reality had struck once I set foot in that courtroom. Now my husband was incarcerated, my marriage no longer existed and my children had been forced to grow up faster than their years. My EFT training had taught me that life is in the here and now. Yesterday is gone, and the only power it holds over us is the power we give to the memories. So with that firmly in mind, I called Aaron and told him to finalize the divorce as fast as possible so I could move on with my life and put the past behind me.

I appeared to be home free with the money I had taken from Jack. No mention of the funds had been made before, during or after the trials. Neither Jack nor anyone from his mob had pursued me for it. I guess my second trip back to my old house in the middle of the night had been successful. By destroying the evidence that was in Jack's file, there was no tangible proof that the funds had ever existed. Jack would never remember the account numbers, so even if he could phone the bank from jail he wouldn't be able to access the account I stole from.

However, I didn't want to overdo it with flashy demonstrations of wealth. So Ben, Cassie and I moved to a nice two-story brick house on Wallace Street. With three bedrooms and two bathrooms, there was plenty of room. We all had our own space and privacy. It wasn't the most exclusive neighborhood, despite the efforts of the real estate agent to convince me otherwise, but it was perfect for us. And I took out a mortgage instead of paying for the house in full, so I didn't look like . . . well, like I had an offshore account in the Cayman Islands.

The house was so close to the kids' school that they could walk, and I allowed them to stay home alone during the summer months, with Cassie in charge. Our house was also close to Marge's, and the kids visited her often, even though, as they said often, they had outgrown the need for a babysitter. I eventually helped Cassie and Ben with EFT techniques, and they began to use them in their daily lives.

Aaron received a request from Jack and his lawyer that Cassie and Ben visit their father in prison. I was adamant that they never saw Jack again, but I put aside my emotions and asked the kids what they wanted to do. We talked it over and agreed to ask Aunt Laura to take them. I figured Laura and I could do some catching up if she came to visit on a weekend. I called her up, and she was pleased to help. I believe she also wanted to gloat at Jack—she never liked him—which would be typical Laura. . . .

. . . Sondra's sister, Laura, brought Cassie and Ben to see me. I thought I'd be happy about it, but I ended up wishing they hadn't come. I felt bad when I looked at Cassie and remembered that I had nearly married her off to advance my career. I really hated what I had done and who I had been, but who could I tell? The Sondra I used to know would listen to me, but she refused to see me ever again. That was the reason Laura brought the kids here. The visit didn't go well, and as they left, I realized that I probably would never see my kids again. But hey, why would they want to visit me? They were brave to have come here even once. . . .

. . . Neither Cassie nor Ben talked much about their visit to their father. I don't suppose it's the happiest moment of a child's life, visiting their dad in prison. I'll leave it up to them if they want to visit him again, but I'm pretty sure I know what their answer will be.

Chapter 10

It seemed a lifetime ago that Connie and I had last sat in the French Café on Bainbridge. It was a favorite meeting place of ours. The coffee was good, and the décor was continental, in a chic, modern way.

"So, what are you going to do, now that you're unemployed and wealthy?" Connie asked me with a sparkle in her eye. Even as the words left her lips I instinctively looked around just to see who might be listening. "I'll tap for this habit later," I thought to myself.

"Well, the biggest thing I had to think about was where to live. The Feds gave me the option of relocating permanently, with their help, or staying here—my choice. I thought long and hard about what to do. I realized that if I run and hide, Jack and his thugs win. But what really helped me decide to stay was I found out from the Feds that the cartel Jack was in—the whole empire—has been brought down in one massive, synchronized sweep across the country and in Mexico, where they had their headquarters. I also heard that they have no further interest in me or the kids—and the way things stand now, they don't have the manpower or the wherewithal to even manage to get anybody to come after us— which makes staying here more of an option. So it looks like we're staying."

Connie grinned. "I'm really glad to hear that. So what are you going to do with yourself?"

"Well, you know how I've always dreamed of opening a retail shop, always thought that would be fun?" I asked. Connie nodded, and I playfully paused for dramatic effect. Then, "I've changed my mind."

A surprised look came over her face and her mouth open slightly to mouth the word "What?" She looked puzzled, then said, "Well Sondra, I can't blame you for wanting to just do nothing for a while and get your life back to how you want it. But I must say, honey, you've talked about this dream of yours for so many years, it would be a shame to—"

209

"Relax, Connie," I interrupted. "I figured out something even better. I just spent six months thinking about my future, and I don't see myself being an owner of a retail shop anymore. When I was in Tucson and studying to get my master's level certificates in EFT, I was fortunate enough also to have been mentored and have had several clients of my own. I can't describe how good it makes me feel to know I'm helping people get over emotional problems. So I was wondering if there was any chance I could hook up with your clinic so I can gain more practical experience. I know I could afford to set up my own clinic, and I plan to eventually, but I'd really rather work where I can be mentored and guided for a while. Do you think your clinic can help me out?"

Connie beamed and said immediately, "I'm sure it wouldn't be a problem. Our place could use another EFT therapist—we're always booked a month in advance."

"How do therapists deal with the issue of competition? I mean, Philadelphia is a large city, so I figure that after I get more experience with clients, I can start my own place far enough away from your clinic so it's not infringing on your clientele. How does that work? I have no idea."

"Oh, there's more than enough work for everybody; I don't think it would be an issue at all. And Sondra, honey, when you start your own clinic, you know you can count on me to help you set things up. You'll need a practice manager, and I can help write the job description and sit in on the interviews, if you like."

"Thanks Connie, I was hoping you'd be able to help me get started. There would be so much to do."

"Oh, my clinic practically runs itself by now, so if it turns out you need me for an extended period of time, I could easily take a few months off. I know the partners wouldn't object to that—they have a very enlightened outlook." Connie sat back and just grinned. "Sondra, I can't believe all this! You've completely changed your life around. I'm so proud of you, and so happy for you. The first thing we need to do is get you into supervised practice at my place. I can ask all the right questions of all the right people and let you know about joining our team. And then, when you're ready to go it alone, we can put our heads together to make plans."

We sat there looking at each other, both joyful about the change that had taken place within me. I thought back on how skeptical I had been, and now I was so thankful that Connie hadn't given up trying to teach me about energy healing in those darks days. I had gone through the toughest year of my life, losing many aspects of my life I had thought were very dear to me. But because of those tough times, I had grown as a person—even beyond my own recognition.

I was happy to be back in Philadelphia, as were the kids. I was divorced and using my maiden name and had two million dollars in the bank. And I still had my kids, for which I was eternally grateful.

Thanks to Ken March and the others at Health Alternatives, I received the supervision I needed to become a very well-qualified therapist. I saw several hundred clients over the course of a year, and it gave me a sense of purpose that my former career, or even my millions in the bank, couldn't.

After that year, I decided it was time to open my own wellness clinic. I continued to use EFT in my own life, and I was constantly amazed by its results and potential. My goal was and continues to be the health and wellness of clients who've come to trust in me and in the EFT skills I bring to my work on a daily basis. . . .

. . . Being in the slammer isn't too bad; in fact, it's almost like being on the outside. I've worked up a decent business in here and I've got influence and respect. Inmates leave you alone if they know you could have their tongues torn out at the roots or be sodomized until life hardly seems worth living.

Being top dog, with a lot of "employees" to take care of my business, gives me a lot of time to think. And when I do, I start to wonder where I went wrong in all this. How could I have underestimated Sondra like that? Somewhere along the way she got herself a backbone. I found out she and my kids did enter the witness protection program. I guess I don't blame her for that, after what I did to her and trying to steal the kids and all. I have to admit that I kind of admire her. Now that's weird, considering it was her testimony that sent me up the river for what's probably going to be the rest of my life.

Truth is, of course, her testimony was just a very tiny part of the evidence against me. There had been a deep cover agent working against me for years, as I found out at the trial, plus I had been careless to leave my prints where I shouldn't have. Her contribution was the icing on the Feds' cake.

But in a strange way, it doesn't matter. I'm alive, for one thing. And I'm sure, deep down, that I never really had much of a future with the life I had been living anyway. I suspect that once the Brothers' children had grown up—we're talking six sons between the two families—they would have been moved into my territory. And then where would I have been? Nowhere, that's for sure.

So am I safe? Yes, I am. I never spoke a word at my trial. I never did turn states evidence. I'm still represented by the best lawyers money can buy, so I'm just going to wait until they get an appeal together that will get me out of here and back in the action. So I'm not holding my breath or anything, but I have the feeling I'll get sprung pretty soon.

In a strange kind of way I have ended up with the result I wanted. Well I didn't want to be incarcerated for the rest of my life, but I wanted to do right by my kids, give them all the advantages I never had. They'll go to college, do things right. Not like me—all the career advice I got from my pop was to be beaten half to death. No, I wanted them to have more—more freedom, more choices, and more affection. Of course, I didn't even know how to give them those things when I was with them—I didn't even know what affection was like when I was growing up; how could I show them something I never knew about myself? Still, they're great kids; they both take after me. They both have my eyes.

And now Sondra has them, and she'll raise them right. I gotta admit, she's smart—and tougher than I gave her credit for. After all, she was bright enough to get her hands on a very large chunk of my cash. I admire her chutzpah; she would have made a good member of Los Archos. I kept quiet about the money. I didn't tell the firm or the authorities. That money will help my kids get the start in life I wanted them to have. And that was the reason I did what I did. So as it turns out, I got what I planned all along. If I die tomorrow, I will go happy, knowing that everything will turn out for the best for my Cassie and Ben. . . .

212

. . . My Healthy Connections Inc. clinic is not far from downtown Philadelphia. The place is beautiful, and large, with enough client rooms for my four wellness practitioners. The clinic is decorated in navy blue with aqua accents, and several nice pieces of artwork adorn the walls. Each piece of art includes the seven colors of the rainbow in order to reach out to clients on the vibrational level they're at when they enter the clinic.

We have two EFT practitioners, a massage therapist and an acupuncturist, and an outside company leases space for a provider to both sell and advise clients on herbal therapies.

The phone rang. It was late, and the reception desk was closed, so I leaned across the counter and picked up. "Healthy Connections, good evening. Sondra Benjamin speaking." A timid voice responded, "Yeah, hi. I read about you in the paper. I found out that my husband is dealing drugs and I was wondering . . . would you help me?"

Epilogue

"Welcome to Healthy Connections. How can I help you?" It was the voice of my receptionist, Elise, booking yet another client for our business.

When the whole story about my drug-running husband and the attempt on my life broke, it was all over the media, but it was still a local story. But then *Newsweek* picked it up as a feature article. The journalist who put the cover story together portrayed me as a champion for all women, standing up to the lies, deceit and abuse rained upon me by my husband. This image, along with the dramatic element of the vicious drug cartel, got me my 15 minutes of fame—and then some—on a national level.

Women from all over the country contacted me and wanted to be treated at my clinic. My opinions were also sought after and then published, and then more people heard my story and more sought me out. Over time, money, success and peace of mind flowed to me easily and consistently, for which I am eternally grateful.

My kids have grown into decent human beings, and we're closer than ever. As an enduring testimony to the human spirit, both Cassie and Ben have grown from their experience, and it's now evident in their strength of character and mature outlook.

When Ken March told me that "we are all more than what bothers us," I didn't get it. Now I do. I can see that we are very much the witnesses of what happens to us, even if at times what happens is a terrifying ordeal. Life is not all blue skies and warm beaches. It is in the bad times of our lives that we grow stronger, although at the time we may not realize it. . . .

. . . So here I am. Just a year into my sentence and I'm at the top of the heap in Graterford already. And all because I didn't think twice about shanking another man deep in the kidney. The choice was simple—I could fall in line like all the other cons in here, or I could do what I had to do to become head honcho. Wasn't even a choice, really. When I

214

think of how 99 percent of the inmates here do nothing more than blindly follow the daily routine, I despise them, and that makes it easy to walk all over them.

To think those idiots actually get up at the crack of dawn when the guards tell them to, eat the slop they're served when they're told to, work at the menial jobs they're assigned to, even take a crap only at certain times of the day . . . that's not living.

I may be behind bars, but I've carved out my own life—my way. I don't eat the lousy chow they call food, and not with all the other inmates. I've got a deal with the warden's cook, and I get decent food served to me privately.

I'm supposed to be an orderly in the infirmary, but I haven't done a day's worth of work there yet. Instead, I use the place as a center for trading and for granting loans and other favors.

I have a cell in an isolated wing, by choice, but I do socialize once in a while—but it's all about business. During recreation time, I like to see my runners trading with the general population. This is when most of my money is made. I see it as important that I take care of my clients by providing only the best quality shit at the most attractive prices. Keeping the clients happy, I've realized, is the best policy for my future well-being.

Still, in spite of my privileged lifestyle in here, I'm not sure I can do it for 30-some-odd years. And what if I get moved? I'd have to start all over again in a new place, which would be tough. No, I've got to make sure I stay here no matter what—keep my nose clean, keep the warden happy. . . .

. . . Now that Jack is in prison for at least 30 years and our divorce is final, I can breathe a sigh of relief. I don't have to worry about my guilty little secret anymore. I can't change what I did, but thanks to EFT I can feel calm and relaxed about it—even enough to record it in my journal for the first time to release my guilt and gain closure and a new beginning. I'll always know what I did, but at least I can deal with it using EFT.

Ever since Jack and I got married, I've been worried that he'd find out—that I'd say something in the heat of anger, or at a low moment when the guilt was eating at me and I felt I had to atone for my sin.

"Sin" isn't overstating it—that's how I feel about the lie I've lived, the deceit I've perpetrated for years. I can't even own up to it in my own mind half the time. Over the years, I convinced even myself of my virtue. If you tell yourself something often enough you'll believe it. I was a virgin when I started dating Jack—I've told myself this so often I completely believe it.

When Laura and I were kids, our extended family usually got together on Sunday afternoons. In summer, it would be cookouts on the deck; in winter, it would be cozy dinners in our small dining room. Most of the time Mom's cousin Bette came over on those Sundays, along with her new husband Stan and his son, Harvey. It was a little strange, getting used to Bette's new ready-made family. We never knew how to treat them, what to call them. Were they family? Not exactly. And yet they were always around, rather like family.

Because of the frequency of these get-togethers, we three kids sort of grew up together; after dinner, when the adults sat around the table talking, we'd hide out in one of our bedrooms, playing music, having fun. When we got older, we'd smoke a cigarette out the window. And, also as we got older, the talk turned to sex—that great mystery we all wanted to know more about, or more like how to do it.

So when we were all preteens, Harvey the oldest at 13, nearly 14, he took to talking dirty. Basically he knew more than us girls and was eager to share. His sharing included the classic "I'll show you mine if you show me yours." Well, we were just kids, and Laura, who was more forward than I was, despite being a year younger, was happy to take

216

Harvey up on his offer. This youthful silliness lasted a couple of years, Harvey always willing to drop his shorts and show us his private parts. Laura was most times willing to lower her panties, and both of them would hassle me to join the party. So as I approached my teens, I knew exactly what an erect man looked like, thanks to Harvey.

As we got older, our family's get-togethers became more infrequent, and we sort of lost touch with Harvey. But then, one Sunday in 2000, Bette and Stan came over a visit, and Harvey came along. By now, he was a handsome young man, and I'm sure plenty of girls found him attractive. I had to admit his good looks turned my head.

While Bette and Stan visited with Mom and Dad, Harvey and I (Laura wasn't home) naturally went up to my room to listen to music and sneak a couple of cigarettes, as we always had.

When Harvey hit on me, right there in my own bedroom in my parents' house, it just seemed right. He was clumsy and, despite all his talk, it was his first time as well as mine. I don't recall it being enjoyable; in fact, it hurt like hell and was messy. And there was no condom. It was over in moments; in less than 60 seconds, I was no longer a virgin.

We joined our families for Sunday dinner as if nothing had happened, but I was convinced they all knew. The guilt I felt and the shame of knowing it was irreversible was stifling. I knew I was blushing and could do nothing to stop it.

A month later I missed my period. I got hold of a pregnancy test; it came out positive.

The last thing on my agenda was to get married—or even tell Harvey. He was a nice guy, but not "the rest of my life" material. And I sure as hell couldn't face my father and tell him I was carrying Harvey's baby, not after years and years of Dad saying over and over what a good catch he would make—that would have sealed my fate with Harvey.

217

There was a guy from the neighborhood, Jack Ackerman. I kind of remembered him from high school, when he chased after Connie for a little while. He was a couple of years older than she and I had been, and when he graduated, I didn't see him much and didn't think of him at all. But since I got home from college and he had seen me around, he had been sniffing after me like a tomcat on the prowl.

He was cute and cocky and really persistent, so, I decided, Jack just got lucky. My coy performance was deserving of an Oscar. He ended up taking me to a wharfside warehouse, where he had access to a shed with a mattress and booze in it. I can still recall the look on his face when I asked him to be gentle, as he was my first—he looked like he had just won the lottery. There was not even a hint of a suggestion he would use a condom, a selfish act for which I was thankful. Jack was half the man Harvey had been—not that you'd know it, the way he bragged. The thought occurred to me, in my naïveté, that maybe Harvey scored a home run because of his size; after all he had impregnated me very easily.

After that, we got together as often as we could, which was quite often. I got very used to the flavor of bourbon. I'll give Jack credit—he had stamina. Jack's lovemaking became more satisfying, lasted longer than Harvey had managed. It didn't matter that Jack was not as big as Harvey; I was enjoying being the center of someone's attention. After a month of being with Jack I delivered the news. "Jack, I've missed my period, and I took a pregnancy test. It's positive." The silence between us was so loud it was deafening. "Jack, I'm carrying your baby," I said to confirm the gravity of the situation. Jack immediately offered to make an appointment for me to get an abortion, and he offered to pay for it, but I absolutely refused. We agreed to tell our parents and see where that would lead.

After we were married, we got along okay. Jack started to be away a lot—for work, he said. Often he was gone for days at a time. I had Cassie, and I stayed close to my mom and dad, who kept the spirit of the extended family alive and well.

A couple of years later, I took Cassie to my mom and dad's anniversary party at their place. Who greeted me at the door? None other than Harvey. I was genuinely pleased to see him. As usual, my mother spirited her precious little Cassie off, and I found myself talking with Harvey for some time. I found him sweet and easy company.

About an hour into the party, he leaned across and whispered in my ear, "Upstairs in about five minutes?" He walked away before I could answer. So I answered him five minutes later. I could not believe what I was doing, but what I did know was that I felt alive and excited to be in my old room with Harvey again.

He took me with a kind of gentle grace and then an exuberant tour of erotic well-being I have never experienced before or since. I was eager for him to love me again, and he hit the spot for a second time, making our love last for what seemed an eternity. It was in those moments of tenderness that I realized I no longer loved Jack. However, I believed in our vows so I wouldn't give up on our marriage, as unsatisfactory as it had become. Maybe in time our love would rekindle, I thought. Time would tell.

Ben is 12 now, and I have rarely seen Harvey since that hour of passion that brought my little man to this world.

I love Cassie; she is so beautiful. Ben is a wonderful child. I'll never tell them who their father really is. I know that Harvey never married, and I do have his number, but I doubt I'll call him. What if he didn't want to hear from me? What if hung up the minute he found out it was me on the line? I would be mortified. I couldn't risk it.

At least Jack's evil seed found no home in me. I now use my EFT skills on this very private yet internally gratifying aspect. I know I cheated on Jack, but now that it has all worked out in the way that it has, I have not a single regret.

I couldn't tell this to another living soul; this is the very private part of me and will remain so.

The A B C of Emotional Freedom Technique

Awareness:
What bothers you? Notice what tension, pain, memory or craving is there. Name it. Be really specific and detailed. How does it make you feel? Can you give it an intensity number on a scale of 0 to 10?

Balancing:
Say three times out loud as you tap the side of your hand (karate place)...."Even though I ...(describe the problem).....I truly and deeply accept myself"

Clearing:
Tap with your fingertips on the seven acupressure points saying a few reminder words about the problem "this problem" to focus your attention.

Now.... Take a deep breath and close your eyes for a moment. Tune into the problem. Notice what has changed or what emerges. Measure again and repeat ABC on the remainder of the problem or on another aspect of the problem.

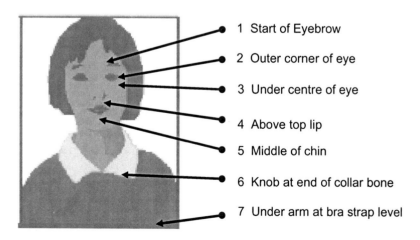

1 Start of Eyebrow

2 Outer corner of eye

3 Under centre of eye

4 Above top lip

5 Middle of chin

6 Knob at end of collar bone

7 Under arm at bra strap level

The ABC of EFT by Gwyneth Moss   www.Emotional-Health.co.uk

EFT RESOURCES AROUND THE WORLD.

Web sites:

Founder of EFT, Gary Craig's web site: www.emofree.com
Association for the Advancement of Meridian Energy
Techniques (AAMET): www.aamet.org
Dr. Pat Carrington (Choices Method) www.masteringeft.com
Ann Adams (EFT Training): www.eft4powerpoint.com
Rue Anne Hass: www.intuitivementoring.com
Till Shilling (TappyBear): www.tappybear.com
Tam & Mair Llewellyn: www.tickhillclinic.com
EFT Masters web site: www.eftmastersworldwide.com
Colin Winston Aldridge's web site:
www.intuitive-therapy-solutions.co.uk
Steve Wells & David Lake: www.eftdownunder.com
EFT guidance site: www.tapping.com
Leon Jay: www.eft-therapy.com
Silvia Hartmann: www.theamt.com
Gwenn Bonnell: www.TapIntoHeaven.com
Sue Beer & Emma Roberts: www.theeftcentre.com
Rick Wilkes: www.thrivingnow.com
Tania Prince: www.eft-courses.co.uk
Gwyneth Moss: www.emotional-health.co.uk
Karl Dawson: www.e-f-t.co.uk
Jaqui Crooks: www.emotional-freedom-technique.net
Andy Bryce: www.spiritcoach.ca
The EFT Vial: www.ehdef.com
Dez Sellars: www.completemindtherapy.com
Jenny Cox: www.eftcambridge.co.uk

Books:

The Heart & Soul of EFT and Beyond by Phillip Mountrose, Jane
Mountrose :Holistic Communications: 1 edition (February 28, 2006)
Tapping the Healer Within by Dr. Roger Callahan: McGraw-Hill: 1
edition (May 9, 2002)
Attracting Abundance with EFT by Carol Look: AuthorHouse (July
28, 2005)
Freedom at Your Fingertips by Joseph Mercola: Inroads Publishing
(April 25, 2006)

EFT Unravelled (eBook): by Colin Winston Aldridge (exclusively at: www.colinaldridge.com)

Emotional Freedom by Garry A. Flint, Gary Craig: Garry A. Flint: Revised edition (August 25, 2001)

The Genie in Your Genes by Dawson Church: Elite Books (April 30, 2007)

Emotional Healing in Minutes by Valerie Lynch, Paul Lynch: Thorsons (January 25, 2002)

Five Simple Steps to Emotional Healing by Gloria Arenson: Fireside (November 27, 2001)

The Promise of Energy Psychology by David Feinstein, Donna Eden, Gary Craig: Tarcher (November 3, 2005)

Adventures in EFT by Silvia Hartmann: Dragon Rising; 6Rev Ed edition (June 1, 2000)

Energy Tapping by Fred P. Gallo: New Harbinger Publications: 1 edition (June 2000)

Freedom From Fear Forever by Dr. James V. Durlacher: Van Ness Publishing: 1st ed edition (January 1997)

Molecules of Emotion by Dr. Candace B. Pert: Simon & Schuster: 1 edition (February 17, 1999)

Energy Medicine by Donna Eden: Tarcher: 1st Trade Pbk. Ed edition (December 27, 1999)

EFT in Your Pocket by Isy Grigg: New Vision Media LLP (June 27, 2005)

The Healing Power of EFT and Energy Psychology by David Feinstein, Donna Eden and Gary Craig: Piatkus Books (March 2, 2006)

Heal Your Body by Louise L. Hay: Hay House; 4 edition (January 1, 1984)

Your Body Doesn't Lie by John Diamond M.D.: Grand Central Publishing (February 22, 1989)

The Power of Intention by Dr. Wayne Dyer: Hay House (December 15, 2005)

The Law of Attraction by Esther Hicks, Jerry Hicks: Hay House (December 1, 2006)

There are many more web sites and books on the topic than could ever be listed here so apologies to those worthy web sites and books that are not listed in this edition. To be included here please email your details to: inclusionDA@colinaldridge.com Inclusions are made on a best endeavours' basis.

About the Author

Colin Winston Aldridge was born in 1948 in Romford Essex, UK. He attended St. Edwards Church of England Secondary School where the headmaster expelled him on the final day of his time there – a useless gesture that was to prove to be a life shaping event and the beginnings of a constant questioning of the ridiculous side of the Establishment and its part in our lives. Holding a vocational degree in Business Management Colin spent till 2004 in business before deciding to change direction and follow his heart by embracing the Healing Professions, in particular Energy Psychology and EFT. He is a qualified EFT Trainer, Hypnotherapist and NLP Life Coach.

Colin discovered his psychic, mediumship and healing gifts around thirty years ago and this along with Energy Psychology have played an important part in creating this fast paced debut novel and its story lines.

www.colinaldridge.com

Printed in the United Kingdom
by Lightning Source UK Ltd.
133168UK00001B/160-165/P